Adaptation
Reborn in the Perfect Fantasy World

Copyright © 2024 Fantasy.Productions L.L.C.

ISBN: 978-1-959098-01-0

Fantasy.Productions L.L.C.
4601 E. Douglas St.
STE 150
Wichita, KS 67218
For serious business inquiries only,
contact cristoph@fantasy.productions

FANTASY
PRODUCTIONS

REBORN IN THE PERFECT FANTASY WORLD

Thank you, to my wife, for supporting me through this series.

And to my daughter for brightening every day.

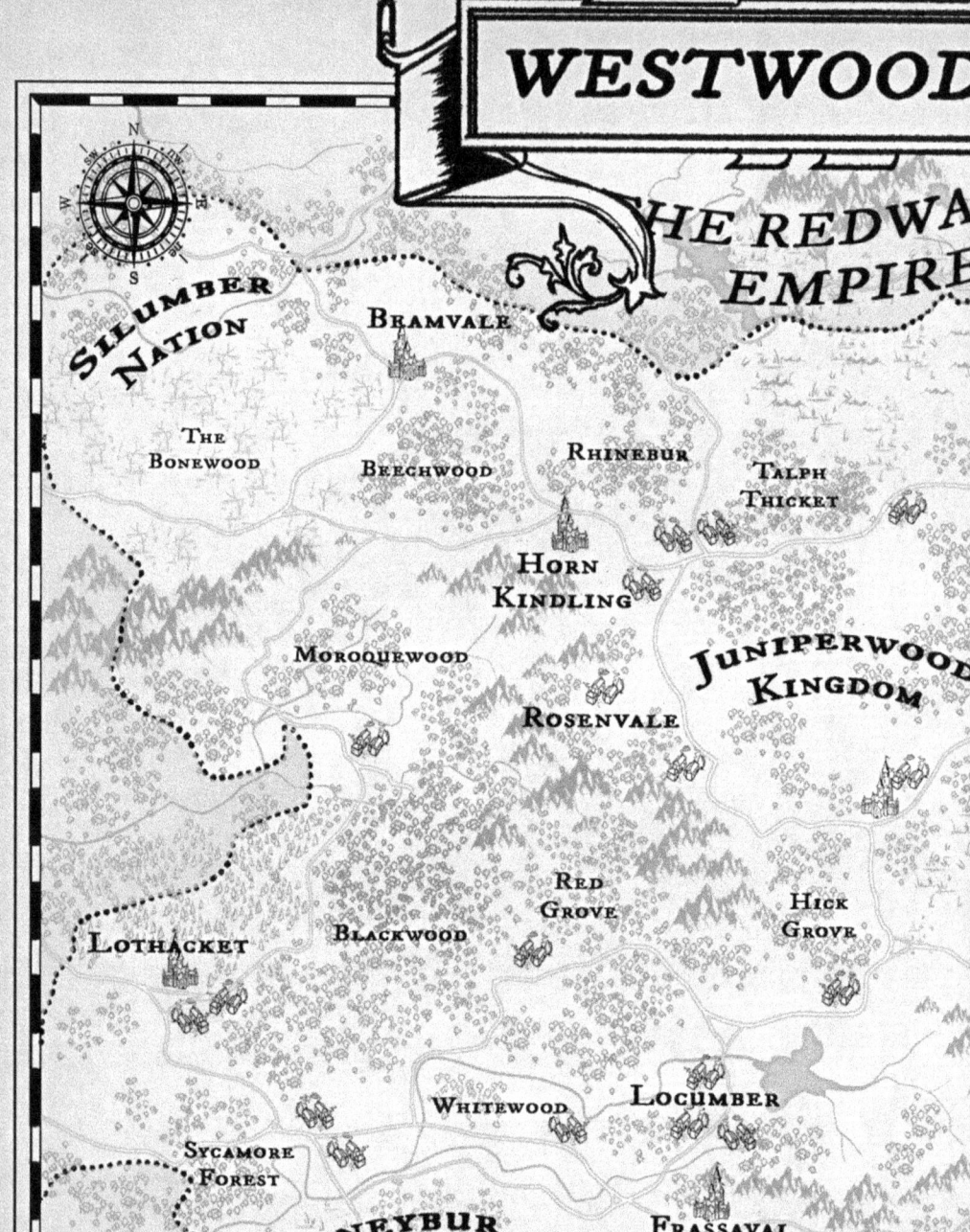

WESTWOOD

THE REDWAX
EMPIRE

SILUMBER
NATION

BRAMVALE

THE
BONEWOOD

BEECHWOOD

RHINEBUR

TALPH
THICKET

HORN
KINDLING

JUNIPERWOOD
KINGDOM

MOROQUEWOOD

ROSENVALE

RED
GROVE

HICK
GROVE

LOTHACKET

BLACKWOOD

LOCUMBER

WHITEWOOD

SYCAMORE
FOREST

HONEYBUR
NATION

FRASSAVAL

THE TANIS REGION

TREANT
FOREST

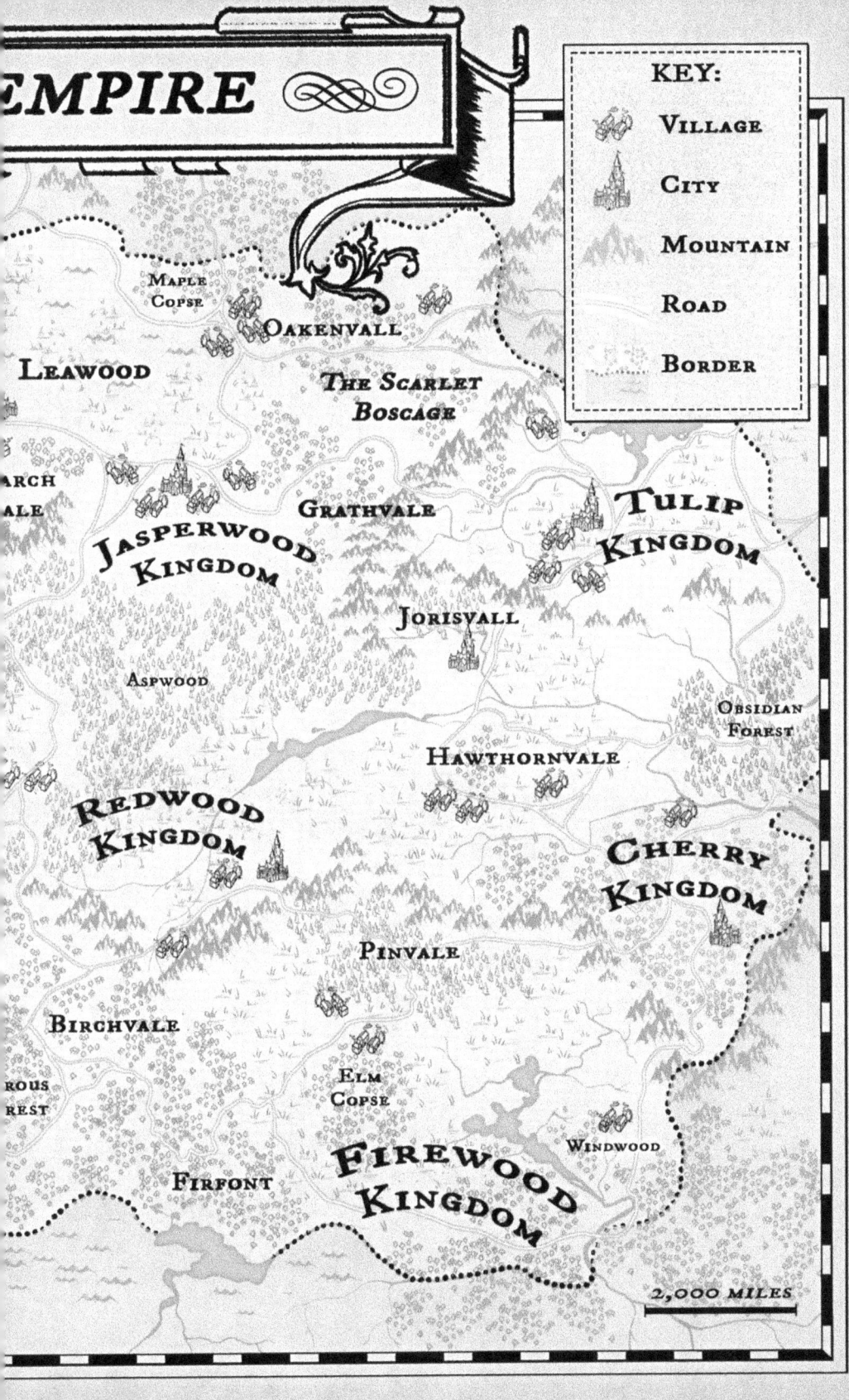

CHAPTER ONE

A NEW DAWN

DEATH, IT SEEMS, is a liar. I expected peace, but found myself trapped and afraid. Bound by the lies that we often tell ourselves, only to discover that the fear and loathing was a side-effect of being reborn.

I, Anessa, came into the world of Anfang strikingly aware from the moment I was born. Blurs of colors and blotches swam across my sight as I was suddenly flooded with light. The blurs cleared, to at least a few inches in front of me, after a minute passed. An almond-skinned mousy woman's face appeared in front of me. Since I had no idea who she was, I thought, *What the hell is going on? Who is this woman and where am I?*

Another woman's voice broke the silence as she asked, "How soon will the others arrive?"

A man's voice replied, "Soon. They were out and about, but when I sent them a message the response was swift. They're about an hour out."

Their conversation made no sense to me, so I chose not to pay attention to it. Instead thoughts of college, my friend Trish, and a white van were all jumbled at the forefront of my mind. I had been walking down the street, and blinked. Then I was surrounded by several strangers. *Large* strangers.

To say it was unsettling would be an understatement. We'd covered highway hypnosis in psychology the week before, which seemed apt, though I knew my current predicament was something far different. The scent of blood marked the air, only furthering my unease. The woman from before wiped me down and she bent down to whisper, "You're an adorable little lady." She started to hum, though it was intermittent and not terribly good. Once I was clean she then wrapped my body snugly.

I was handed over to someone else, a woman with sweat-covered brows and dark brown, wavy hair cascading down the sides of her face.

Though I had the thought that she was pretty, despite the circumstances, I couldn't help but wonder, *Who are these people?*

The words were clear as a bell. "It's a girl," a man's voice said. "She's got such vibrant red hair. Does that run in your family?"

"No, not really. Her name, Anessa Jean, came to me in a dream. Does that work for you?"

I'd had enough. That these giants were passing me around like a football set me off. "You can't give me something that's already mine," I protested in a voice that could only be described as coming from a chipmunk. A light sensation of weightlessness overtook me as the woman's grip relaxed in shock. It firmed up less than a second later, much to my relief.

"Roland," she said. "Pinch me, I swore I just heard our baby talk."

The man, who was too far away for me to see clearly, apparently did as he was asked and the woman chided, "Ouch! That hurt, you know. My point was to confirm what I said. Did you hear it too?"

"I did," said the tall imposing figure just out of my visual range. I later learned he had spiky jet-black hair and similarly dark eyes which had flecks of white in them. At the time he was just a light blob topped by a dark blob. "Can you understand us little girl, or I suppose I should say Anessa?"

"Of course," I said with a mind full of questions. *We're not speaking English. My mouth isn't moving the same way as it should have when I said "Of course." They act as though I'm a baby…* It was then that I decided to take stock of my situation. Looking down at myself, I was shocked to find my epic female frame of six feet in height had been replaced with, if I were lucky, seventeen *inches*. They were treating me like a baby because I *was* a baby. *Crap.*

A flood of pinpricks and tingling hit me at once. *Did I die? I must've.* My breathing began to hitch as I hyperventilated. *What happened to there being an afterlife? Is it just one life after the next?* A torrent of tears filled my eyes. I bawled, and I said, "I'm scared! What's going on?"

"Oh," Mom's soothing voice consoled, "It's okay, baby. You're going to be okay." She stroked my cheek with her finger. "I'm your mommy, Lily." She held me up for the giant to retrieve me.

His deep resonant voice added to her words, "And I'm your daddy, Roland." It seemed as though he wasn't all that comfortable holding me as he swiftly placed me back in Mom's arms. He tapped my nose though with his finger, and said, "Do you remember anything from before now? The fact that you're able to talk is curious, to say the least. You shouldn't even be able to form words, let alone understand us."

Memories of stories where a reborn child is seen as a curse and was cast out came to mind, so I lied, "N-no, not that I'm aware of." A bit of cynicism reared its head. *Doesn't the main character usually wake up after the baby arc? It would be so much easier to have some knowledge of this new world before "I" woke up.* Soft chirping crickets made me nervous about how he took my words.

That was, until he said, "Yeah that would be too convenient of an answer. It also doesn't exactly explain *how* you can talk. Most people who are reborn don't know the new native language." His blobby outline turned, and asked, "Has Oliver said anything?"

His prompt dismissal of me being reincarnated made me sigh in relief.

A third figure, who I assumed was the mousy woman from earlier, stood and answered his question, "No sir. He has not said a word."

"Roland, please be a dear and put Anessa next to Oliver," she said and offered me up.

In a few moments I was lying next to a chunky redheaded boy. At least I assumed he was a boy by the name they were using. He had to be at least twice my weight.

The view from here was terrible, but I could hear everything just fine. Mom was clearly trying to get up by the sounds she was making. "Thank you Fan, but let me get up on my own."

"As you wish," said Fan, the woman who had cleaned me off.

Though she sat on a chair at the end of the table we were lying on, she was just close enough to me that I could still see her. Her eyebrows were upturned and she seemed to be losing the fight she was having against her tears.

I'd lost my previous Mom and Dad early in my past life, and never had the pleasure of a sibling. The contrast to my new situation was stark, and I found myself mirroring Mom's emotions as my vision blurred even more with tears of my own.

"Welcome to the Carlyle family, Anessa," rumbled Dad's voice.

Though it wasn't apparent in my initial confusion, being reborn is quite stressful for your body. The moment I relaxed, sleep overcame me. When I awoke, I found myself in a completely different room. At least I assumed so based on the vertical lines stacked up all around me. They bore a striking resemblance to the bars of a crib, which they turned out to be.

I took stock of my situation. I was still, clearly, a baby. Born to a new family, with a brother. My former life remained clear in my head, although I couldn't remember anything about my death. I knew something else though, and I could not explain why, but wherever my new life had dropped me, it wasn't Earth.

I looked over. Oliver was still at my side. At twelve pounds, twice my weight, my new brother was quite the chunk. He was most certainly adorable though, with pinchable rosy cheeks, vibrant curly red hair and light brown eyes. Having a brother was going to take some getting used to, but I was warming up to the idea every moment that I was around him.

A part of me wanted to cry when Mom noticed he was hungry and he dove into his "meal". It meant almost assuredly…

"Fan," Mom called to the entryway. "Be a dear and hand me Anessa."

Fan was apparently a maid who seemed to follow Mom around almost everywhere. A lady's maid, if you will. She wore a French maid outfit, if there ever were one. Not the stereotypical objectifying outfit that's seen in many depictions, but a conservative black and white outfit, complete with a remarkably frilly headpiece. Her complexion was more middle eastern, though I immediately realized that was me projecting my Earthen sensibilities onto a new world. The concept of the "middle east" was likely absent or entirely different here. As was, presumably, the origin of the "French maid" look.

Once I was passed over to Mom, I yearned for the obliviousness of a regular baby. No one wants to be reminded of nursing. Though it's natural, and perfectly normal, experiencing it with the wherewithal to comprehend it is another story.

Afterwards Fan's attention turned to Oliver. She asked Mom, "Is it true he is already in the Ascended Realm?" She pushed his hair out of his eyes.

What on earth is the Ascended Realm? He never left or disappeared. He's right there! Never mind that – Oliver has incredibly long hair for a newborn. I hope he doesn't lose it like most babies do!

Mom's smile softened with affection. She replied to Fan, "He is. If you change him, make sure to mind the anklet he's wearing. It makes sure he doesn't tear through his swaddle," She looked down at her blouse, "among other things."

"How would he tear through his swaddle?" I asked.

Mom covered her mouth as though she'd slipped up, and handed Oliver to Fan. Then she held me like a football. "Well, I'm not allowed to tell you that." She stroked my cheek, making me close an eye. "At least, not until you've had your first … Ceremony in church."

Ceremony? Is it some kind of religious thing? Does it have something to do with being reincarnated, and how common is it on Anfang?

"Needless to say your twin brother is special, and his future is bright," Mom continued while beaming at him. Next, she laid me down next to him. "Sleep well, you two."

Leaving the room she paused and my instincts said she smiled lovingly at us both. Though I couldn't be sure, because my eyesight still sucked.

Isn't she going to put me back in my own crib? I thought as I drifted to sleep.

Intrigued with the notion of being a twin, I had always dreamed of what it might be like to have one. Would we like the same foods, have similar interests, personality, or a "twin connection"? I had enjoyed parts of my life on Earth, but it had been a lonely home life, with no family. I was nervous and excited about starting a new life with a sibling.

When I woke again later, Mom had returned and was dealing with Oliver. An unwelcome aroma bit at the air. Worse still, I had a sneaking suspicion the origin was not Oliver. My brain may have been more or less in control of its faculties, but my body was not. I felt my cheeks flush with embarrassment. *For heaven's sake. Can things get any worse?*

At that moment, Mom piped in, "Did getting sick wake you Anessa? I'll get to you shortly."

Sick? Taking stock, I noticed the crib was dirtied where Oliver was. *Oh brother. T-that's not what I think it is, is it?*

Mom returned to me and sat Oliver in my crib. She took me over to a changing station and started to clean me up while Fan changed the sheets.

"I don't feel sick," I said.

"That's good. Must be a baby thing." She didn't bat an eye at the *other* situation.

"Is there a reason Fan didn't take care of this?" I asked.

Mom smiled and her voice was warm, as though she were remembering something fondly. "Fan has long been a friend of mine, but she's not 'taking care' of it because you're my babies. This is the least I can do for you two."

I blushed again. "Oh. I suppose so."

"Why are you embarrassed?"

Giving her a teeny sigh, I said, "I'm just glad Oliver won't remember any of this when he gets older."

"Oh no!" Mom said and pulled back in surprise.

"What!?" I pulled my now free hands up to my chin.

"All cultivators remember everything, from the day they are born."

Tears welled up and I covered my eyes.

Mom chuckled and gently pulled my hands away. "I'm sorry. I was just teasing you. Maybe I went a bit far. It isn't every day someone has a newborn with your level of awareness."

"You were joking, right?" I put my hands around Mom's fingers. "He won't remember me… puking all over him?"

"No, he won't remember." Mom nuzzled her cheek against mine. She whispered, "I'm sorry for teasing you."

Complex comforting emotions of warmth and adulation that didn't seem to reflect our brief amount of our time together swirled around in my head when Mom pulled away. This was confusing.

Why do I want her to hold me?

She resumed her efforts, and held me up once she was done.

A smile may have broken across my face as she held me close enough to identify her face. Which was quickly dashed with longing when she laid me back down.

"What's wrong?" she asked, seeing my smile vanish.

"Nothing," I lied. I wasn't ready for her to lay me down.

Fan whispered something to Mom.

"Oh. Right." She picked me back up and held me to her chest. Then she began rubbing my back.

I'll admit, I may have let out a squeak of contentment.

The next thing I knew I was jostled awake once more. I was back in my crib, apparently hours later judging by the dimness in the room. Sighing happily, I thought, *Why was something so simple, like a back rub in Mom's arms, so epic?*

A light snort made me turn my head.

Oliver was eerily close. But rather than being bothered by it, instead I found his scent calming, and fresh.

Being a baby again is weird. But I guess it's not so bad. Using what little muscle I had, I tried to nudge myself closer to him, to no avail.

As though there was an unseen connection between us, Oliver did the same, with much more success. His cheek squished mine severely.

Okay buddy. Love you too. We just need to set some boundaries.

He nudged even closer, tearing through his thick cotton swaddle as if it were tissue paper. The hug he put me in was like a vice grip. His tiny chubby arms felt like iron bars. It wasn't just because I was small myself.

This can't be normal. Oof. Suppose I should be careful what I ask for. A small surge of anxiety rose in my stomach, but I pushed away thoughts of him doing me physical harm, since I knew if he hurt me even a little, it wouldn't be on purpose. *I wonder what being a cultivator is all about. Is that why Oliver is so darn strong?*

So much about Anfang seemed similar to Earth. But I lay in my crib, a talking baby, inexplicably with the mind of an adult. I squirmed uncomfortably in the unnaturally strong embrace of my brother, and I wondered just how much of my new life would be different. What it would cost me to find out.

CHAPTER TWO

INTO THE LIGHT

A DAY OR so later, Mom was humming around me while changing me, energized by something or other. Her voice was soothing, and Mom's light honeyed perfume, always-kempt appearance, and graceful poise made her seem almost magical to me.

She's like a Disney princess.

At the edge of my vision, Fan was busy tidying the room, rapidly buzzing around like a bee. She was far enough away from my young eyes that I struggled to track her. When she came close enough to get a clear image I could see that she was a small mousy girl with big glasses that highlighted her ash-gray eyes. Her shiny black hair blended in well with her improbable outfit.

Folding something near Mom, she asked, "I hear Oliver's test went well."

Mom smiled in satisfaction. "Yes. Quite well. The proctor was a little shaken up though. He said Oliver could even advance by the time he's six-Standard-years-old."

"No way!" Fan said in disbelief.

Mom bumped Fan's hip with hers. "It's possible." She paused. "Though I can hardly believe it myself."

Based on the shapes I could make out, Fan looked my way. "Do you think Anessa will do okay?"

Mom gave a curious hum. "Not sure." She tickled the end of my nose with her finger. "She is special in her own way, regardless."

Since it was about me, I asked, "What test?" I wanted to ask about Oliver "advancing," but hearing my name put that to the side.

Mom's eyebrows waggled with an ornery smile. "You'll see."

Evasive. Though it isn't as though I can refuse to take the test. Looking down at the diaper on my lower half I thought, *I can't even control my bowels.*

Having your every need tended to sounds like a dream to many. However, finding yourself *unable* to do anything for yourself turns that dream into a nightmare.

Mom lifted me and held me close. Her delightful warmth contrasted with the nippy air. Her touch was so soothing that it took every bit of my focus to not close my eyes right there.

Suppose not everything is bad. Taking advantage of my lofty perch in Mom's arms, I tried to make out more details about our bedroom but was disappointed by my unformed eyes. *I hate being baby blind.* Wondering if there was a god or goddess out there. I thought, *Can we skip ahead a few years so I'm not so helpless?* Only to sigh at nothing happening. I didn't expect it to.

Mom moved me into a safer position in her arms and gave me a loving smile. "You're actually going to have a test in just a few minutes." She carried me out of my bedroom for the first time in a few days. Her voice fell to a stern whisper, "Do not talk to the proctor, okay?"

"Okay," I tried to whisper back but it came out as its usual squeak.

She teasingly placed her finger over my mouth. The click of my bedroom door was stark as she moved us through the house.

Weird how I notice sounds more since I'm effectively blind. Will that awareness fade when my vision comes into maturity? Mom must not fully trust the proctor if she wants me to be quiet. Though I can certainly see that a newborn shouldn't be talking, either. An involuntary shiver hit me, and I gripped Mom's blouse.

"Are you cold?" She held me closer, and covered me with her arms.

What do you expect? I've got only a diaper on! Then I remembered when Mom took Oliver for his test. Mom had to sit him next to me for a moment before she left the room. He was just as lightly dressed.

What exactly are they testing?

We entered a dark room lit by what I'd guess was candlelight – at least that's what I thought the tiny flickering orbs in the distance must be.

Mom held me facing outward, like a prize pumpkin. "Renault the Sensor, meet Anessa Jean Carlyle."

A middle-aged man's face entered my focus and he rubbed his chin. He looked straight down at me. "She looks normal enough," he said in a whiskeyed monotone, disinterest clear in his bored expression.

"Sit her in this seat," he tapped some black object as he walked away, "and I'll get started."

Mom laid me down next to the curious thing. It was lined with what appeared to be traces of a circuit board. However, before I could think further, Mom removed the one snippet of clothing I had remaining, making me fuss wordlessly. *Are you trying to shame your daughter? I don't know this Renault fellow!*

Mom pulled in close. "It's okay Anessa," she said, as if reading my thoughts. "This exam is clinical. He won't hurt you."

Her honeyed words calmed me, so I stopped resisting.

Thankfully, my dignity was restored by the harness of the "chair". *Odd how they're using candlelight, yet here I sit in a circuit-laden baby seat. I don't know where Anfang is, but it's sure not anyplace I've heard of.*

Renault began to set out some, what appeared to me to be, polished stones on teeny protrusions that sat around me.

It was then that I realized Dad was in the room; his signature baritone voice mixed with ire came booming from the shadows. "I asked you to bring your highest-leveled set."

My proctor seemed disinterested in Dad's complaint. "There is a way to things Roland." Ignoring what I imagined was a glare from Dad, he continued setting things up. He touched the far edge in front of me, which lit up very briefly. Then, every stone around me vanished in a near-silent pop.

The effect startled me, and I let out a squeak of protest. *What was that all about? Where did all the stones go?*

"Unexpected," Renault admitted. He placed a single, slightly larger stone in front of me, but Dad's hand landed on Renault's shoulder.

"Use your highest set," Dad insisted. "I have somewhere I need to be."

Oof. I barely know Dad and he's wanting to rush off.

"Fine," Renault growled. He removed the stone and put a large vibrant red one in its place. "Just know, if she doesn't react to these it will take longer, and you'll be even later to your appointment."

I stared at the red object before me. Even though I knew it was a mere stone, its interior seemed to roil and pulse.

Its siblings put on a show of their own: a caged storm, a serene light that warmed the room, the deep blue of the sea, and the icy blue that chills you to the bone. Though, I didn't see all of them, I wished I could. Were they all as fantastical as the ones I could see? Was this a side-effect of my bleary baby vision?

Before returning to the front the proctor stopped and turned to Dad. "This is the highest set I have, but it is finicky. If it imprints on her..."

"I'll pay for replacements." Dad's voice was harsh. "Get on with it."

His ire, though not directed at me, caused me to shiver.

Maybe he doesn't like Renault? I must be missing something.

With an air of resignation, Renault repeated his earlier gesture. The light from all of the stones vanished. His surprise was instantly eclipsed by irritation.

"Damn it," he snapped. "At least one resonance must be far above Perfect." He picked up the once red stone and sighed. "And I just bought these."

"I already said I'd replace them," Dad chimed in. He folded his arms. "Don't you have a simpler affinity test you could use?"

Renault collected the remaining stones and pocketed them. "Yes. But I can't be sure of the quality of her actual resonances. You'll need to see my master in Aspwood for that."

"Noted," Dad said.

Renault pulled out squares of paper with intricate markings on them. Their colors matched the earlier stones. He placed them on my forehead one at a time. Each of them flew off in a flit of flame. It was weird, to say the least.

To act the part of someone my age, I laughed and put my hands up each time it happened.

Renault's annoyance and disinterest faltered before this display. "I-impossible," a whisper escaped his lips. "All ten elements?" Turning to Dad he regained his voice, "It's no wonder you called me. After your son's middling resonance in fire, I didn't have high expectations for this test." He paused and looked down, clearly in thought. "If there's even a chance that she's above Perfect in all ten elements, that's huge. You know I have to report this."

"My resonance was enough to garner the attention of Anfang's major Earth spirit, Juno. It tested her last evening." Dad gave a half-smile. "Her Earth resonance is greater than mine." His arm went around Renault's shoulders. "Let's talk about that report some more in my study."

"Roland—" Mom said.

Even I could see Dad's glare left no room for argument. Obviously, Renault saw this too.

Is Dad going to threaten Renault?

Minutes later Dad returned, alone.

"What was that test about?" I finally asked. "What do the stones and the papers mean?"

Dad rushed to me and whispered, "Shh. He isn't gone yet." Unstrapping me, he then picked me up and held me. Unlike Mom, Dad smelled like... absolutely nothing. However, he was a lot larger than her, making it seem like I was being held by a giant.

Am I really sure this isn't a dream? Everything seems so fantastical and odd. Though I suppose it beats being reborn as a spider or something.

Dad graced me with a rare genuine grin that tore down the tough exterior I'd built up in my head around him. "You're going to be a great cultivator in the future, just like Oliver." He handed me over to Mom. "Even if you aren't as strong as he is, your Earth resonance is unmatched."

I wish I knew enough to know what the blazes he's talking about! I'm guessing when he says "cultivation" he is not talking about farming. His comment specific to Earth made me wonder. *Surely it's nothing so convenient as The Last Airbender.*

He started to poke at my cheeks and nose and mumbled in a babyish voice. Apparently, I was more interesting to him now.

Renault soon returned to collect his testing apparatus. He regarded us as he did so. He didn't seem particularly pleased, and he said nothing, not even goodbye.

Once he was out of earshot Dad's entire demeanor changed. "That man is irritating," he growled. "He tried to fleece us over being quiet." His focus turned to Mom. "Tell the staff nothing. Oliver is merely at the 'beginning' of the Ascended Realm, not its peak."

Mom's face showed confusion for a second before her soft gaze straightened and she nodded. "If you wish, but I've already told Fan what I knew."

Dad placed his hands on Mom's shoulders. "That's fine. Just tell her to keep it quiet. I know she's not one to blab." He chuckled. "Well, except to you."

"Will we be okay? Money won't be an issue for their education, but I'm concerned about what others might do to them if Renault doesn't keep this quiet."

Dad exhaled. "Don't worry about it. I've already started drafting a letter to him. He'll ensure no one bothers us."

Him? Him who? Why are they being so evasive!

"What are you two talking about?" I said crossly. "I'm a bit lost."

Dad looked down at me. Every time I spoke his face betrayed him and said he couldn't believe it. "You know, you might be more surprising in the future than Oliver."

CHAPTER THREE

QUESTIONS ON CULTIVATION

THE DAYS PASSED swiftly. Having little else to do, it was easy to sleep the day away. My gentle frame didn't seem to mind it much.

Nonetheless I still had unanswered questions nagging me for answers. After several days of hearing whispers about it in the halls, I gathered the courage to ask Mom, "Can you please tell me what a cultivator is?"

She was busying herself in the corner with a book. My question gave her pause, but she didn't answer. After I repeated myself a few times and she still didn't respond, I turned my attention elsewhere, stomping down my urge to scream at her willful silence.

Oliver was his usual adorable self. Light rhythmic purring accompanied his chest's rise and fall. He'd managed to pull his arm out of his swaddle and was sucking his thumb. He was even bigger than before. Already, he'd gained three pounds to my paltry six ounces.

Turning on his side, a faint tearing noise accompanied him freeing his other arm, followed then by his legs.

Something is definitely different about him. That *is not normal... is it?* Using maximal effort, I tried to do the same. Succeeding in doing little more than exhausting myself.

Mom snapped her book shut and went to Oliver's crib. With a sigh she picked him up, and I tracked her to our changing station. One blue swaddle later, another red for extra hold, and the old one in the bin, he was snugly wrapped like I was.

Once she had him back in his crib she stood. Placing a finger over her mouth she said, and pointed to Oliver. "Cultivator."

Oh. So his superstrength is due to being a cultivator?

She then pointed to me and smiled. "Cultivator."

It wasn't much of an explanation, leaving me with more questions than answers. And I sure didn't have superstrength yet.

Mom motioned toward herself. "Mortal." She then moved closer and whispered, "You'll find out more later. That's a promise." A quick peck on my forehead was the last she said of it. She wrinkled her nose with a sniff. "But first, let's take care of that."

It's embarrassing every single time!

With "that" taken care of, Mom left the room and me to my thoughts. *I don't really want to wait to learn more about this world, and cultivators.* A flash of anger made my face and chest heat up. *Though it isn't like I have a bloody choice! I'm stuck here in this blasted feeble form. I can't even sit up without assistance.*

As though he heard my thought Oliver sat up enough to look around, seemingly ignoring the restraint of the double swaddle, his eyes tracking the room in a daze. He saw me and smiled. Then he fell forward against the spindles of the crib and was out like a light.

His upper lip inverted and his puffy cheeks flattening around the bar made me giggle.

It really is as though you can hear my thoughts.

Seconds later his face began to slide down, eliciting another round of laughs. It was the best show around. Hey: life in the nursery was pretty dull. Oliver was generally the best entertainment I had available to me.

Time passed, and though it took some time, I was finally able to see pretty clearly up to six feet away. From what I could make out, the nursery was fairly gaudy. Other maids besides Fan would enter and tidy up the room. The fact that it was a new maid every day suggested we had a large staff, indicating we were pretty well off.

Stranger still, a few of the maids wore even nicer clothes than Mom did. The style was still reminiscent of Fan's, but there were more frills, gilded stitching, and the parts of the cloth seemed to be woven from silver. It didn't seem like very practical attire for cleaning and such, but they seemed to manage. Sadly, Mom had warned me to talk to no one but family.

Carlyle, I thought, musing over my new last name.

I'd found myself thinking of "home". Though there was a kind of void within me when I think about having died, it didn't stop the lingering thoughts of what I left behind.

It wasn't much.

"Oliver," I said. His chubby face turned to me with his eyes closed and a light smile.

"Can I tell you a story?" I asked. Hearing no complaint from him, I continued. "I used to be older."

He gave off a gentle sound.

"It was a world far different than this. It was run by AI." The next words were difficult to get out. "Created by my mother."

A tear fell from my face, and I realized, "She's a story for another day. My best friends were named Trish and Zia. Trish and I were super close." A strange vertigo made me blink my eyes a few times when I thought of Zia.

"Zia was… different. She was an AI. Though it was impossible for us to meet directly, she knew my every secret." Though I said the words, they seemed hollow to me, I couldn't actually remember telling her anything, which I found odd. *Must be part of being reborn? I think some stories of reincarnation talk about your memories being "washed" – is this what they meant?* My instincts told me that wasn't quite right, since I remembered so much about my prior life.

"At least I'm not dead," I finally said.

Our bedroom door clicked open. "Hello?" a maid said looking around the room. "Is someone here?"

Without hesitation my eyes snapped shut.

"Huh," the woman said. "Must've imagined it. Maybe it was a rogue elemental?" She went over to Oliver's crib. "Goodness, that can't be comfortable."

A few minutes later, Oliver was adjusted, the maid was gone, and the room was silent once again.

That was close.

"Where was I? Right. Earth was all technology. Elementals, cultivation, super strength, those were squarely in the realm of fantasy."

Oliver made a cooing noise. It seemed he was awake now and looking over at me. He then moved back to the edge of the bars and leaned against them. With a little more grace, this time. A tearing noise accompanied him trying to reach for me as the swaddle failed. Again.

"You're so lucky," I grumbled. "Let's see... Artificial intelligence, or AI. The Government AI, Zero did what no human could do. It ruled Earth peacefully. Though if you ask me, it..."

Never interrupting, and always keenly watching me, Oliver made the perfect sounding board. Even though I was sure he couldn't understand me, he leaned forward and made noises as though he was following me at key moments.

"As I mentioned, Trish was my best friend. We were closer than most. No matter what guy I dated, she was there when things inevitably fell apart."

Oliver looked at me with furrowed brows.

"Are you upset that I brought up dating?"

Did he just nod?

"Don't be jealous, silly. You'll find some girl you like, I'm sure of it. We'll look out for each other. Just like Trish looked out for me."

I can't believe I'm having this conversation with a newborn. Though the fact that I can speak is equally unusual.

"Being alone is scary, and I'm glad I'm not alone. Everything I've been through so far in such a short period – being a baby again, being 'tested' as a cultivator. It's all alien to me. I don't have your strength, but at least I have something special that shows I'm meant to be here.

"I'm eager to learn what resonance and being above Perfect mean. Given that the literal definition of Perfect cannot apply here, I'm guessing it's an old term found to be untrue, so they probably had to extend the vocabulary?"

A glance to Oliver showed he had nodded off.

Guess my thoughts on Cultivation bored you.

"Trish and I were more than friends. We weren't like sisters, really. On occasion we would—" Looking back over at Oliver showed he was once again awake. *He was either faking it earlier or he's a light sleeper.*

He made a soft noise, and nodded.

"Hold hands and lie in bed together to gossip." The image of us doing so entered my mind's eye, making me blush. *Why am I blushing?*

Oliver didn't have the slightest clue what I was saying. *At least I hope so.*

"We would hang like that to relieve stress. At least that's what I thought. Trish would always tell me, 'I'm always here if you need me. For whatever reason.'" The part I didn't say out loud was, *Did she mean that in some deeper way?*

"Trish was a very patient friend. She never had a boyfriend. But she was indeed… 'there for me'." The pieces fell into place, and my mind was effectively blown. "Huh. It only took dying for me to realize she 'liked' me. I'm such an idiot." A cloud of emotion brewed inside me. "I'm not sure how I would've responded to her." A snort-giggle escaped. "That's assuming I'm not imagining all of this."

My eyes stung. "I'm laughing at myself, so why am I crying?"

A brief glance at Oliver showed he was sniffling and threatening to go into an all-out bawl.

"Don't you do it," I warned him. "It's hard enough for me not to cry."

But he did, and I joined in. Though I had the mind of an adult, I was bawling like a baby.

▼ ▼ ▼

Though we bawled loud enough to garner attention from Mom, Oliver was easier to soothe than me. After saying to Mom that I didn't know why I was crying she let it be.

Our door clicked shut again, and I breathed a sigh of relief.

That was close. I don't mind telling Oliver about a past life because he won't remember… I hope. Mom, on the other hand, might react differently. She was already shocked by the fact that I can talk.

"It's strange, but talking to you has made me feel a lot better. You're such a good listener."

My brother gave me an affirming nod and grunt.

I really hope he doesn't remember these conversations. Suppose I'll cross that bridge when I come to it. I'll just need to be careful not to say anything to anyone else.

CHAPTER FOUR

WALKING THROUGH A NEW LIFE

"WALKING SUCKS," I said, sitting on my rear. My legs had finally buckled as they had been so desperately wanting to do.

"Don't be like that," Mom said in a sweet voice. "You're getting closer. You can crawl almost as fast as Oliver can…" She lightly bit both of her lips.

Narrowing my eyes at her, she averted her eyes.

Oliver ran past Mom and me, giggling as he chased Fan.

"As fast as Oliver can run?" I finished her sentence and jealousy bit my chest.

"Yes. Don't get distracted," Mom said and held out her arms. "Come to Mommy!"

Her stereotypical line made me roll my eyes. "I can't believe he can run already," I huffed. "It's not fair."

"I'll have none of that, young lady," she chided. "You have your gifts, and Oliver has his."

Her abrupt shift in tone made me flinch. *Yikes.*

Mom's voice softened. "Now come on. You are making good progress. You're able to stand, that's a big step."

Oof. Her choice of words left me frustrated.

Standing once again, I cursed that my legs were so jellylike. *I'm barely able to hold my weight!* The memories of my former tall, strong frame were almost intolerable.

Mom took my hands into hers. "Okay, I've got you."

"This is awfully reminiscent of someone in rehab," I said.

"Yeah?" Mom asked. "How do you know those words, 'reminiscent' and 'rehab'?"

Urk. My flub made me stumble. "I don't know. Why do I know any words?" I countered.

She squinted at me. "Good point, though it's still odd."

I'm going to have to tell her one of these days. I just don't want her to think differently of me.

"Bwa!" a voice shouted behind me, making me jump.

It startled me so much that I turned around and griped, "Don't do that! You scared the daylights out of me!"

Oliver backed up a step then went on to run around the room while laughing.

"So," Mom chimed in. "Should we use Oliver to scare you into moving forward?"

"What?" I asked turning back toward her.

She gestured expansively at me. "You took several steps away from me, all on your own."

Then I took note of the distance between us. *Holy crap!*

"You didn't even notice," Mom cooed. "Try and walk back towards me."

Taking the next step I face-planted right before I reached Mom.

"Ow."

Mom lifted me up and held me. "Are you okay?"

I tried pushing away. "Yes. I'm fine. I'm not a baby."

She relaxed her grip and held me at a distance. "In point of fact, you are."

Lowering my face in defeat I thought, *As much as I hate to admit it, she's right.*

"Don't fret. You'll grow up in a flash." Her voice dropped to a whisper. "Not that I'm looking forward to that."

Slapping my own cheeks for motivation I said, "Let me down, I want to try again."

She obliged.

I took a tiny exploratory step. *I don't know how I got here, but there's no going back.* Another stumble left me on my rear and I looked at my tiny hands. *Before this, I didn't even know a soul was real. Electronics, AI, and technology tend to make anything beyond what you can see difficult to grasp.*

Out of the corner of my eye I saw Mom moving toward me, so I stood on my own.

"Mommy," I said to get her attention. In my head I thought it would be difficult to say, but it was quite easy, "I love you. Thank you for being here for me."

Before I could react, she swooped in and pulled me into a hug.

Oliver dashed over to us and joined in, hugging me from behind. His grip hurt more than Mom's.

"Carlyle squeeze," She smiled, clutching us a bit tighter.

The experience left me wanting somehow for those in my past life. It was odd that I couldn't remember them well save for Trish. *I hope they live full lives.* It then made me wonder whether the world I was on, Anfang, was part of our galaxy, or if it was even in the same universe. But the warmth surrounding me pushed these questions aside. *Who cares where Earth is.*

▼ ▼ ▼

Although I was emboldened by my early success, walking was a tough nut to crack. It had been two weeks and I realized that it's one thing to take a step or two, and a whole other to keep upright. Memories of my past life weren't doing me any good. After all, do *you* actively think about walking? I sure didn't.

"Okay Oliver," Fan said with her hands on her hips. "Stop jumping around like that."

A nervous laugh accompanied the thought, *Then there's that brother of mine.*

"Mom, you say that we each have our own talents, but he's exactly my age. It doesn't explain how he can jump, and touch the ceiling! You can't keep saying he's 'special', what's that make me?"

She pursed her lips and looked away. "It's complicated." With a sigh she crouched before me. "Our scriptures are very clear about what can be said. I'm sorry, but I can't tell you yet."

"Scriptures. You mean church scriptures?"

Mom nodded.

So, we're religious. That's new for me. I was agnostic on Earth. Wondering how I arrived on Anfang, the name of the new planet I found myself on, and my new parents aside, I started to speculate about the outside force that brought me here.

"When will we go to church for the first time?"

She touched my shoulder. "When you're an Anfang-year-old."

Wait a minute, though. How old am I now? I've heard people talk about Anfang years and Standard years.

"When was I born, and what's the current date?" I grabbed her hands. "Oh and how does the calendar work?" For a few minutes I prodded Mom with questions about my new world. I learned that I was barely five Anfang months old, which worked out to ten Standard months. Minutes, hours, days, months. All of them were different than what I remember.

I'm going to guess that the words being the same has something to do with me knowing how to talk. I highly doubt that I'm speaking English.

Septaday, Fandariae 21st, 1733
[May 4th, 2025]

Though it had been ten months. Or more accurately, ten "Standard" months. That's how long my new life had been. In simpler terms, three hundred and ten Earth days. The math was difficult to work through, but I had a lot of time on my hands to figure it out.

It seemed like an eternity.

In that time the most I'd been able to do was learn to walk. Since I'd been talking from day one, that didn't really count as an accomplishment.

"Oliver, it's frustrating that I've been able to talk from birth, yet I'm still treated as a baby."

He was sitting up in his crib and furrowed his brows at me as though I'd lost him.

"Well, they seem skeptical of me for using words that are beyond my age." Letting out a sigh I said, "Although since babies don't usually talk, I don't know how they're deciding what's unusual and what's not. It's as though they're only seeing part of me."

The chunky little guy nodded, and his hand went to his mouth as he shook his head.

"Right. You can't speak at all yet."

He retorted, "Mama."

"Right. You can ask for our mommy. What I mean is even though I understand almost everything they're talking about, it's not enough for them to open up to me." I threw up my hands in defeat. "Especially about cultivation! I get that Mom said there are religious reasons to keep quiet about it, but to give me nothing is just unfair."

Oliver blew a curl out of his eyes in a huff.

I snickered. "What have you got to be upset about?"

He pointed to me, then to himself and grumped again.

Is he telling me my problems are his, too?

"Thanks."

Straightening his back he tapped his chest with his fist and nodded.

"I don't suppose you could tell me about cultivation?"

"Guess not," I lamented. "I just need to trust Mommy."

He nodded, an oddly sage motion for a chubby little infant.

"I want them to trust that I understand topics an adult might, but I don't want them to think badly of me. It'll bring up questions of how I died. And I don't really have any answers."

Oliver leaned forward.

"I don't know. There's nothing there when I think about it." Hugging my body I looked down. "It's scary. Something important is missing."

He gestured toward me through his bars.

Taking his hand he squeezed it.

"You are the best listener," I beamed.

Then he pulled me hard, hurting my arm a little.

"Hey!" I complained. "What's the big—"

His efforts pulled our cribs closer together and he was hugging me. "Here."

Oliver, you're scary bright. Especially emotionally. I was nowhere close to as aware as you are, at our age, when I was on Earth.

When I was able to pull away, I said, "My memory is a bit fuzzy about it all, but I know that my friend Zia was originally made to help me. I had a condition called autism. It affected the way my brain worked. Though I was high-functioning or more accurately I had low-support needs, which made dealing with people difficult. That's where Zia came in."

His look was puzzled, not that I could blame him.

"I suppose the closest parallel on this world is a fairy," I said, then realized, *of course, assuming such a thing exists.*

A moment later our door opened, startling us both.

"Are you two talking in that made up language of yours again?" the older maid said.

Made-up language?

While she moved about the room and cleaned up, I ignored her entirely.

Closing my eyes, I replayed my conversation with Oliver. Whatever magical method I used to talk seemed to turn everything into English, though if I slowed my thoughts down enough, I could recognize the differences in the syllables. However, I hadn't been using the local language with my brother.

I've been talking to Oliver in English! To her it must sound like nonsense. Did I start doing that subconsciously? The first time a maid had almost caught us talking, I remembered being on edge.

"What's your name?" I asked in English, playing a hunch.

She came over to my crib and smiled. "Sorry little one, I don't understand you. Maybe when you've grown up some more."

"Cultivation?" I then said in our native tongue.

"That's not something I can answer. I'm a mortal and a lowly head maid, so I don't know anything about it." She smirked at me. "I've heard you can talk, but even if you know a few words, that doesn't mean you'd understand, even if I did know."

A voice came from outside our bedroom, "Yllia."

"They're calling for me, I'll see you two around."

Crap. The few who know I can speak well cannot tell me because of "scriptures". Those who don't know think I'm unable to grasp the concepts involved.

I don't think anyone will be explaining things to me anytime soon.

CHAPTER FIVE

INTRODUCTION TO THE FAMILY

Deuday, Fandariae 25th, 1733
[May 13th, 2025]

TAILS WERE SOMETHING humans had lost millions of years ago. On Earth, at least. But Oliver and I were now face to face with two people, a woman and a girl, who still had one. Though, strangely, they did not appear to be descended from primates, as their tails were fluffy, and they had cat-like ears. This, more than anything else I'd seen here, made me feel like I was truly in a different world.

"Good morning, Lily," the woman said and nodded to Mom.

"Morning Mama Lily," the girl added and curtsied.

Mom, while holding Oliver, smiled at the girl and returned the woman's nod. "Good morning Veronica, Kristine." She paused. "Did you have any luck?"

The woman pulled a rolled-up parchment from what seemed like thin air and said, "Yes. He was able to make one without too much trouble." She walked over to Oliver's crib and placed it in the center. A moment later the scrawlings on its surface flared to life and the paper went up in flames. Oliver stared curiously at the bright spectacle.

I asked, "What was that?"

"She is an inquisitive one," the woman said, surprised.

"Anessa," Mom added, "say hello to Kristine."

"Hi."

Mom grinned and placed Oliver back in his crib.

"You can speak freely. Kristine and Veronica are family."

Oh. I looked at the two.

Kristine was poised and calm with her tail in a smooth arc behind herself.

Veronica was bouncing on the balls of her feet, swinging her tail behind her.

"How do you do, my name is Anessa Jean Carlyle, Lily and Roland's daughter."

The girl squealed and practically jumped on me, pulling me into her arms with a hug. "She's so cute!" Holding me on her hip she continued, "I can't believe she speaks so well for a ten-Standard-month old! It's nice to meet you, I'm Veronica, daughter of—"

Kristine bopped the top of her head lightly with the end of her tail. "Mind yourself Veronica. You are scaring the poor dear."

Veronica laughed and sat me back in my own crib. "Sorry Mama." She went and stood by her mom and folded her hands in front of herself.

"It is fine, just try to act like a lady of your standing. I know it will take some getting used to."

Kristine doesn't use contractions, how odd. Is Veronica acting like a proper lady something new?

Veronica nodded.

"Please forgive my daughter, she is young." Kristine rubbed my cheek. Her hands seemed a bit calloused at first, but then I realized they were more akin to paw pads, though her hands were definitely human. "You may call me Mama-Krissi."

Oliver was patting the spindles of his bed which made them emit a faint light. He laughed and began to whack them harder, to no avail.

"It seems the Art is working well," Kristine said.

"Art?" I asked.

"Yes, Art. I am sure you've noticed Oliver has…" She pursed her lips, "Broken a few cribs. This should curtail that some."

Yeah, I'd be surprised if it were fewer than ten cribs already.

Growing tired of hitting them, Oliver tried next to jump out, only to find himself smack into an invisible wall that rebounded and shot him back into his cushion.

"Oliver!" I cried.

The seemingly stoic Kristine chuckled, then coughed to cover it up. "He is fine. It is merely a means to curtail his escape efforts."

As if to prove her point, Oliver hopped up and looked toward the invisible wall. He planted his feet and his foot pawed the bedding, determined. Again he decided to dash toward the empty space, only to find himself right back where he started. He doggedly tried another half-dozen more times before he sat down in a huff.

I'll admit, I may have giggled myself the fourth time when he tried to fool the Art by moving slower, only to have him slide down the invisible surface with his cheek and lips squished up against it.

"M-mama-Krissi," I said. "Are you a cat girl?" Calling the woman *mama* made me blush.

Veronica chortled, making Kristine glance her way. The girl's ears and head instantly dropped.

"Cat girl," Kristine said, placing a hand on Veronica's head, allowing her to relax. "An amusing construction, but no. Veronica and I are called demi-humans. Our distant ancestors are indeed cat-kin, but the further we are from our bestial lineage, the fewer traits of our ancestry we exhibit." She held up Veronica's hand and pointed to her fingernails. "Note how Veronica has her claws extended. This is something she is unable to control as she lacks the anatomy to retract them. Further, she has no whisker lines."

Kristine's hand moved to her own face, then she extended a claw next to her nose. "Where as I can retract my nails, and have lines on my face where whiskers once were. My father had a full set of bristles."

She seemed starry eyed talking of her father's whiskers. How odd. Does she want facial hair?!

"It was nice to meet you Anessa and Oliver; however, I must return to my previous task." She nodded at Mom before turning to leave.

"Are you my aunt or something?" I asked before she could leave.

She grinned. "No. I am the second wife of your daddy, though Veronica is not actually your sister."

Polygyny maybe? The thought struck me as odd, and I was curious to why Kristine said Veronica wasn't my sister, when her mother is married to Dad.

"He has three wives. Julilah, his first, myself, then your mommy." She approached my crib with a serene smile. "Is there anything else you're curious about?"

"So you're all married to only our daddy?"

Mom answered for her. "Not quite. Julilah is currently engaged to His Royal Majesty, Bal Blackwood from the Blackwood Kingdom. She's also married to another."

Just "another?" At this point I was used to the occasional evasiveness. Perhaps they were afraid of losing me, or that Oliver wouldn't understand, or both.

"Mama-K," Oliver said with a smile.

Kristine picked him up and tapped his nose with her padded finger. He grabbed onto her neck and she held him while closing her eyes.

Three moms. What will I call Julilah's future husband, once they're married? Shaking my head I briefly thought, And *what would having more than one husband be like?*

Before my mind could veer too far into impure thoughts, Kristine put Oliver back down on his mattress. "I get the feeling this one will be a little lady killer."

Her thought made me think of Oliver in a Chucky outfit until I realized that she meant popular with the girls. *Oh, that makes more sense.*

He shouted an excited affirmation.

"You'll need to wait a few years before you're engaged, I'm afraid. At least two."

"Two? He can get engaged before he's even three-years-old?!" I shouted.

"You *are* surprisingly astute for one so young. Engagements tend to happen early. A chance to intermingle with other families, build relationships, and form bonds. Spiritual resonance happens after your first—"

"Kristine!" Mom interjected.

"Ah." Kristine gave Mom a light bow. "My apologies, you and I were raised under different traditions. I meant no harm."

Mom sighed. "It's fine. Those old dodders drilled me incessantly when I got married to Roland."

Kristine put her hand on Mom's shoulder. "There is a current book in our library, I will be sure to read it before the morrow."

Mom pursed her lips and simply nodded.

This is a lesson in clueless 101. Worried about my future prospects I asked, "Will I be required to have more than one husband?"

Kristine ushered Veronica out the door and smiled at us before she closed the door.

"Not necessarily," Mom said. She went quiet and chewed on her bottom lip. "It depends."

I said, "I'm not sure what I think about that."

Mom whispered, "Or wife."

Her commentary made me sputter, internally, as I thought it through, *N-not touching that topic with a barge pole.* My cheeks heated up and I shook my head.

Oliver clamored with his hand raised in a fist, "No husband!"

Mom grabbed his hands and beamed. "You're saying you don't want a husband?"

He pulled his hand away and pointed at me. "No husband!" Then moved his finger to Mom and said the same.

She looked like her hopes and dreams were dashed.

Was she hoping Oliver understood well enough to follow along? In honesty, I was envious of my brother. He was in fact a genius, through and through. Not only was he able to run, jump and do some things even most adults could not do on Earth, but his language skills were advancing far faster than they ought to. *I only understand things because of a past life; what's his excuse?*

After Mom left the room I started to talk to Oliver.

"I'm not ready to start a relationship." I shook my head. "No way."

He mimicked my words, and I couldn't help but smile. *You're far too cute.*

"On Earth, it was typical for people to start relationships at fourteen or fifteen, and then only with people their age." I went on to explain what was generally acceptable. "It just doesn't sit well with me for kids to be engaged so young on Anfang. Maybe there's more to it than that?"

Looking to Oliver for a response was for my own peace of mind, at best.

"No husband!" was his response.

I couldn't help but ruefully laugh at my incessant chats with someone who didn't understand me. "Yes, for now, that is exactly correct."

CHAPTER SIX

BONDING WITH OLIVER

ELEVEN STANDARD MONTHS of being cooped up in our bedroom has made us a little stir-crazy, especially as we napped less often than we used to. Sure, we would occasionally eat with Mom and Fan, or be taken outdoors by maids for fresh air, but by large, we were stuck in our gaudy nursery. I'd found myself playing with Oliver to pass the time. Not that I minded.

"Sissy," Oliver said, using the nickname he gave me.

"Yeah?" I replied crossly. *His penchant for calling me "sissy" is aggravating.*

He pulled a bright blue, thinly-woven blanket out from our dresser drawer, and tied it around his neck. "Sky reml!" Then he leapt up onto my crib and then jumped out, falling to the ground. He landed on his chest. "Ow."

"You okay?" I asked.

"Yeth," he said and held his mouth.

"Did you bite your tongue?" I asked and pointed to my own, and took it between my teeth.

He nodded. It seemed he understood more if I gestured to my intent, versus the words for it.

Giving him a hug, I said, "Don't do that. You can't fly." Attempting to ruffle his hair I added, "I didn't have any siblings before, did you know that?"

"Daddy. Sky reml," he said.

Thinking about his odd words I asked, "Do you mean Realm?"

Nodding, he rubbed the end of his tongue with his hand.

REBORN IN THE PERFECT FANTASY WORLD

Though I didn't know its significance, it seemed Realms were important for cultivators. Fan and Dad had let it slip early on about Oliver being Ascended, whatever that meant.

"Wait, you said Sky reml, I mean Realm, and tried to fly by jumping. Can daddy fly?"

Tilting his head to the side he said, "Sky rem—"

Our door opened and both of our parents came in together, a rare sight.

"Daddy!" Oliver said as he rushed him.

"Hey there big boy," Dad said and picked him up.

"Sky reml."

"He means Realm," I said.

Mom sighed. "I told you not to tell him." She looked at me. "I'm not sure what to tell Anessa," she whispered.

Mom isn't very good at being discreet.

"The truth, for starters," Dad said and looked at me. "The Sky Realm is an important steppingstone for cultivators. Few are able to make it to the Realm."

"Why was Oliver trying to fly?"

"Uh," Dad hesitated, looking at Mom.

"See what I mean Roland? If you were around her more, you'd understand how perceptive she is."

He coughed. "Right. Point taken. Yes, I can fly." Looking at Mom he added, "If you want to know more ask your mommy."

Great, so I'll get no answer, since Mom has been stonewalling me. Scripture something or other. Though... my curiosity was piqued. "Can daddy take me flying?"

"No," Mom said resolutely.

Damn.

"Imagine if you were to fall."

Yikes, yeah, no thanks!

48 ADAPTATION

"Hey!" Dad protested. "I wouldn't drop her. Reaction makes sure of that."

Mom's eyebrow twitched as she glared at Dad.

Is Reaction something other than reaction time? That word alone seemed to upset Mom.

Oliver had grown tired of the conversation and wiggled loose from Dad's grip. He then started zooming around the room with his cape behind himself.

I wonder why Oliver would think to use a cape, isn't that trope based on Superman? Then I had a startling thought. *Is Oliver also from Earth?*

Mom chuckled. "He's pretending to be you."

"Yeah, when I took him flying last week I was in my formal attire. The cape is stifling, though."

"Hey!" I said and pointed at Dad, with my other hand at Oliver. "No fair!"

Dad smiled and whispered to Mom. "This one's all yours."

"Why can't you tell me anything, and why is Oliver allowed to go flying with Dad, but I can't?"

Mom exhaled deeply while closing her eyes. "It's complicated."

"Scriptures?" I said, a bit snarkily.

"Yes." Her body language said my tone didn't go unnoticed.

"Please promise me that you'll tell me everything when you're able to."

Mom squatted in front of me. "I promise. Though when the time comes, I might not need to say anything. Oliver goes flying with daddy for similar reasons."

With a sigh I walked over to Dad and held up my arms.

The Goliath picked me up and gave me a bear hug. I swear my back popped.

Once I managed to pull away, I looked him in his gruff face and asked, "Will you take me flying after whatever Mom's waiting on is cleared up?"

"Yes," he said without hesitation.

Giving him another hug, I said, "I'll hold you to that."

"Oliver, why do you have blood on your shirt?" Mom asked.

"He told me he bit his tongue," I answered for him.

"Is that what happened?" she asked him.

Completely misunderstanding what Mom was asking Oliver stood still for a moment before dashing off with his arms out.

Dad asked, "How did you ask him, exactly?"

"Gesturing and talking. He jumped off my crib's ledge and fell to the ground. Saying 'Sky Realm!'" I may have gestured like he had, making both Mom and Dad stare at me bemused.

"Must be a twin thing," Dad said and sat me down in my crib, then wrangled my buzzing brother, doing the same with him.

"Now, I'm here today to tell you both about some decisions we've made. This is earlier than it would usually be, but you're both…" He stroked his chin as if searching for the right word, "…unique. Starting tomorrow, I will begin giving Oliver some personal training." His eyes landed on me. "And Anessa will start lessons with Julilah."

Though the statements were simple, Mom's demeanor and posture stiffened at hearing the name Julilah, turning her face away from us.

"She will teach you history, maths, and some other subjects." He waved his hand. "I honestly don't partake in such studies myself, so I do not know exactly what is involved. When Oliver is able to control his talents," he then muttered, "and can speak," Dad spoke louder, "he'll be trained in the essentials of reading and writing."

Seeing as Dad was being serious, I felt it necessary to raise my hand.

"Yeah?" He seemed somewhat amused.

"What will he be doing with you, daily?" I asked.

Dad glanced at Mom and said to me, "Learning to not damage everything he touches. His restrictive anklet will be removed once he has some control. The rest of your answer, I'll leave for later."

"Is Julilah a teacher or something?"

My question made Mom fail to hold back a smile.

Mom's smile dropped when Dad looked her way.

"No," he said, a bit surprised. "She is merely responsible for the Carlyle family children's early studies." He closed his eyes and went silent for a handful of seconds. "While we could certainly find the money to hire a tutor, that's something we only do when there is merit. As I recall your older sister Nicole had her own tutor. Though that was largely because Julilah was busy in the Blackwood Kingdom at the time."

"Is that when she met her fiancé?" I asked, and also wondered why we'd need to *find* money to hire a tutor given the number of maids we had running about. *Maybe we were one of those house-rich, cash-poor families living beyond their means.*

Dad coughed. "Yes, though we're getting off topic. Put simply, if we find Julilah cannot be your teacher for some reason, we'll hire a tutor. You might go to a school when you turn five-Standard-years-old." With a shrug he said, "Depends on how things progress."

Oliver and I sat there in silence for a minute and Dad finally asked, "Do you have any questions?"

Oh, so now he asks that. He was worried about going off topic a few minutes ago.

"What is Julilah like?"

"Polite, but stern. If she gives you a task, or homework," he smiled, "be sure to complete it."

"Mama-Krissi mentioned Julilah was married to you, engaged to Bal, and was married to another. Who's the other?"

Dad's reaction startled me. He pinched the bridge of his nose. "Anessa," his stern voice bellowed, making me jump. "When referring to a king, be sure to call that king His Royal Majesty."

I nodded fearfully.

"Since I like my head attached, when referring to the emperor, you must say 'His Imperial Majesty.'"

His warning made me nod emphatically. *He'd cut off our heads for not calling him the right honorific!?* It made me miss my time on Earth before AI took over.

"As for who her third partner is, I think you've met them," Dad looked to Mom who nodded. "Kristine."

My jaw may have fallen off for a second before I recovered my wits. It wasn't that I was opposed to two women being together, but I certainly wasn't expecting my new family to include a polyamorous styled relationship, nor was I prepared for him to tell me details about it.

Wondering if Kristine had another husband herself, and recalling her earlier words, I asked, "Why did Mama-Krissi say explicitly that Veronica isn't my sister?"

"Veronica is Julilah and Kristine's daughter."

I blinked. "How exactly does that work?" I asked disbelievingly.

"I'm not sure you're ready for the full details," he said with a smile.

Did they use a donor of some kind? Or maybe they adopted her? Then something I'd wondered often entered my head. "Why aren't you around very often?" I asked bluntly. It was why I didn't get overly excited when he was here. There wasn't much time for me to grow attached to him. Oliver saw him more often than I did, so of course he had a different reaction.

"Work," was all he said.

I stood and crossed my arms. "That's all? You're at work so much you can only see me once every few months, if I'm lucky? You're my daddy!"

Dad took a step back and looked at Mom, who turned away.

Looks like you're on your own.

"Surely I see you more often than that?"

"Not really." I held out a hand, and counted on my fingers. "I saw you when I was born, when I was tested by that Renault guy, *after* I walked for the first time, and today. That's it." I wiggled my four fingers. The gesture might have been more dramatic if my fingers weren't so small and chubby.

When I said "That's it" each word seemed to strike him. He sighed. "I'm sorry. How often would you like to see me?"

His words made me smile. "I'd prefer daily, though I realize that may not be possible. But at least a few times a week maybe?"

"That seems fair." He picked me up and put me on his arm, like I was a doll. "Would you like to eat lunch with your mommy and me now?"

"Yes please!" Seeing him react to my request to see him more made me happier than I realized, and I was acting like the little kid I was again. I didn't remember my previous Dad much; he was such a distant memory. I couldn't even remember his name.

"Let's go. We're having roast meat, with fish, bread and honey. Cooked greens and…" He laid out everything we were having, in exhausting detail.

His words didn't detract from my excitement at being included. Oliver was frequently taken into other rooms without me, so it was nice to be a part of it for once. I took it all in as he carried me through the house.

As we approached the dining area, I saw Kristine, Veronica and a few others I hadn't met yet. Mom sat down next to Kristine.

Kristine said, "Oh. We have a different little visitor today."

My heart sank a little when I realized how often my brother must have been here.

"True, Oliver doesn't make much in the way of conversation, but when he escapes his highchair, he is quite amusing," said an older girl with dark brown hair.

"Can Anessa really speak well?" asked a cat-kin woman with light brown hair. Her ears flicked on occasion, and she was even more energetic than Veronica had been when we first met. She dashed around Dad several times looking up at me, before Kristine chimed in.

"Settle down Nicole. You will scare her."

"She's fine," I said. "Nicole, was it? I'm Anessa."

Nicole's eyes visibly brightened at my greeting, and her whiskers quivered as she asked, "Oh! Can I hold her?"

"Yes, you can hold your sister. Just be careful with her. She isn't as robust as Oliver."

Who is? I thought.

I was whisked away and twirled around a few times before she sat me in my highchair.

Kristine was holding a young baby in her arms, and it seemed the child was sleeping.

"Right. Anessa, you already met Veronica, your mommy, and Mama-K. That little fellow in her arms is your younger brother, Lom." She pointed at the darker haired girl from before and said, "That's your older sister Lana." Pointing to herself she added, "And I'm your eldest sister Nicole."

"Where's Julilah?" I wondered aloud.

Smiling wider, Nicole said, "Mama-J is eating separately with His Royal Majesty Bal and their baby boy Marcus."

Interesting. She's very clear about who my siblings are. Marcus is not my brother. Also, either there are other suitors I'm unaware of, or Dad wants a big family.

Looking around at my new siblings, I added to my thought, *An even Bigger family maybe.*

CHAPTER SEVEN
LESSONS WITH JULILAH

ELORIA. THE NAME of Anfang's goddess of Death resonated in my mind when Julilah spoke it for the first time. Stranger still, I was learning that gods on Anfang were very much real.

"I saw one as a child," Julilah said, tapping her fan against her hand. Our lessons began at dawn, but the library didn't have any windows, being in the interior of the house.

I admit I couldn't quite believe what she was saying, so I answered, "Saw one what?"

"A god. He floated to the ground as though he were a feather." Julilah's deep green eyes reflected the candle in the room along with the books neatly lining the outer wall. A model globe-sized planetarium of Anfang and its moons sat in the distance.

I rubbed my nose. The faint musty smell would make my nose twitch every so often. "Can't daddy fly, too?"

"Yes, Roland can fly." She had been pacing around the room, her dark brown hair pinned back by the sides of her face, and sat in the chair next to me. "But he met my father, and the lack of reverence he gave Roland is a stark contrast to the blond-haired god I saw." Looking away she continued, "When my father met Roland for the first time, he punched him."

I gasped. *Why would her dad punch mine?*

"But when father met the god, he scraped and bowed, as though he were the lesser." Our eyes met. "Never before had I seen my father bend knee to anyone, and never again after."

My eyes fell on the black diamond set in her brooch that sat on her neck. "If gods are real," I said, pondering whether I should ask this question, since it could make my family question my life before this one, "are there souls and a punishment after death if you are vile?" I asked. *I'm sure souls are real; how else would I have a mental continuity between lives? But I also need to know what they think on Anfang.*

Julilah regarded me for a time. The subtle shades of blue-gray and the filigree patterns on her dress gave her a prim, proper, and somewhat snooty look. "Yes to both." Gesturing at me with her folded-up fan she said, "Every action you make is recorded. If you do good and are good, you're rewarded in your next life. Most of your memories are washed away, as to not hinder your next life." She leaned closer and her voice deepened, "But should you be evil," her enunciation of "evil" made me gulp. "Your soul will be sent to the Nether where it will be tormented in accordance with your sins. As you go, your memories are stripped away."

That's a scary difference. Evildoers don't have their memories washed, but stripped. I don't even want to imagine how. It made me wonder, many times later, how it was that I remembered so much. Whoever or whatever had washed or stripped my memories hadn't done a very good job.

She flicked her fan open in a smooth soundless motion. "Back to the topic at hand. Eloria was once revered as the principal goddess of craft. As for why she's now viewed as the goddess of Death, that's unfortunately a lesson for another day." Turning her head toward the orrery at the end of the table, she gestured towards the moons around Anfang, and she said, "Lokar and Fandar, after whom our moons were named for, are the deities of War and Hope, respectively." She went on to describe several other gods and goddesses.

When I asked her what makes a god, she said she didn't know. There were at least ten major gods and thirty minor gods, with Eloria as the only high goddess.

"Mommy refuses to talk to me about several things, because of some scripture. Why is that?"

"Well…" Julilah began in her signature low timbre, drawing out the word. "Our scriptures dictate that only those who are initiated can discuss those topics. For someone who has never had their first Ceremony, they aren't permitted to have any information on certain topics." Snapping her fan shut again she held it up, in her white-gloved hand, to her mouth. "Gods are always watching everything, so we'd best listen to their warnings."

I sighed.

"You aren't going to tell me anything about Cultivation, either, are you?"

"Anessa, it isn't that I don't want to tell you. I cannot, because I myself do not know. I'm a mortal, like your mommy."

"So, you've gone your whole life not knowing simple things, about how daddy can fly? Isn't that frustrating?"

Julilah closed her eyes and breathed out. "Divine scriptures are absolute." She opened her eyes. "That's all I can say."

When I pressed for more information, she'd repeat those four words. The gods had a tight grip on Anfang. My gut told me it explained why she knew the blond man from her memory was a god, but couldn't say for certain. No one had told her.

This pisses me off. Why would they control information like that? It's not fair.

"Now that I know you are excited to know more, let's focus on what I can tell you." She then began the monotonous background of the gods. Valuable information to be sure, but I may have checked out a few times.

Once the pantheon lesson was over, I asked, "When will Oliver and I go to church for the first time?"

"After your first Anfang birthday."

"That means…"

"Yes, in a bit over a Standard year from now," she nodded. "It's not so much you that is the issue, but your brother. As twins you are responsible for one another. Were Oliver to go as he is today, he wouldn't be ready, and you'd get in trouble, too."

I crossed my arms. "That's hardly fair."

"You're right. It isn't. But Roland is an important man. If Oliver were to cause a scene, and you don't, people will assume it's because we treat you differently, or that you are favored." Pointing her fan at me she said, "You were born on the same day, and sleep in the same room.

Therefore, if one of the two children behaves better than the other, people will conclude that we did something wrong. It would reflect poorly on our family."

That kind of makes sense, I thought, then asked, "But Oliver *is* treated differently than I am. He's spent a lot more time with daddy than I have. They go flying together, and—"

Julilah's gaze made me stop. "And?"

"N-never mind," I said sheepishly. *Man her glare is scary. It's nothing like Mom's glare when I do something wrong.*

Julilah's voice softened, "It's because you are treated differently that we cannot have Oliver misbehave. Roland is partly to blame for that, but I hear you convinced him to see you more often."

I nodded.

"As to how your daddy is important, some of it has to do with," her voice shifted as though she loathed even saying the word, "Lily."

"Lily is from a very influential family," Julilah began as she stood. "Enough so, that in marrying Roland, she had to give up something."

Seeing her face had relaxed from its previous death glare, I dared to ask, "What did she give up?"

"Her right of inheritance," Julilah said. For a moment I thought I saw a twitch in her lip as the edges curled up, but it passed so quickly I thought I must've been mistaken. Her expression was neutral.

Though I knew inheriting money is a big deal, I pretended like I didn't know. "Is that a big deal?"

"It's a bigger deal than you can hope to imagine. She didn't just give up money. She gave up status, power, and her future."

So Dad is important because of what Mom gave up? I suspect that sentiment doesn't go much beyond our family.

"Who is mommy's family?"

Julilah continued on as though my question was heard, but not worth answering in full. "You might find out some day if the worst comes to pass."

"That's ominous," I said before catching myself.

"Indeed." She paced around the table. "There are six in the line of succession before you. Seven, if you include Oliver."

Oh. She really meant that other people would have to die *for me to inherit whatever Mom's family has to offer.* My mind shifted to my brother. *I hope nothing happens to him.*

"Those aren't thoughts for a child, much less a mere infant."

With a snort, I said, "It's not like I want to be a baby."

"Treasure what you have, for you never know what tomorrow brings."

Huh. She was right. Julilah's insight on the obvious was keen, but I couldn't get a bead on her. She seemed aloof, cool, collected, and a little *cold.*

"Now let's move onto the protocol and go over how you should behave in church." She pulled a book from the stack she had made before our lesson started. "Church begins with a prayer to the gods, and goddesses of Anfang. This is a silent, personal prayer. Most opt to choose a god or goddess they wish to curry favor with." She snorted. "While others try to pray to everyone." A whisper caught my ear, "A foolish endeavor."

How different that is from Earth, I thought and nodded.

"Even as a child, you are expected to be quiet. It may seem dull at your age, but I think you can handle it based on your nature." Her tone on "nature" annoyed me a little. "The issue comes with Oliver. I haven't seen him sit still for more than five seconds. Even lunch is a challenge for him."

She pressed her lips together. "If we are seated next to others, and they do not follow protocol, you are to ignore them."

Julilah went on to cover a litany of finicky rules, most about what we weren't supposed to do. It was a stifling lecture.

Before our session was done, making sure to raise my hand politely, I asked, "Who is mommy's family?"

"That is something for Lily to tell you, not I. Just know they are powerful and wasted no time casting her out when she chose love," she paused and added, "over duty."

"Is that a bad thing?"

Julilah tilted her head to the side.

"To choose love, I mean."

She gave me a calculating look. "That depends. There's a chance you may not have a choice in the future, and duty will choose you before you find love." She shrugged. "Or perhaps you'll marry up. Don't worry yourself with that, for now." She brought out a chalk board with a chalk stick. "Now it's time for a quiz. Let's see how well you were listening." A smirk found its way across her face. "I saw your eyes drift on many occasions."

Crap. What followed were questions that highlighted only when I wasn't paying attention. *She watches me well while tutoring me.*

Later that evening, Oliver and I joined the family for dinner. Julilah was present and seated next to Kristine, who was to Dad's left. Mom sat on his other side.

Everyone bowed their heads and prayed, though I opted not to, focusing instead on those at the table. Oliver was equally disinterested in the prayer and was smacking his steel highchair. The heavy metal chair was a stark contrast to the other furniture in the room, which was made of wood and elegantly carved.

When they were finished, Dad said to Julilah, "How was Anessa's lesson today?"

"It went well. She's a good student." Looking at me, Julilah allowed herself a little smirk. "Easily distracted though."

"Sorry," I said and laid my arms over my highchair's surface. "There's so much protocol at church to learn."

"Don't worry, we'll go over it as much as we need to until you get it all."

I let out a groan of dissatisfaction making the adults at the table chuckle. I guessed that the dreary details weren't fun for them to learn either.

A wet nurse was feeding my youngest brother Lom to the side, and another was feeding Julilah's youngest, Marcus.

Strange to have them in the same room. I suppose they want to bond with them? Wait a minute. The sudden realization that I was treated differently made me exclaim, off topic, "Why wasn't I allowed to eat dinner with the family, until recently?"

Dad looked at Mom who looked to Kristine. Finding no help there, Mom said, "I wanted to see to your care myself. It was a bit selfish, and Roland said it's improper to expose myself at the dinner table."

"Hey!" Dad said. "We talked about that." His voice dropped to a whisper, which I could hear just fine. "There were other reasons that I can't say to Anessa."

At the same quiet level Mom replied, "Yes, I know." Her voice grew stern, "*That* topic is hardly dinner talk."

My penchant for speaking out of turn reared its ugly head. "Oh, daddy's a pervert?"

"Anessa!" Mom replied, unable to hide her smile.

Kristine and Julilah shared their own hushed giggle before going silent.

"Julilah," Dad said with bright red cheeks. "Please make sure your lessons with Anessa cover impropriety."

CHAPTER EIGHT
DISCOVERING ANFANG

"KNOWLEDGE IS POWER" is a famous quote from Francis Bacon. Anfang has always been a huge unknown to me, and my lack of knowledge bothered me to my core. I decided it was time to do something about that.

"Fan," I said, attracting the mousy maid's attention. "Can you take me to the library?"

Her face was full of skepticism. "I don't know. It's not really a safe place to play." She went back to dusting the overly intricate cribs Oliver and I slept in.

"I don't want to 'play'," I said with air quotes. Crossing my arms I added, "My intent is to learn."

She put her hands on her hips with the feather duster sticking out almost like a tail. "Will you need me to stay there with you?"

Thinking how I probably couldn't reach any of the books, with a nervous smile, I said, "Maybe."

"Okay, but you need to help me if I get in trouble for not doing my duties."

"Deal." I held up my arms, knowing she'd have to pick me up.

"You're not going to walk?"

Heat rushed to my cheeks. "I suppose I could, but I figured we'd get there quicker," I ducked my head in defeat, "if you carried me."

Before I could think further Fan whisked me out of the room. Her highlighting my desire to have her carry me made the curious looks of the other staff even more judgmental than they usually were. By the time we got to the library, my face was hidden in her shoulder.

"We're here. What book did you want to look at?" Fan sat me in a chair. She went over to the shelves and started to pull books out, flipping through them. "How about this one?" She came over to me with a book titled "The King's Last Hurrah." She continued, "It's got nice pictures in it. I can't read the words, but I'm sure I can come up with a story that suits them."

My previous blush came back with a vengeance. "I was hoping to pick one without pictures, maybe one on Anfang's history."

Yesterday Julilah said that the section she took the book from was off-limits. Saying the books were for the women of the house.

Turning my head away from the book I said, "Also, maybe flip through the whole thing before suggesting it."

Fan looked down at the book, then back up at me. She pulled away and scanned through the pages. After a few seconds of this she closed the book with a crisp thump, and robotically placed it back on the shelf.

Her tone went rigid, "Have you been looking at these?"

"No, but Julilah warned me about them."

She visibly relaxed and breathed out. "Okay. I'm not sure how I can help you with the history book."

"I can read them."

"How!?" she said.

"I don't know," I admitted.

Pointing behind herself at the bookshelf she said, "What was that book called?"

I told her the title and she face-palmed, realizing she shouldn't have asked about that particular book.

She once again picked me up and said, "Okay, let's go pick out a book."

We picked out five volumes, covering history, literature, religion, and other topics. While I was in the middle of reading the first book, I noticed she was lingering over my shoulder.

"Yes?" I asked.

"What's that one about?" Fan asked a bit longingly.

On the exterior of the book was a black leather, trimmed in gold, titled "The Politics of Westwood and its Leaders."

When I told her this, she seemed concerned. "When was it made?"

Flipping to the front revealed a similar dating system to what Earth used. "1717, why?"

Her hand went to her chest and she nodded in apparent relief. "Okay."

Her continued presence stopped me again. "You're hovering."

"Sorry, excuse me." Looking toward the door she said, "Could I ask you to read it to me, too?"

Oh. The fact that she couldn't read meant that she didn't have many opportunities to gain knowledge. Her apprehension reinforced that. "Sure."

I started over and gave her a breakdown of the ruling class of Westwood. It was strange; the book only seemed to cover what they called Imperial nobility, which had sovereignty over several kingdoms, save for baronets, which were the *Kings* and *Queens* of their region. Seeing them reduced to the lowest form of nobility from the Earth systems I remembered made me think I was missing something.

"Fan, this book covers Imperial Nobles. Are there non-Imperial nobles?"

"Yes, an Imperial noble is someone in the second caste nobility, which is beneath the first caste, the Imperial Royalty. Non-Imperial nobles are in the third caste above commoners, like myself, who are in the fourth caste. There are other castes, but I don't know much about them."

"That's complicated." I shook my head. "Why would they make such a complicated system?"

"Yllia made sure I studied that. I've heard Master Roland say that Imperials are mostly about timely reports to His Imperial Majesty."

I was surprised that she shared this information with me. *Is she allowed to tell me what my dad says when I'm not around?* Then I realized it likely wasn't anything sensitive.

We moved onto the next topic in the book titled "Noble Visitation."

I read aloud, "When an Imperial noble visits other lands, their rank shall drop by two, but not so far as to fall to the lower caste. However, should two Imperial Nobles meet at the same rank, one visiting, the other in their own territory, the latter shall have 'Droit de Seigneur'." That quoted text was oddly not in the native tongue, but I could still read it. I immediately knew it meant "Right of the Lord," which I told Fan.

"Having the Right of the Lord shall edge out those of equal, visiting, rank." I stopped realizing Fan's eyes had glazed over. I had to admit that the book was a bit complicated in its phrasing.

Puzzling over it a bit, I said, "Look at it this way: Yllia is the head maid for the Carlyle family, right? There are also senior and junior maids, and each has their own responsibilities in this house."

"Right, okay," Fan said.

"If we were visiting another household that already had its own maids, you might come with us, but your status would drop, though probably not as much as in this book."

She nodded.

"If Yllia were to meet the head maid there, she'd still be the head maid, but the house's head maid would likely have a bit more authority. Yllia's position is like the Imperial Nobility; she can't not be a head maid, but she won't always be in charge."

"That's the 'but not so far as to fall to the lower caste'?" she asked.

"Exactly."

"Fan," an older, familiar, and cross voice called from behind us.

Fan dipped and her breathing hitched for a moment. "Yes Yllia?"

Crap, speak of the devil.

Thankfully Fan didn't get into any trouble, perhaps because I spoke up for her. Yllia was initially doubtful that I had come here to peruse the books, and had me prove it by reading from the books, which I did. Yllia hid her surprise well, and gave us no more trouble.

It also appeared that I automatically carry a title a rank beneath my parents when they aren't around, or "Rang en Absentia", but it's contingent on their absence. Otherwise, people would defer to them alone.

Shortly after, Oliver and I had our first Standard birthday, which passed with little fanfare.

"Do you ever feel like you don't belong, Oliver?" I asked to the room. My brother's light snoring interrupted the monotonous silence. "Day in and day out… it's like I'm living in a dream, or I'm an impostor."

Tears threatened to fall, but I battled them back. "Trish would say to 'Fake it until you make it.'" The salty water finally won the fight. "I miss her. I miss Trish, Zia, and going to college."

Sitting up I said, "How did I die, even?" Every time I tried to remember it I drew a blank. Then I took a different approach, focusing on my last Earth memory. I tried and tried to follow-through on what happened after the white van stopped next to me.

The vehicle doors closed shut, drawing my attention. *It was someone I knew, but who? They wanted me to go with them, but I refused.* Pain then lanced through my head in the memory, and everything went black. *When I came to…* The memory, unlocked, caused sensations to fire through my new small body. Hugging myself, I began to scream, finally remembering the horrible truth of my Earthly end.

Someone entered the room and promptly fetched Mom, who held me until I calmed down.

Once I was merely sniffling, she asked, "What happened Anessa?"

"I had a bad dream," I said, still not sure if I should tell her about my past life. I dearly wished that I could.

"It's okay." She pulled me into a hug, and started stroking my hair. "You're safe."

I mumbled in her blouse. "Mhmm."

Oliver called from his crib, clearly awoken by my clamor. "It's okay Sissy."

"Anessa," Mom called.

"Yeah?"

"Who's Trish?"

My mouth wouldn't function, and I didn't say anything as I just stared at her. I must have screamed her name.

I guess I'll have to tell her the truth. But still, I hesitated.

Mom squeezed me and said, "That's okay, you don't have to say."

"She was my best friend," I blurted out.

Mom didn't respond in words, but she sat me in a chair and kneeled to look me in the eyes.

Looking down at my lap I added, "Before here, I mean."

She took my hands and squeezed them.

My next words were barely a whisper. "I remember who I was… before being a Carlyle."

Mom nodded, as if confirming a theory. "Are you sure Trish was a friend?" she asked gently.

"Yes," I said, wiping my eyes. "Why?"

Pursing her lips, she momentarily looked away. "You were telling her to stop, because she was hurting you."

"I—" My skin ran cold as I remembered. *Gods. Why would Trish do that?*

"Anessa."

Snapping my eyesight back to Mom I saw her eyebrows were furrowed and nervous.

"I'm sorry to have alarmed you further. You don't have to talk about this now if you don't want to."

"I want to," I said. Keeping who I was from Mom had been eating at me. It was a relief to actually talk about it.

"How old were you?" she asked quietly.

Realizing she was asking how old I was when I died, I said, "N-nineteen-Standard-years-old." It didn't seem prudent to say Earth years. Discussing a past life seemed seismic enough. I wasn't in the mood to explain a whole different world.

"What was your name?"

"It was the same as it is now, Anessa."

Her eyes widened in surprise.

"Is [reincarnation] normal?" I asked.

"I'm sorry, is what normal?"

Huh. I wondered briefly why my inexplicable vocabulary didn't include this fairly relevant term. Moving past the fact that I'd apparently said "reincarnation" in English, I changed gears. "Is it normal to remember your past life, I mean?"

"Sometimes," her eyes went vacant, as though she were thinking of something, "I may have read a story or two about such a thing." She gave me a weak smile. "All those who remember are cultivators."

Guess it's official. I am one. It was little consolation.

"Do you remember your nightmares?" she inquired.

Nightmares? Her use of the plural was curious. "Have I had others?"

She nodded. "Since the day you were born."

This was disturbing news to me.

"I didn't even know I was having bad dreams," I admitted, "let alone so regularly. If I'm honest, what triggered this now is I was trying to remember how I died." A humorless laugh left me. "Bad idea, I guess."

"Would you like some warm milk and honey?"

I nodded silently.

She stood to leave and I held onto her night dress. "What's wrong?"

"Can you take me with you? I don't want to be alone right now." Looking to Oliver I said, "No offense Oliver. I... would rather have my mommy right now."

"Sure thing," she said, and held me tight.

As we exited the nursery I spied no fewer than four maids, and my stepmother Kristine. Telling Mom about remembering my past had helped relieve the weight that'd been sitting on my shoulder.

Anfang was a strange and wondrous place. I needed to accept what had happened to me and move on. Having a twin was exciting, and knowing there were powers akin to magic, even if I wasn't allowed to learn about them yet, made me optimistic.

One thing was for certain: I wasn't going to try and remember my final moments again. Fortunately, young minds are resilient and before I was laid back down that night, after a soothing drink of milk and honey, the memory of the experience had all but faded.

CHAPTER NINE
MORTALS / CULTIVATORS

IN MY NEXT lesson with Julilah she didn't say anything about the nightmare I had the night before. Given the fact that her wife had been standing outside my door, I'm sure she knew.

Our library had three levels to it. Today we were on the second level as many of the books Julilah wanted to use were on it.

There were stairs to each level off on both sides of the room. The intricate reliefs carved into the handrails were gilded. The place was almost gaudy. It certainly showcased that our family had money, which begged the question, *Why were they worried about coming up with the money for a tutor?* Something didn't add up.

"I know you don't know anything about cultivation, but can you tell me what the difference between a cultivator and a mortal is?" I said, probing her for more when our lesson hit a lull.

"The differences are stark. Physically, it's said that the weakest cultivator is as strong as your average man. That includes children." She turned to me. "Most children."

Ouch.

"You've seen how destructive Oliver can be. He can already lift a carriage." Julilah shook her head. "He was looking for shiny rocks, and the carriage I was in happened to be in the way."

"That's unfair in so many ways."

She intoned, "Agreed."

"I'm not even allowed outside," I complained.

"Oliver was kicked by a horse last week. Do you know what he did?"

My gut instinct was to panic, but I'd seen him this morning, fit as a fiddle. "No?"

"He got back up and kicked the horse. It was our dinner that evening."

Visualizing his retaliation made a wry smile slide across my face. Until I realized the implications of what she'd said and chastised myself. *Don't smile, they had to put it down, if Oliver didn't kill it outright. Surprised they ate it though.*

"Is Oliver going to be important in the future?"

"Very. Roland said that a talent like that boy's is unheard of." She picked a thick tome from the shelves and dropped it onto the table. "If…" Julilah said tapping the book cover. "If you wanted to know more about the difference between mortals and cultivators, Kristine would be a better source to ask. She's a master with the scriptures and might know how far she can push the rules about what you can be told."

"Could you ask Kristine for me? It's not like I have free reign over the house. Yllia made sure Fan isn't allowed to take me to even the library anymore."

"Did she now?"

I nodded. *Please don't yell at Yllia.*

"I'll talk with Yllia. She means well, but she's a bit by the book." She looked over at the section of the library I'm not allowed to read from and gestured toward it with her folded fan. "But be sure to stay away from that section, okay?"

"I will. Fan thought they were picture books. Until I told her to flip through it on her own first."

Julilah smiled. "Fan isn't allowed in that section, either. Remind her of that."

"Yes ma'am." Remembering Fan's reaction I said, "She seemed more scared than anything. I will tell her, but it shouldn't be a problem."

"Now then, back to the topic of exponentiation from yesterday. I'm surprised you're able to grasp the concept so quickly. Would you like to try tetration?"

The entirely blank look on my face made her smile, which made me scowl.

"It's simple," she said, writing out a small equation on my chalk board. "You take a number and take it to the power of itself, repeated by the number of times noted here." She tapped the black slate and drew a circle around it, showing what she meant.

Those numbers would grow fast. I asked, "What's this useful for?"

She shrugged. "I honestly don't know. It's said to be the method to calculating how sharp a cultivator is mentally by their Realm, but that's beyond me."

"That makes no sense."

"Agreed. But put that to the side." She erased the board. "Let's do a few problems."

After our lesson was done I asked Julilah, "Why is Oliver being taught by daddy directly?"

"Roland is the only one in our family who is capable enough to teach him," she said simply.

Wondering about her words, I asked, "Isn't Mama-Krissi a cultivator?"

"Yes, well, she is not," her voice dripped with contempt, "'qualified' to teach Oliver."

"I'm sorry."

"What for, child?"

"I don't think it's a bad reason that daddy wanted to teach him personally. Mama-Krissi didn't do anything wrong. You trust daddy, don't you?"

Her face made a small "o". It seemed I made her think about it differently. With a smug snort she said, "Perhaps you're right."

Bringing up Kristine made me curious. "Mama-Krissi said she's descended from cat-kin. What do you know about them?"

"Cat-kin is a more colloquial term for a kind of beast-kin. Since our lesson is over for today, that can be our topic for tomorrow."

Fan and I continued our late-day rendezvouses.

"I was worried I wouldn't be allowed back in here," she admitted.

Looking up at her from on her lap was a little odd, but it seemed to be comfortable enough for us both. I said, "Yllia didn't get in trouble, did she?"

Fan gave a nervous laugh. "Well…" Her eyes darted away from mine. "Maybe a little."

I protested, "She was only doing her job!"

"Maybe. But she should have asked you. At least, according to Julilah."

Pointing to myself I asked, "Why, I'm just a little kid. Do I rank above Yllia?"

"Of course you do. That's obvious. You're the head wife's daughter."

Head wife? Shaking my head internally I said, "Isn't it weird for there to be multiple wives?"

"No, why would it be?"

"What about monogamy, and jealousy?"

Fan said, "Hmm. Things like that are tricky. As long as they talk to one another jealousy doesn't tend to be a problem. But what does that other word mean?"

"Monogamy? When you only have one spouse."

As though a light bulb went off in her head she said excitedly, "I heard about that from Yllia. It's really rare."

Monogamy is so atypical as to be rare? As I had that thought, I glanced in the direction of the "forbidden" section. All I was able to spy from that glance was the word "Cultivation". *Could they be lying to me?*

On the second balcony was a curious sight. My "sister" Veronica was crouching with her tail and rear in the air as though she were ready to pounce. Her tail was moving slowly to an unheard rhythm.

"You asked about cat-kin yesterday." Julilah turned toward the silly girl and placed her hands on her hips. "Enough of that now, young lady. Come down here and say hi to Anessa."

To our surprise, she launched herself from the second floor and landed at the bottom, a few feet away from the stairs. The small rug beneath her feet bunched as she slid forward a few inches and she held her hands in the air as though she were proud of herself.

Julilah sighed and shook her head. "Veronica," she chided, "what did I tell you about acting like that?"

Veronica's ears flattened, "Sorry On-pa."

On-pa? I instinctively knew, thanks to whatever allowed me to speak the local language, that this meant female-father, which was even more confusing.

"You were asking about cat-kin." Julilah put her hand behind Veronica's back and said, "Since Veronica seems to have some extra energy today, why don't we go outside?"

"Okay." I said, glad to be given a chance to leave our home.

Once we were outside Veronica stood as tall as her five feet of height would allow. She was evidently excited about something.

"Now then," Julilah said. "You've seen her evident features – non-retractable claws, a tail," she rubbed Veronica's fluffy ears, "and her ears."

Veronica leaned into Julilah's efforts, clearly not minding the attention from her on-pa. My ears caught a faint purring, though it was deeper than a house-cat and closer to the sound of a snore. When she playfully put her hand on her on-pa's arm, Julilah stopped, placing her hand on the girl's cheek.

Motioning towards the distance, she added, "She's also very agile."

The girl took off like a bullet, reaching the white barn-like stables in the distance in two seconds. They were about sixty feet away. She then climbed to the top of the building in about the same time.

Julilah sighed. "I didn't ask her to scale the building. Silly girl, always wanting to show off."

It seemed the building was too high for even Veronica's adventurous spirit to jump off of, as she climbed back down and rejoined us in under ten seconds.

Veronica was barely out of breath and she recovered in under a minute. Her silver-green eyes were brimming with pride.

While I was left speechless, Julilah said, "While most might consider her feats comparable to those of a cultivator, for a cat-kin her efforts are about average for her age."

My not-sister crossed her arms and turned away from her on-pa. Her tail flicked back and forth.

"Don't be upset, it's the truth." Julilah walked over to Veronica and kissed the top of her head. Julilah whispered, "I hope you awaken on your next ceremony, just as you do."

Awaken? Did Julilah accidentally slip there, or does she not realize I can very clearly hear her?

Julilah broke me from my thoughts by saying, "Kristine was even more physically adept than Veronica, before she became a cultivator. The more human a cat-kin is, the fewer traits they exhibit from their kin." She looked down. "In the past, her ancestors were closer to their cat-kin kind, but Anfang used to be much more volatile than it is today."

Veronica went from seemingly proud, when Julilah mentioned Veronica's kin, to looking around and pensive when her on-pa mentioned the past.

Julilah said, "Anfang used to be a world filled with miasma, monsters and bandits. However, all that changed. I won't get into the specifics of how, as that is related to specific scriptures, but cat-kin exist today only because the broader beast-kin do not."

"What happened?" I asked, knowing she would likely refuse to tell me anything.

"They died."

That's… vague.

Before I could ask her to clarify, she held up her hands. "That's all I can say, truly. When you're older perhaps you'll find out more. Saying anything else could be… problematic."

"Can you at least tell me what miasma and monsters are?"

After hesitating a bit, she nodded. "Miasma was a nasty amalgamation of evil, a sort of malevolent mist. If it touched you, you'd be driven mad and killed or empowered. Nobody knows what it truly is. Most people weren't crazy enough to study it, and those who were generally met an untimely end.

"Monsters, on the other hand, were creatures born of miasma or cultivating animals. Neither exist today."

It sounded like that was a good thing they were no longer around.

"And how long ago did things change?"

"A thousand Anfang years."

Over two millennia! That's so long ago.

Julilah's tone improved. "That's the distant past, though. Beast-kin were aptly named. More beast than human. It's sad that they aren't here today, but had they never existed at all…" She looked at Veronica. "I would be missing a big part of my life."

Veronica looked at her on-pa and smiled, breaking out of the funk the conversation had put her in.

My ears caught a faint clanging noise. I turned to try and find its source. "What's that noise?"

"What noise?" Julilah asked.

"I hear it," Veronica chimed in.

I asked her, "Where's it coming from?"

She sped off toward the house and got nearer to its edge, slowing as she approached. Her ears rotated as she went. Rounding the corner she stopped and her ears perked up. Motioning toward us we joined her.

On the side of the house was Dad and Oliver. Both were holding a dagger. Occasionally, Oliver would dart forward and attack, but his jabs were effortlessly deflected.

"Good job," Dad said, and held up his hand. Holding his blade out he added, "But try to change your angle of attack." He gave a few swipes at the air and shook his head, then he gave a few alternating motions and nodded.

Gesturing toward himself to continue Oliver shot forward like a bullet, leaving a cloud of dust in his wake.

Yikes. Veronica was fast, but Oliver was on another level.

When our lessons were over for the day, my mind was brimming with more questions than ever.

Noticing the book in the forbidden section had the word "Cultivation" on its spine had piqued my interest. When I'd returned from the library earlier, I decided, *I'm going to the library at night!* I hadn't planned on going quite so soon, but I was unable to sleep.

Fandar, the moon of hope, cast our room in a dim blue light; our crib's jewel-studded bars drew long shadows and a rainbow of light spots along the far wall. I climbed up to the crib's edge and "helped" open the curtain over our window enough to improve my sight, but not enough to disturb Oliver.

Going over the edge of my "cage" was difficult, mentally at least. Looking down made my head spin. Probably something to do with being a massive two and a half feet tall: at that size, everything is bigger than you.

I'd almost made it over when I my foot slipped off of the crib's spindle, and I tumbled to the floor.

"Ouch," I yelped, before I remembered that I was trying to be quiet. My impact silenced the crickets outside our window for a brief spell. Stalking over to the door, I stopped midway, "What am I doing? Who am I sneaking from?" Looking to Oliver's crib I saw he was sound asleep.

At the door I was pleasantly surprised to find it hadn't been fully closed. That made things easier for me. I used my fingertips to try and pry the door open further. Looking at the hinge I noticed the small rolled up ribbon I'd placed there to make sure the door wouldn't completely shut.

It made me hitch when the door clicked as it opened enough for the latch to come free from the catch. Hearing nothing, I opened the door further and peered down the hall. It was darker than black.

Come on Anessa, it's just darkness. I told myself, though the more I looked down the hall the clearer it was. *My eyes must be adjusting.*

Mostly closing the door behind me I noticed Oliver standing up and waving at me. *Great.* I hoped he wouldn't call out or anything.

The library was fairly far from my room, but it was almost a straight shot. It seemed the house at night wasn't as still as I thought it would be. There were actual guards walking the halls. Thankfully, for me, I could hear the measured tread of their footsteps and was able to evade them by hiding behind bits of decor along my way. Luckily, since I was so small, there were plenty of objets d'art large enough to hide me. *What would they do if they saw me?* I didn't have a clue, but I didn't want to find out.

Near the library I heard a number of voices. The door was ever so slightly ajar and I dashed past the beam of light that it let out, afraid it would spell the end of me if I were seen.

They weren't talking about anything that interested me. People's names I didn't know, and what I assumed was gossip about who was dating whom and what guard they found dashing.

Once I was past that room the floor creaked and I froze. *Crap.*

One of the female voices said, "What was that?"

Silence reigned, and I held my breath. Those few seconds were an eternity. Only when their voices resumed did I continue my trek. I was a few feet away now, and I faced my next stumbling block: the library door was closed.

The problem was that, try as I might, I could barely reach the latch. It was a large metal rod with a metal loop on it to help slide it. Pushing it up as far as I could go, I was able to get it somewhat vertical, but not enough to get it over the small protrusion that prevented you from just sliding the latch to the side while it was facing down.

My fingers were barely able to keep the bar up. Taking a chance, I jumped with it in my hands and tried to shove it over. I gasped when the bar crashed down into the metal plate on the door, and looked behind me.

A voice came, "Did you hear that?"

Followed by, "Yeah, go check on it."

"No! What if it's a thief?"

Their then hushed voices made me hide behind the nearest plant. Their door opened and a cat-kin maid stepped out, looking right at the library. I swore her eyes locked onto me, but I was sure I was well-hidden.

Her tail flickered slowly behind her and she turned back into the room and said, "There's nothing there."

Relaxing my muscles I breathed a sigh of relief. Going back over to the door I cheered voicelessly. It seemed my efforts weren't in vain, and the door was unlocked. Or so I would believe. The door was uncannily heavy, and pulling against it left me out of breath. By the time I was able to get it to move, I found myself with my feet planted against the door's frame.

When it finally pulled free I ungracefully tumbled alongside the door. To my surprise, there was no further reaction from the room of maids. I don't know how they failed to hear me, but I wasn't complaining.

Testing the waters, I nudged my foot into the room and promptly hid behind the door. The instant I toed into that space an otherworldly light popped above my head. Its light was quite unlike Fandar's, and seemed more like Cherenkov radiation, a soft bluish glow. Since it didn't follow me out of the room, I gathered my courage and peeked over and up at it. Anyone watching would think *I* was the cat with how I pawed at it.

I'd decided to ignore the strange new development and enjoy its friendly company in the dark expanse. Without it, I was sure it would be difficult to see much beyond my hands. *Maybe it's how they read at night?*

Though I'd made it here, I decided to tread cautiously and went straight for my target. The book I'd seen earlier was titled "A Primer on Cultivation." Fearing my illuminating companion would draw too much attention at the table, I decided to read it there.

Much to my surprise I found myself instantly lost. Though I could read the words, many of the passages seemed to rely on an intrinsic understanding of what cultivation was. It was like picking up a college textbook in a subject I was unfamiliar with, when what I needed was the grade-school primer. It was a wet blanket for my enthusiasm and I instantly yawned. Knowing I might not get another chance to access the book, I decided to hide it somewhere in the normal section that Fan and I read from.

Maybe I can read it when Julilah lets me study on my own later. She leaves the room then, so it might be as good a chance as any.

CHAPTER TEN

CULTIVATION CONVERSATIONS

THE NEXT DAY I woke bright and early, going so far as calling for one of our many maids. But instead of doing what I asked her, she fetched Mom.

"What has you so excited?" she asked.

After relaying what happened yesterday with Veronica, I said, "Today we're going to cover the pre-cultivator era in history." My mind went to the book I'd stowed away, *and I have something else I want to read.*

Mom gave me a half smile. "Is that so. That sounds fascinating. Did you call for me just so I could hear all about it?"

I spoke with a slightly bitter tone, "Actually I called for a maid and asked her to take me to the library, but for some reason they thought it was necessary to get you."

"Don't be mad at them. They're only doing their jobs. The only maid allowed to accompany you to the library is Fan, and she's busy today." She held out her hands. "Are you ready to go?"

"Yes please!"

Inside, Kristine was sitting near the stairs, rubbing a spot on the floor with her fingers.

"Kristine," Mom said, "Could you watch Anessa until Julilah gets here for her lessons?"

I replied, "I'm not a ba—" stopping to realize the fallacy of my next word, "baby," which made me growl and continue, "I won't cause any trouble."

With a light chuckle Kristine smiled and said, "Yes. It would be my pleasure."

After Mom had left I walked over to Kristine. The area she was focused on had some light scratches in the floor about two feet long. The damage looked new. "What happened here?"

"Veronica was a little overzealous yesterday, and gouged the floor with her feet."

An image of her racing around flashed in my mind. *Ah, right.* Looking around I saw a rolled-up rug. The end of which was shredded.

"Is Veronica in trouble?"

Kristine looked up long enough to say, "A little. She has to write a letter of apology to the owner of the rug."

Odd. Does that mean she has to write it to Dad, Julilah or Kristine? Forgetting that, I asked, "What about the floor?"

She smiled. "I am taking care of the floor."

A faint green light glimmered underneath her hand. She waved it over a part of the scratch. The damage vanished, leaving pristine wood.

"Cool!" I said, astonished.

"Isn't it?"

"Yeah," I gushed, "The green light was neat. Is that magic?"

The briefest of frowns crossed Kristine's face. "No. It is not magic. Magic is—" She shook her head. "Never mind. You saw the green light?"

Thinking it an odd question, one of my eyebrows rose in confusion. "Yeah? I mean, why wouldn't I?"

"Cultivators, such as myself, can influence elements they are attuned to and can perceive related energies. Even mortals know this, though rarely the uninitiated, such as yourself." She raised a finger. "I am allowed to tell you that, *because* you saw the light."

"That's weird," I admitted.

"Oliver does not understand language well enough to have these conversations. But suffice to say, he would be privy to the details, as well. The only allowance for breaking the scripture-ban for the uninitiated on cultivation knowledge, is a clear sign of either an awakening or a partial awakening."

Julilah chimed in. "You're here early."

Kristine turned to her. "Love, I will take her session today."

Julilah wrinkled her brow in puzzlement. "Is that so?"

"Cultivator stuff. I am certain she is at least partially awakened." She placed her hand to her chest. "If I am wrong, I will bear the responsibility."

The two stared at one another for a full half-minute before Julilah said, "Fine. But tonight you're with me, and I get the ring."

"Deal," Kristine said.

I didn't understand what that was about, but given the conversation was between a couple, I felt it wiser not to ask.

Julilah exited the library and she even locked the door.

"Now then," Kristine turned to me. "How much do you know about cultivators?"

"Very little. Mom's very strict about the topic. She spouts something about the scriptures, but doesn't give anything more than that."

I went to explain about Realms and the terms I had heard up until now. Since Kristine was easy to talk to, I even added in that I heard Julilah whisper about Veronica awakening.

"You do not know much. That is good. Lily is an ardent supporter of the scriptures. Do you know why?"

Shaking my head no, Kristine said, "A goddess has spoken to Lily, personally."

Kristine had my complete attention and I moved closer, sitting down on the floor.

"The uninitiated. Children who are neither awakened nor have they gone to church to hear the scripture." She stood and walked over to the table. She patted the chair at the head of the table, for me to move. Then she perused the bookshelf until finding a specific book, "Fundamentals of Essence and Energy".

I'm still annoyed that they made me believe that section was off-limits due to the mature content. My back tingled as I saw "A Primer on Cultivation," sitting next to it. *Shit, they found it!* Sweat formed on my palms and I did my best to look innocent.

Kristine said, "This rule is made to guard the world against magicians."

Oh. That's why she frowned when I said magic.

Opening the book, she sat it in front of me. "Magicians are non-cultivators who aspire to be something they cannot be."

On the page was a person sitting in a lotus position. A series of arrows were drawn to their body. Marking some things I'd read about in fantasy novels, and others I had not.

She pointed to the figure's chest. "The nexus is an organ that lets us control essence." Motioning to the seven orbs on the figure, she said, "These are dantians, used to store essence. The more of them you have, the more powerful you will be. All cultivators have at least one. Most have two. The odds of having more beyond that are vanishingly slim."

On the page was the same figure with a series of what appeared to be veins, but the coloration was neither blue nor red like you'd see in medical textbooks; instead, they were yellow. "Your meridians transport essence throughout your body, like your arteries carry blood."

No wonder that primer didn't make any sense. This book is a prerequisite.

Kristine turned the book several pages forward to a diagram showing five swirls of colors on the left, matched with five on the right. Nebulous gray specks were sprinkled throughout the page.

"Cultivators have elemental resonance through the ten known elements. These colors relate to the possible elements. Tell me: how many colors do you see?"

"Including gray? Eleven."

Kristine's ears swiveled toward me and her vertically slit pupils constricted, as though I'd had her attention. She tousled my hair, giving me a deep, quiet purr that came through in her voice. "Very good."

Later, on one of the chairs in my bedroom I sat in the lotus position trying to meditate. It was the same pose I saw in the book Kristine showed me. It was also the pose I used when I meditated with Trish, back on Earth.

I'd been trying to focus on the good memories with Trish. The nightmarish waking vision I had where she ended my life unsettled me. In my gut it didn't seem right. Yet, the more I tried to deny it, the stronger the images and sensations became. Instead, I decided to focus on the good times Trish and I had together. Doing so made me feel at ease.

When Trish had first pulled me to the wellness class, I told her learning meditation was like cultural appropriation. She'd countered with, "Cultures are meant to be shared and unite, not divide us."

Sitting in the lotus position, on Anfang, made me smile a little at the memory.

I'm excited to be here, and for once, it doesn't bother me that I'm so young, or small. Dantians seem an awful like chakras were on Earth.

Oliver had been doing his usual "training" with Dad, and entered to say, "Sissy. I three danchin." He was holding up three fingers with a goofy grin plastered across his face.

"Danchin?" I asked.

He kept smiling obliviously.

I questioningly asked, "Do you mean dantian?"

Looking at me with puzzlement he pointed to himself and said, "Danchin?"

I spent a few minutes trying in vain to correct his pronunciation.

"You were saying that you have three dantians?"

Nodding emphatically he said, "Rare."

"Zero so far for me," I said and slouched. "They said I have dantian buds in the places where I can get them, but none have come in yet." Whatever a "dantian bud" was. Their commentary was a big reminder that I was indeed a baby.

Oliver's dantians sprouting early was just chance.

He then put his hand toward me and said, "Whoosh!" His simple gesture conjured a gale-force wind that blasted me head-on, knocking me on my rear.

"What was that for!?" I said and crossed my arms.

He came over to me, and helped me up. "Sorry sissy. You okay?"

Though I knew it was his age, I was a bit annoyed in my response. "I'm 'fine'."

Oliver continued to smile, but his blast of air had put me in a foul way and I unloaded on him.

"You're so lucky. Dad spends more time with you than me." His smile dropped, but I pushed on, "Lifting entire carriages is child's play to you," I said, failing to notice him sniffling. "And now you're going around blasting off your wind, and all you have to do is say," I shouted, "'Whoosh'." I stretched my hand towards the doorknob; I could barely even touch it. "I can't even open a damn door!" Kicking the blasted thing, and irrationally hoping it would disappear, led to instant regret as pain flared through my foot and I started hopping on it.

Bounding over to the small couch I was sitting on I buried my face in its pillow. On top of the pain in my foot, I could hear Oliver crying, only adding to my shame of losing my temper with him.

"Oliver!" Mom said from our door. "What did you do? You know you're not supposed to damage the house."

Looking at what she was referring to, I saw to my surprise, that there was a circular hole in the door, floor and the frame. Curious about it, I hopped back over to it, and saw the edges weren't burnt. The wood was simply gone. Like someone had deleted it.

Oliver bawled loudly at the accusation. "Not me!"

My stomach turned in knots and I spoke up, "Mommy, he didn't hit the door. I did." It was difficult to look Mom in the face. "I think I upset Oliver, too."

Her focus turned to me and her hands went to her hips. "Explain. Also," she added, her expression shifting to one of puzzlement, "what happened to your shoe?"

Looking down I noticed the end of my shoe was missing, much like the chunk of the door.

What the heck? While Mom calmed Oliver down I said, "Oliver came in here bragging about having three dantians, then he blasted me in the face with wind, knocking me over. Then I kind of… went off on him.

"It's just so frustrating." My eyes stung a little. "He has everything I don't, and daddy still treats him differently than me."

Mom's next question hit me hard, "Were you not close with your parents… from before?"

I paused for a moment, taken aback. "T-they both died when I was young. Dad was stabbed, and Mom died in an [airplane] crash." *No word for airplane on Anfang, I guess.*

Mom pulled me into a hug with Oliver. "It's okay Anessa. When you're feeling upset, you can tell your mommy all about it."

Instead of pushing her away, I held her tight. Naia Rovenal, my previous mother, was always on the move and we had rarely talked. I lost her when I was four, though I wasn't ready to share that with Mom yet.

"Okay," I said. Giving Oliver a hug I added, "I'm sorry."

He sniffled and wiped his face on Mom's blouse, making her sigh. Oliver said with a smile, "It's okay sissy."

"Do you two need me any more?"

We both shook our heads.

Mom stood. While leaving, she shook her head at the new hole in the room. "I'll have to tell Fleure about that."

"You were telling me about having three dantians?" I asked my brother after Mom was gone.

He smiled. "Three danch... dantians."

"Did daddy teach you about meditation?"

"Meditachon?"

"Meditation. I guess not." I took two flat pillows off our furniture and sat them down for us to sit on. "I don't know how relevant it is here," I sat down in the lotus position and gestured for him to do so, as well. "But the idea is to control your breathing and help [qi] or something flow through you." Realizing I had used an Earth word, I corrected myself, "Sorry, and help essence flow through you."

CHAPTER ELEVEN

THE SPARK WITHIN / SHATTERED BOUNDARIES

OLIVER HAD A hard time focusing, which was not especially surprising for such a young kid. Before he sat down, he had to tell me where his dantians were. He pointed to his chest, abdomen, and then said, "Down here." He motioned around his groin. The blush on his face made him pinchably cute, but he hates when I do that.

"Show sissy big whoosh?" he asked.

I started to say, "Okay." But before I could tell him not to target me this time, he had pushed both his hands forward onto my shoulders and sent me flying across the room. What stopped me was the wall. For three seconds, I was pinned there and my cheeks were flattened by the intense pressure on my face. It was like being hit with a firehose of air.

When I finally dropped to the floor, I was more glad it was over, than upset that my foot was throbbing once again.

A few shrieks outside our room told me the gust had found its way into the hallway through the convenient hole I'd given it.

"What happened!?" Mom burst back into the room her face manic, and her hair was disheveled.

I was still a bit dazed, and I said, "Big whoosh."

Several dozen minutes later, Dad joined us, looking none too pleased. He was dressed in his military garb, cape and all. Short golden tassels hung off his shoulders, giving him an even wider appearance than normal.

Mom was holding me with an ice pack to my head, and the dizziness had finally faded. My ankle and foot were wrapped, she'd assumed I sprained it. "He blasted her with so much wind she hit her head on the wall." She hugged me tighter. "He could have killed her." A sigh left her. "Not to mention that it stripped nearly everything from the walls outside their rooms." She paused. "As you saw, even the wallpaper."

Dad asked, "Oliver, do you want to explain yourself?"

The boy gave his side of the story to our giant of a Dad who looked over at the door, then to the Anessa shaped impression I'd made in the wall. Once Oliver was finished Dad failed to suppress a chuckle.

"Roland!" Mom protested, and pulled me into her chest.

"Sorry, sorry. We're raising cultivators, Lily," he said with levity, "If this is the worst trouble they get into, consider us lucky."

His voice dropped. "Now Oliver, you need to understand you are a lot stronger than your sister right now. Do you like your sissy?"

"Love sissy!" he said and tried to dart toward me.

Dad scooped him up. "Alright. Calm down. You didn't mean to hurt her, right?"

Trying to lighten the mood, I said, "I guess that makes us even."

"Hm?" Dad asked.

After I explained our previous encounter when I made him cry, he took a closer look at the door, then sat my brother down. He glared at Oliver, making it clear he should not move.

"Interesting." Dad turned to Oliver. "Will you be a good boy?"

"Yes daddy," he whispered with his head toward the floor.

"I couldn't hear you," he bellowed.

He straightened up, looking Dad in the eyes. "Yes daddy. I be good!" Oliver shouted back.

"Alright then." Dad looked at Mom. "I need to get back to it. Though," he paused and looked at the door. "I'm taking this with me." In what could only be described as tearing a sheet of paper from a book, he plucked it off the wall and snapped it in half, taking the section that I had damaged. The other parts he dropped to the floor, I guess for someone else to deal with.

Mom glared at him, like she wanted to protest, but said nothing. When he was out of earshot she sighed. "Really." Her voice gained a hint of annoyance, "He could've at least taken the two seconds needed to remove the pins on the door."

Did Dad just casually hulk out on the door? He snapped it in half like a twig. I said to my brother, "Oliver, would you like to do something together?"

"Is okay?" he said, trepidation evident in his voice.

"Yes. We're okay. I thought you'd like to meditate."

Unlike last time, Mom didn't leave us to our own devices and sat there on the couch as I slid off her lap.

We sat on top of flat cushions that he'd flung here and there in his previous display of wind. Our meditation lasted a massive two minutes before he shot away from his seat and out of the room.

Mom followed him, making sure to avoid the hole in the floor.

In the silence after their departure, I gingerly approached the void in the wall and floor. *How exactly did I do this?* Beneath the hole was the actual ground. Whatever I'd done had eaten right through the boards, cement, and – to my surprise – steel rods going through the concrete. *I'm surprised they use rebar. This world is a mishmash of tech from different eras, but life is largely simple.*

Running my finger against the edge of the wood, I realized that it was smooth where it was missing, without a single splinter sticking out. *Very strange.*

Barely a minute after moving away from the mess, a trio of maids arrived to look over the damage to our room, writing notes and cleaning up the mess of splinters from the door that Dad had casually broken. They also put our room back in order.

Returning to my seat I decided it best to try and meditate again. In the class I took in the past we'd learned a handful of breathing exercises. They were probably useless here, but it wouldn't hurt to try.

Taking a few breaths with my eyes closed, I was surprised when I saw a few flashes of light in random colors. Opening my eyes showed nothing was around me, so I continued. It seemed it wasn't any single color, but several at once, like static on a television.

Breaking myself out of the lotus position I cleared my mind and pushed meditation out of my head. Breaths without that focused intent seemed to have no effect. *Weird. Should I ask Dad about this?*

One of the maids commented, "What caused this? It ate through everything. Thankfully no one got hurt."

The word "hurt" resounded in my head, and my scalp tingled as my skin went cold as ice. *Gods, what if I had kicked Oliver?*

If Merlin had an older, grumpier, and wrinklier unkempt twin, I'd believe it was the man sitting across from me. When I told Dad about the static I saw when closing my eyes, he said I'd have another test coming up, and shortly after appeared not-Merlin.

He's just been staring at me for the past five minutes. Every time I try to talk, he asks me to sit still.

This went on for another minute before he finally said, "Interesting."

"What is?" I asked impatiently.

"The elements around you are."

"Can you be more specific?" I asked, but he just stroked his beard. I added for clarity, "I'm not actually versed in the elements."

"I'm proficient in wind, water and earth. Yet, even when I try to increase my focus, like so," he held out his hand toward me, "the earth essence directly around you fails to heed my call."

Blinking at him a few times I said, "What does that mean?"

He grumbled. "Seriously, have they taught you nothing?" He started to run his fingers through his beard.

"No, sir."

Whispering under his breath he said, "Backwater nursery plane—" he cleared his throat, "Backwater empire."

"What's a nursery planet?" I asked.

The old man, who had been leaning back in his chair, pushed forward toward me with new focus. "When did you awaken?"

I sighed. "I haven't yet. My dantians are only buds yet, though I don't really know what *that* means either."

He chuckled. "I suppose it's my fault you didn't understand my question." Underneath his scraggly beard I think I caught a smile. "What I meant was, when did you first remember your past life?"

Looking down at the table, I stammered out, "W-what do you mean?"

"Anessa, I will not harm you. Your dad, Roland, called me to test you. You're far too mature for a child your age."

When the old man asked that question, my palms started sweating. His calmer voice and insistence that he wouldn't harm me was little consolation.

Perhaps seeing my panic, he spoke more gently. "Let's start over. My name is Gerald Orris of the Bahamut Clan from the planet Rath. Most people from Westwood call me Sir Orris." When I looked up at him in surprise he winked. "Few know where I'm really from, but given that you likely remember your past life, I figured you wouldn't be surprised by it."

Wouldn't be surprised by it!? I was sure my eyes were the size of saucer plates. "So you're an alien?"

Sir Orris let out a bellow of laughter. "Alien? Hah! That's a good one. No, child, I won't turn into some monster. An alien is a non-human person from a different world. Though from your reaction, it meant something else in your past life, right?"

Nodding I said, "Yeah. It just meant anyone from a different world. Some stories would depict them as inhuman looking, but most of the time people preferred to show them as humanoid." Fiddling my thumbs I said, "As for your question of when I remembered, it was immediately after I was born."

"How were you as a cultivator? Is that the part of your memory that is missing?"

Tilting my head, I thought his question was odd. "It's not that I don't remember it. There was no such thing as cultivation on my old world."

"Fascinating," he breathed. "A dead zone."

"A what?"

"Sorry. Dead zones are regions where cultivators are severely weakened. Most who awaken their past life's memories are ignorant of cultivation." He leaned back once again. "Most souls on nursery planets are new souls, or those souls who weren't strong enough to remember."

"Were you called here to ask about my past life?" I asked.

Sir Orris shook his head. "No, I merely got off track. I'm actually here to test your resonance with the elements."

"Oh." I remembered Renault the Sensor, mostly because of his breath. "I was tested by someone before that said I had all ten elements."

Rolling his eyes he scoffed and pulled what looked to be a magnifying glass from his sleeve. "That's..." Looking through it his voice changed to that of disbelief, "debatable...?"

"What?" I asked and stood on my chair's bottom rail. Though at my height I appeared shorter than when sitting down on the chair. "What's wrong?"

"Nothing's wrong, per se." He sat the handled loupe to the side and pulled out another. Then another. By the time he was done he had close to twenty laid out on the table in a neat line. Halfway through he had stood and rounded the table looking more closely. Placing the final looking glass on the table, he returned to his seat.

"That's a first for me," he said incredulously. Dropping his voice to a whisper he said, "Anfang is aware of ten elements. How many do you think resonate with you?"

His odd behavior and close observation had me on edge. It sort of seemed like a trick question. "Um... ten?"

"Sixteen," he replied. I just gaped at him. "Remember this is a nursery planet. The final six elements are hyper rare. You could scour a galaxy and find only a handful of individuals with one of those elements. Having all six?" He shrugged. "I've never seen it." He blew through his teeth. "Your resonance levels are nothing to sneeze at, either."

"What are the elements anyway? I know of wind," remembering Oliver blasting me point blank soured my tone, "because of my brother. Earth because of my daddy. I assume water and fire are among the others, but as for the rest, I haven't got a clue."

"I could tell you, and in most cases I would. But…" His voice trailed off as his eyes went distant. "Doing so might influence you negatively. Also," he shook his head. "Some of the elements are *very* dangerous. The 'scriptures' of your planet are a bit provincial, and old-fashioned," he said quietly, "but perhaps it was a good thing your parents followed them so strictly."

CHAPTER TWELVE

OF BIRTHDAYS AND BONDING

Septaday, Lokandae 21st, 1734
[July 8th, 2026]

KINGS AND QUEENS carry monumental power in their respective sovereign states. Enough that you'd be hard-pressed to see any of them leave their territory without good reason. Today was Oliver's and my first Anfang birthday, and royalty from across Westwood had come to celebrate. To see and hear dad dropping several such people off in our courtyard was quite the sight.

He was "carrying" what amounted to little more than a yellow tube with rounded ends, not unlike a stubby airplane fuselage with no wings. It looked like a giant Twinkie filled with people. On his approach he would arrive in a careful manner, but on departure he would create a sonic boom, going Mach something in an instant.

One of the arrivals, His Royal Majesty Bal Blackwood, Julilah's second husband and third significant other, walked past Oliver and me without so much as a glance. While I didn't really expect a man of his standing to stop and say hi, all of the other guests, regardless of their status, had done so, and I had the impression he was kind of rude.

Julilah greeted Bal at the Twinkie departure platform, and was equally distant to us. She took Bal's left arm, while a blond woman I didn't know took his right.

The blonde said, "Should we wait for the boys?"

"The attendants will see to them," Bal said as they entered our home.

"What a butthead," Oliver said as the door to our home closed behind him.

His insensitive commentary had me looking around us to make sure no one of note heard him. "Be careful! He may be rude, but that doesn't make it okay to badmouth him."

"What's the big deal?" he said stubbornly. "He *is* a butthead."

I sighed. "Be that as it may, I like having a brother." Giving him a tap on the shoulder with my fist, I added, "So please don't push *our* luck."

He huffed. "Fine. But you have to listen to me vent later when I get frustrated."

"Deal," I said, and admired the fact that Oliver's speech had improved by leaps and bounds in the past several months. He'd made astonishing progress for someone without memories of an adult past life to help him along.

As interesting as watching Dad jet off was, after the eighth time it lost its luster. "I'm going inside. You?" I asked.

"No, I'm going to keep watching. Daddy said we'd spar later."

Shaking my head I smiled. "Suit yourself." While I walked in I wondered again about our family's odd background. We're considered "poor," yet our house is enormous and gaudy, and here Dad is carting in several people of high status. *Are we merchants? It might explain the opulent surroundings and lack of funds.* Dad returned with another batch of nobility. *There's the appearance of wealth we'd have to keep to attract people like these.*

Inside, I decided to find Veronica. As I approached her room, I noticed it was quite lively, with some of the guests' daughters circling about her.

Veronica was sitting at her dresser as Lana and Nicole were plastering deep blue makeup all over her face. Were the other girls not chattering about, I might have found it funny.

She caught a glimpse of me in her mirror and turned to say, "Hi Anessa!"

Nicole forced Veronica's head forward again and chastised her. "Sit still. The makeup won't dry smoothly if you talk before we're done." She pointed to Veronica's lips. "Look, it's already got wrinkles in it, and it's uneven!"

Veronica groaned as Nicole reapplied it to the affected area.

One of the other older girls saw me and said, "Oh! Isn't she cute?"

When she moved to try and pick me up I dodged her and hid behind Nicole's legs.

"Don't pick her up," Nicole said. "She doesn't like being treated like a little girl."

Another of the girls said, "Um—" Before she could say more I glared at her.

I looked up at Nicole and asked, "What's the makeup for?" The blue, near-plaster looking stuff, looked thick and uncomfortable.

Without even looking my way she replied, "This is bridal makeup. All women wear it on their wedding day. This is the base layer. We'll be adding more soon."

As I continued to watch, the deep blue colored paint seemed to rapidly dry into a sky blue. *Is that an Art or something that makes it dry so fast?*

Veronica moved her hands up to her face, but Nicole stopped her hand.

"I know it itches as it dries, but bear with it. You'll have to apply this yourself later."

Lana hugged her half-sister Veronica. "This makes me excited for my own marriage in the future."

A girl asked, "Yeah, who are you getting married to?"

Lana scratched her cheek. "N-no one yet."

"Perhaps not, but your reaction says you have someone in mind!"

Lana blushed and whispered something to her, making the other girl cover her mouth.

"Who is Veronica getting married to?" I asked.

Nicole's voice shifted down an octave. "She will be married, but to whom, I cannot say." Seeing her words garnered the interest of the room her tone gained some levity, "But I can drop some hints. If you guess on your own, lucky you! Please don't press me for details though, since it's not necessarily set in stone."

The girls nodded emphatically, and I found myself following along, though I wondered.

"Will be married." That... seems like it's not her choice.

Nicole moved on, and opened a can of black paint next. She brushed it over Veronica's left cheek, making a perfect five-point star. I was secretly impressed.

Lana mirrored Nicole's efforts creating the star's pair on Veronica's right cheek.

"No way!" one of the girls said enviously. "You can have ten children?"

"What the nether's she talking about?" I asked bluntly.

"Each point is a possible future child. It's Veronica's Genesis Number."

"Her what?"

Nicole looked down at me. "The number you heard before your birth?"

Looking at her blankly I said, "I have no idea what you are talking about."

There was a stark silence after I said I didn't know what she was talking about on the "number you heard before your birth."

Nicole brushed it off. "Oh well, I'll talk to Mama later and she'll help us out." Though it did little to dispel the awkward atmosphere my response had created.

Hoping to move on, I asked, "Why is everyone here today anyway? Daddy keeps dropping people off, and they're all kings or queens and their families."

Nicole gasped and looked at Lana. "Didn't you tell them?"

"I asked Veronica to tell them."

They both looked at their shared half-sister who waved her hands in front of the mirror. "On-pa said she'd tell them."

"Tell us what?!" I asked peevishly, feeling completely left out.

One of the noble girls turned to me and smiled. "We're here for your birthday, silly. Oliver's too."

"Why? We're just little kids!" I said.

"Important little kids," the same girl said with a giggle.

Seeing as everyone was now focused on me, again, I decided it was my cue to exit. Instead of saying bye I just ran off, with my face blushing. *Why did I run off? I didn't do anything wrong!*

Fan's voice caught my ear and she seemed a bit distressed. "Come on now, please do *not* do that."

When I rounded the corner, I saw Fan surrounded by four young boys. One of them was lifting Fan's dress and throwing the hem up into the air. She seemed distressed, trying to maintain her modesty without directly opposing the boys.

The boy responsible yelled at her, "Stop holding your dress down, this instant, commoner."

Fan reluctantly removed her hand after her hem fell once again. She balled her fists up at her side as the boy grabbed for her hem again.

"Stop that," I snapped.

"And just who are you?" he said, standing before grabbing the cloth again. "I am Prince Rhis of Blackwood. This commoner whelp should feel lucky that I have taken an eye to her."

"You're what, five—no four-Standard-years-old?" I asked.

Rhis snorted. "What of it?"

With my hands on my hips I said, "Maybe you should wait for your balls to drop first."

I heard Fan gasping at my comment.

His age was evident in his response. "Huh? What do you even mean? Who are you to talk to me in that tone, anyway?"

"My name is not important." I stepped forward toward him making him flinch. "Leave Fan alone."

"You refuse to give me your name?" His face became red. "I'll find out in my own way." Turning to the other three boys he said, "Let's go."

Once they'd left I wondered, *Why did his face turn so red? Did I make him that mad? Serves him right for picking on Fan.*

"Thank you, Anessa," she said and smoothed out her uniform. "I should be getting back to my duties." With a nod she trotted off. Before she left I caught the briefest of smiles cross her face.

Figuring I'd go and watch Oliver and Dad practice I headed outside, though I had to make a pit stop first. Instead of the usual training, I saw the same boys, with a few others that were a bit older. They were surrounding Oliver. Though he was my age, two-Standard-years-old, he was by far the oldest looking of the eight.

Oh, here we go. I groaned.

"I asked you to do something, carrot top, so do it. A lowly baronet family should understand their betters."

These kids were clearly looking for trouble, and didn't seem to care where they found it. Recognizing they were trying to bully Oliver, I thought, *Why are these boys such idiots? Nice to have someone confirm we're part of a Baronet, now I wonder from which one.* Then I noticed Oliver's outfit. He was wearing a crest on his jacket's shoulder. *What the heck? Oliver gets a crest on his outfit, but I don't?*

Rhis chimed in, "By your crest, you're barely a noble." He made his stance wider. "Dad's even thought of removing their status in our kingdom. So do as he says."

"No," Oliver said. "I don't want to lick his boot. That's gross."

What the devil could've happened that makes them think Oliver should lick a boot? Looking at his crest I knew I'd seen it, then it hit me. *Cherry Kingdom!* It wasn't so much I recognized which Baronet of the kingdom, but each sovereign state had its own rules for making family crests.

The tallest of them stepped forward. "Then you need to be taught a lesson."

I'd moved forward by this point and stood outside their circle. Enough that I could see. The boys didn't seem to take notice of me.

"Get him Wyn," Rhis said.

Wyn strode forward to Oliver and threw a handkerchief at him. "I challenge you to a duel, son of a baronet."

"Okay. That sounds fun!" Oliver replied and picked up the handkerchief. He threw it back at Wyn, hitting him in the forehead hard enough to make his head snap back.

"You'll pay for that!" Wyn said and charged at Oliver.

Oliver laughed at the boy as he dashed forward.

Wyn was nowhere near as fast as my brother, and I knew the outcome here was a foregone conclusion.

"How old is Wyn?" I asked Rhis who stumbled back a step in seeing me.

"H-he's six-Standard-years-old, as of yesterday."

Six? It's nice to see I'm not the only one Oliver is leaving in the dust. Seeing I made Rhis uncomfortable I moved into the space Wyn had stood in, in their circle. The hot-headed boy Rhis took a step back.

"Wyn's fast for a kid," I commented.

"You're a kid too!" Rhis said and stomped his foot. "Wyn will beat him soon, and then he'll see to you."

"Him?" I asked. "Beat *my* brother?" I laughed. "Doubtful."

The older boy chased Oliver around. Each swing he took winded him a little more and he was sweating.

"Stop dodging and let me hit you!"

Oliver complied, and Wyn smacked straight into his opponent, bouncing off and falling on his rear.

Oliver didn't even budge. It was like Wyn hit a brick wall. Oliver's movements were smooth, and as though he was skating across the ground. The odd patch of dirt here and there, where his foot would step on, was untouched. That sealed it. I understood what was going on. *He's so unfair.*

Oliver was in the Sky Realm.

He wasn't walking, he was *floating*, though his movements made it look natural, effortless.

Whatever skill Dad uses to fly is what Wyn smacked into. And Oliver can do it too now. Wyn doesn't have a chance.

"Forget this!" Wyn said and jumped back. He did a few odd gestures with his hands, and a small flame appeared above his hands. Seeing it, the boy smiled, and continued to make symbols in the air. The ball grew in size until it was about the size of a bowling ball.

Uh-oh, I thought. *Maybe I spoke too soon.*

CHAPTER THIRTEEN

TIES THAT BIND /
MYSTERIES UNRAVELED

WYN CONTINUED HIS laborious efforts, making two more spheres.

As he worked, fire essence would coalesce from thin air, and was given form. Though the ponderous rate at which he moved made me think, *If this were a* real *fight, it would be over by now.*

Once all three orbs were fully formed, he was sweating profusely. An odd sight for a child of six Standard years. He held his hand forward and the fireballs launched toward Oliver. "Let's see you dodge this!" he said, adding to the ludicrous drama of the situation.

Oliver grinned. "No need." With a wave of his hand a matrix of wind essence flared to life and began to move forward.

When he'd blasted me nearly a year ago, I didn't have the time to see what he had done, as I was too busy flying into a wall. I had a better view of his powers manifesting. I took a few cautious steps to the side, to make sure I was out of the line of fire.

Wyn's efforts hit Oliver's slow-moving wall of wind and simply winked out. Then the wind-wall ran into the kid. It was sort of slow, for wind, but it was still fast enough to reach him as fast as I could run.

The boy went flying, along with the two others who were caught up in its path. They seemed taken totally by surprise.

Strange, couldn't they see it? Oliver even made it really slow. It made me wonder if something about me seeing the essence in action was unusual. My thoughts went back to that interview with Sir Orris.

Before they could hit the ground, an older man caught Wyn and Rhis, though he let the third boy hit the ground behind him. It was His Imperial Majesty Bal Blackwood.

"What's going on here?" he demanded.

Oliver put his hands together and gave him a curt bow. "Senior Wyn asked to duel me, and I obliged."

"He did now, did he?" The man's demeanor became even more severe as he sat the two boys down. "Is that true?"

"Yes Papa," Rhis said.

"Rhis, I was asking your brother."

"Y-yes Papa," Wyn finally said.

Shaking his head Bal muttered, "By the gods." Then he took both boys by their hands and pulled them along. "You two know why we're here, and you still had to go pick a fight with one of the twins."

Rhis turned toward us with wide eyes. "That's Roland's son?"

"Yes. That's Oliver Carlyle. Consider yourself lucky, Wyn, that he saw this as a game."

"B-but that means," Rhis's eyes locked onto me. "She's Anessa?" His face went red again and he turned back around, letting his father pull him away.

Oh crap, not only does he know my name, but... He wasn't mad earlier. He can't seriously be crushing on me, can he? It made a shiver run down my spine. *I really hope not. Thankfully he's just a little kid.*

Turning back towards the other boys, their tune had completely changed. They were all talking cheerfully to Oliver as though their previous behavior never happened.

Okay, we're seriously missing some information here. Those two boys were heirs to the Blackwood throne, which means these boys are the same rank for their regions. Why are they being so nice now?

"Anessa, Oliver," Mom said. "Come along now."

At her arrival the boys scattered, seemingly attracted by some unheard voice.

"Once the adults come by their bravery evaporates, huh?" I said.

"What's that?" Mom asked.

"Nothing. Just find it funny that the boys ran off when they saw you."

Mom's voice became playfully stern. "Are you saying I'm scary?"

I laughed nervously and gave her a smile. "You can be!"

She picked me up and hugged me, then whispered, "I know it's your birthday, but don't grow up too fast."

"I won't," returning her hug I continued, "you'll always be my mommy."

"Where we going?" Oliver asked.

"It's time to celebrate your birthday, silly."

Oliver dropped his shoulders. "Is it like last time?"

Mom ruffled his hair. "No. Everyone is here for you two. That means they brought gifts."

He perked up. "Do you think they brought meat?"

Mom tittered. "Yes, they brought meat. Other things, too."

He ran in front of us. "Come on, let's go!"

Mom just waited. "He doesn't know where to go."

"Let's wait here for a few seconds. He'll be—"

"So," Oliver said, he laughed and put his hands behind his back. "Where are we going? No one is in our dining room."

We went through our house to a part that I'd never seen.

"Just how big is this house?" I asked.

Mom said simply, "Big enough."

As we proceeded, the decor became even more extravagant than in the parts I was familiar with. Here, there wasn't a single surface untouched by gold, and while it was pretty, I guess, I let slip the word, "Gaudy," before stopping myself.

Mom was still carrying me and she replied, "A bit, but this area is only used to receive important guests. They expect a certain standard of living." She lowered her voice, "The Aspwood palace is much more extravagant, and is much less overdone."

How can you do more than this *without overdoing it?*

When we arrived in front of two large doors, easily twelve foot tall, I admired the white paint and gold inlay. *This part isn't so bad.* Mom opened the door and we found everyone Dad had been carting around in front of us. Including their kids.

On seeing us everyone said, "Happy birthday!"

The hall reverberated with deep thumps sounding outside the room, and I realized with a start, *Were those cannons?*

My brother seemed equally enamored. "Wow!"

Our guests parted and two tiny thrones sat before us. Oliver hopped up into one as though it were the most natural thing in the world, and Mom placed me in the other.

This is so embarrassing! I couldn't help but cover my face for a moment until I calmed down.

"Everyone is here today because it's your birthday," Dad said. "Anessa Jean Carlyle and Oliver Sil Carlyle." He started to sing what amounted to "Happy Birthday", only in our native tongue, which I had learned was called Estar.

It brought back a memory I had on Earth of my fourth Birthday with my previous mom, Naia. My eyes filled with tears.

Crying on your birthday is awkward enough. Doing so in front of a room of nobles on your birthday is even more awkward. A few of the nobles began to chat among themselves wondering what happened.

Mom kneeled before me and asked in a quiet voice, "What's wrong honey?"

I shook my head. "Nothing, just a memory."

Mom's eyes widened in understanding. "Ah. Do you need to leave the room?"

"I'm okay. Can I tell you later?"

She smiled. "Please do."

After I wiped my eyes Mom stood up and moved away.

Mom whispered the details to Dad, based on what she said, he knew about my past life.

He simply nodded and stepped forward, he motioned to my brother. "Why don't we start with Oliver?"

Bal Blackwood urged his oldest boy forward.

"Here you go Oliver," Wyn said and presented a pair of white bracers. "These were crafted from an…" he paused and the blonde that came with Bal dipped down and whispered something to him. The boy said, "Elder Treant's wood. They should help you until you reach the Sky Realm."

Oliver took them in his hands and tried one on. He smiled. "I like this, thank you Wyn!"

The older boy moved back in line and Oliver slipped the second one over his wrist, and almost skipped back to his seat.

He really likes them.

Since our seats were next to one another, I got a good look at them. Though I tried not to ogle them since there were plenty of eyes on me. They looked like you'd expect wooden bracers to be, though the intricate pattern carved into them added a lot of appeal to them.

Another nobleman called out for Oliver and he went to receive their present. This went on for a while until someone escalated things and gave him a sword.

Before he could gleefully receive it, Dad placed his hand on Oliver's shoulder.

"Be sure not to take the sword by its handle. Accept it by the scabbard and carry it back here, slowly."

Oliver tried to move but Dad's grip was firm.

"Understood?"

The boy nodded and Dad let him go.

Once he'd returned he handed the sword immediately to Dad who placed it carefully to the side.

It wasn't until a moment passed that I realized. *Ah. Don't draw a sword in polite company. That would be awkward if he did, given everyone here are sovereigns. Good call, Dad.*

Oliver's final present was given to him by a flashy lady in a shimmering dress. It hurt my eyes to look at her silver kirtle and what seemed to be pure gold-stitched overcoat with puffy shoulders, accented with a mixed gold and silver mantle.

Ugh, she's as overdone as our home.

She presented a perfectly straight smile and offered Oliver a box. Inside was what looked like a simple rock, though others seemed to gasp when it was revealed.

Okay, a rock. I thought, then saw Dad's eyebrow was twitching and he was gripping his bicep.

"Rhinebur gifts you the heart of a Wandering Mountain."

This set a few voices chattering further until she closed the lid and handed it to Oliver. He didn't seem to understand what it was any more than I did, and bowed to her, returning to his seat. It was clear that he'd been much more excited by the sword.

Dad sighed and said to Oliver, "That's a good gift. If it grants you resonance on par with your wind element, you'll surpass me someday."

"Does the rock give you resonance?" I asked.

Dad winked at me and said, "And now onto Anessa."

Crap.

Rhis stepped forward holding a child-size lute. His face went red as a tomato when he accidentally touched my hand as he handed it over.

Oh brother, I really hope he doesn't take a fancy to me. Looking at the instrument I thought, *What am I going to do with this? I was tone-deaf on Earth.*

I returned to my seat and the next person gave me a seashell. A bloody seashell. It took all of my presence of mind to not lose my cool. The same family had given Oliver something sensible, a whetstone that had a filigree silver inlay on its box with his name on it.

The trend continued. Oliver's presents were largely militaristic in nature, whereas mine were more focused on my gender and intelligence.

The flashy lady from Rhinebur was the only one to make another splash. When I stood before her, she kneeled to me.

Aren't queens supposed to kneel for no one?

"This is from all of us," she motioned around the room and said, "I don't have a separate gift, because I covered most of this." In her hands was a box that was the size of my two fists. Inside was a gem that looked like a diamond, glimmering with all the colors of the rainbow. Something most diamonds did when you rocked them back and forth, except she wasn't moving it at all.

Wow, that's pretty.

She sat the box in my hand, but before I could touch it Dad interrupted, "We can't accept that. It's a treasure from His Imperial Majesty's vault!"

The queen before me said, "Please let us do this. His Imperial Majesty agreed to our terms."

Hearing her words I took the gem in my hand, delighted by its sparkle, and Dad yelled, "Anessa!"

His sudden alarm made me bobble it in the air, to a collective series of gasps. I was able to catch it at the last second and place it back inside the box.

However, before I could close the box and breathe a sigh of relief, the stone crumbled to dust, leaving the container empty.

CHAPTER FOURTEEN
A PUZZLE OF LIFE

A LOW MURMUR broke out among the adults and I returned to my place next to Oliver, cheeks burning. Bits of surprise and disbelief caught my ear about the reason the stone disappeared. I didn't know what had happened, but I was pretty sure that a royal treasure disappearing into dust wasn't good.

Oliver said, while kicking his feet, "What's next Daddy?"

Dad said, "You two are free to leave now, but be sure to thank everyone personally for their gifts first."

Oliver and I did as he asked. It was especially awkward with the queen of Rhinebur. She had what seemed like a false smile on her face. Perhaps it was me.

"I'm going to my room to polish my sword," Oliver said.

He really shouldn't say that to his sister, I thought, but decided not to say anything right now. *I guess he is only two-Standard-years-old. I doubt he even knows why that sounds odd.*

Julilah caught me before I was able to escape the room of adults idly talking to one another. "Anessa, I have someone who wanted to meet you."

"Okay."

"Gray, meet Anessa," she said as we arrived in front of an ancient woman. She was the oldest person I'd ever seen. The wrinkles cascading down her face made Sir Orris look like a spring chicken.

"Ah, what a cute little dearie," she said, arching her eyebrow up, like an enormous grizzled caterpillar.

"How do you do. I am Anessa Jean Carlyle. Why was it you wanted to see me?"

She pulled a small scroll from her sleeve. "I've been told you don't know your Genesis Number. A most unusual thing."

Oh, and just who told her? My eyes went to Julilah who smiled innocently. *Seriously, this is suspicious.*

"This is an Art specially made to reveal someone's Genesis Number." She brandished a needle. "All it needs is a drop of blood."

Taking a step back I thought, *Isn't this how every fairy tale ever ended with the girl in a coma, or straight-up dead?*

"It won't hurt, it's just a little prick." She reached for my wrist at a speed that belied her age.

Before she could touch the tip of my finger, Fan piped up, "Wait." She took the needle from Gray and added, "Sadly, if anyone is to do this, it should be a staff member, at the very least." Without much fanfare, she obtained what Gray needed, and handed it over.

"Thank you." With a little tap, the droplet of blood vanished into the paper, making the scrawlings on it momentarily ripple across the page. A second later the page burst into flames.

"I knew it!" Julilah said with a grim smile, and my stomach churned.

"Knew what, exactly?" Mom said from behind us. "What's going on here?"

Before I could say anything, Julilah said, "She has a genesis number of zero. Anessa will inherit nothing!"

That's her play? What the hell woman!

Gray coughed. "Sorry to disappoint you, but you are wrong."

"Excuse you?" Julilah replied, in words that came out as almost a growl.

"If it were zero, the page's edges would have frayed but it would've stayed in one piece. If it were one, the paper would have burned away to the writing. For it to vanish entirely..." She shrugged and a smile crept across her face. "That means she has no number. No limit on her future kin."

"Either way," Mom said, "You and I need to talk. Who is this old crone—"

"That was uncalled for," Gray interrupted and pulled out a black bar from her robe and dropped it, to Julilah's shock. "You can have this back." She gave me a curt bow and said, "It's not every day I get to test someone without a number." Sliding the bar toward Julilah with her foot, she added, "I won't be needing this payment. Meeting someone of such rarity is a treat in itself."

Looking at the little black thing that Gray dropped, Mom's eyes widened. Before she could lay into Julilah once again, Kristine stepped between them. "Now is not the time Lily," she murmured.

Fan took my hand and ushered me away from the women.

Kristine continued, "It is Anessa's first Anfang birthday, truly a special day." She looked around them and Mom noticed there were a few onlookers, "Please leave this for later."

Before I could even come to grips with the argument those two were about to get into behind closed doors, I heard Fan say in a cross tone, "That sly old woman."

"What?" I asked.

"I switched the needle she was using because I worried for your safety, and slipped it into my cuff, but it's gone." Fan was looking at her unfastened sleeve. "When did she take it?"

I stared. "What were you worried about?"

"Um," She paused. "Never mind that for now. Why don't you go find Oliver, or play with some of the other kids?"

"You mean the same kids that tried to look under your skirt?"

Fan's mouth dropped and she shook her head. "Not them. There were about five to ten girls around your age or a bit older that are playing with Lana in the great room."

Her words made me sigh. "Okay. I'll go and try to play with the little kids."

"Don't put it like that. That's why you don't have any friends—" She covered her mouth as though she'd spoken a cardinal sin. "Sorry," she said and bowed deeply.

Her words made me realize she was right. "No offense taken. I don't actually have any friends." I smiled. "Maybe one of them will have something interesting to talk about. Maybe they can tell me about those 'Awakening' Ceremonies everyone's been hinting at but never speaking of."

Fan gave a nervous laugh. "Yeah, maybe."

Oof. Nice way of hinting "fat chance".

Picture nine children going wild in a room filled with fragile, valuable objects. That was the sight before me. Lana was frantically running around trying to prevent anything from being broken.

At Fan's request I tried approaching one of the tamer girls in the group and said, "Hello."

She looked up at me and nodded, then went back to staring off into space.

Okay, this one's a nutter.

I went to another girl who seemed to be more interested in standing on her head than anything going on around her. My guess was she did this often as she wore a pair of shorts along with the dress she was flipping up for all to see by being inverted.

"Want to join me?" she asked in a playful tone.

"Ah, I was hoping to just talk. I don't have any shorts on, it might be a bit embarrassing." I instinctually held down my dress, though I wasn't sure why.

"Suit yourself," She flipped up onto her feet and moved to some other location to repeat the process. It seemed not joining her meant that I was not welcome.

Kids my age are weird, I thought, after helping Lana corral a few of them and trying to talk to them while doing so.

After we'd managed to get them all settled down to eat a snack, which I didn't mind sharing with them, I decided the best person to talk to was my half-sister. At a whisper, I said, "These girls are a handful!"

"You're telling me!" she said, a bit above a whisper, making all eyes focus on her. She exhaled with her eyes closed and then turned back to me. "Once everyone was done with giving out your gifts, Mama found me and said, 'Take care of them.'" Patting the floor with her hands she added, "Then just walked off, like that was all I needed!"

Her flummoxed state made me giggle a little. "Weren't you looking forward to getting married earlier?"

Her face erupted into a rosy red. "What's that got to do with these kids?"

"What usually happens after you get married?" I asked.

Instead of replying, her ears and chest joined her face in an amusing display of embarrassment. "T-that's not something you should be talking about!"

Oh, she might be thinking about something other than kids, I thought, then said, "Maybe not. But how many kids might you have in the future. What is your Genesis Number?"

Lana pretended to swallow something and kept her eyes closed for a few minutes. Her full-on blush faded and I admired her ability to control that so well. "Seven," she admitted, looking across the children in front of us. "Though after today," she sighed, "I'm not so sure I want to go for that many."

"I can imagine having seven of your own would be hectic," I agreed. A few of the girls had taken Lana's offer of a nap and were already asleep after their tiny snack. "Though they probably wouldn't all be this age at the same time, unless you had septuplets."

"Thank the heavens for small mercies."

"Speaking of the number, what's it mean to not have one?"

Wrinkling her brow, she asked, "What do you mean? Do you mean about earlier, when you said you couldn't remember yours?" She shook her head. "You most certainly do have one. Everyone does. It's uncommon to not remember it, but there are ways to find it out."

When I told her what had happened with Gray, Lana's face became crestfallen and she looked away from me.

"What's wrong?" I asked.

"Sorry. I may have told Mama about you not remembering your number." She looked my way for a brief second and turned away. "It seems that may have been a mistake."

Seeing she was bothered by it, I put my hand on her knee. We were both currently sitting and watching the other children. "Don't apologize. You didn't do anything wrong."

Lana put her hand on mine. "Thanks. But it was unkind of me to speak of such a thing carelessly. Based on how Lily reacted…" She trailed off and didn't finish her thought.

"It's okay. Really. I'll talk to mommy. I don't think she'll be mad at you."

Lana gave me a weak smile. "Thanks, I'd appreciate that. Sorry Mama caused you trouble."

Standing I lamented that her eye line was above the top of my head still. "Again, don't worry." I gave her a hug. "After all, I learned something important about myself today."

A thud came from the acrobatic girl. She'd apparently fallen asleep while doing a headstand. She was currently clutching the bedding we had put out for her.

The sight made Lana laugh and she returned my hug. "Thanks sis."

It was the first time she'd called me that, and a warm fuzzy sensation spread through my chest. Instead of returning her sentiment, I redoubled my hug.

"No Genesis Number. How many kids will you have in the future?"

I barked a laugh. "Like I'm thinking about that right now."

A soft knock came from the door, and Lana called softly for them to enter.

It was one of the sovereigns. They saw most of the girls were asleep and quietly picked up their own little princess and left. Over the next thirty minutes this process repeated itself. When the girl who preferred to be inverted was picked up, I was shocked. Her mother was a petite woman with a grace and poise that rivaled my own Mom's.

When it was just the two of us, Lana asked, "Did you get anything good?"

In telling her about the stone that turned to dust, she covered her mouth. "Goodness. Since Dad was so grumpy, I imagine it was priceless."

Her words hit me like a freight train. "Oof, thanks." *I'm sure I'll learn exactly how valuable that thing was. And I'm not sure I want to.*

CHAPTER FIFTEEN

PARADOX OF OTHERNESS AND BELONGING

UPON RETURNING TO our bedroom, I found Oliver sitting on the side polishing the sword he received during our gift giving ceremony. He seemed entirely familiar with the task, as though it was just any other day. I began to suspect that some of his training with Dad had involved swords.

"Do you like your new sword?" I asked.

"Yes. Rufus is a great sword. We really get along."

Really? Rufus? That's different.

Seeing as he was focused, I decided to go through the things that I'd received. Someone had already dropped them off in our room.

I picked up a small tome with an ornate binding. "My first breathing technique," the book's cover read. *Interesting that they'd phrase it that way, as though it's made for children.* Inside the book was a diagram of someone, once again, sitting in the lotus position. The method depicted in the book was very similar to what I'd already been doing. Though, there were a few key differences, and the language was a little simpler. It was still much closer to that of a college textbook than Dr. Seuss. Knowing that it would take some time to go through, I set it to the side.

"Oliver," I said, since he seemed to be focused on Rufus.

"Hm?"

"Are you interested in any of these books I received?"

He shook his head. "I can't read, sissy."

"Would you like me to help you learn?"

Shrugging he replied, "I guess. What's the point, though? Will it help me hit better?"

I sighed at his disinterest in basic knowledge. "It might. One of them is a breathing technique that's supposed to help you understand how to cycle essence. I'm not sure exactly what makes you so strong, but I'm pretty sure it has something to do with some kind of essence, or other."

He sat Rufus down. "Maybe. It might be useful if it helps me finally land a hit on Daddy."

You want *to hit Dad?*

"You know, Daddy also told us to show an interest in one another's specialties. We never know when it might come in handy. We're twins, you know?"

Oliver smiled. "Yeah, good point. I'll always protect you though."

"Thanks. So you named your sword Rufus?"

His mouth dropped and he covered "Rufus" as though my words had offended it. "No I didn't." Pointing to the sword he said, "He told me his name!"

Right. Walking over to the steel, I tried to pick it up, to no avail. "I can barely lift part of this up. No way I can wield it."

With a smile Oliver said, "Rufus said you aren't worthy."

"Really?" Oliver's rejection made me try harder, and I was just barely able to lift it before I started to lose my breath, I managed to get out "This is… heavier than a normal sword… isn't it?"

"A little I guess, though it's hard to tell the difference between ten and a hundred pounds."

His lackadaisical way of insulting my strength made me drop the sword back onto the shelf he had it on.

"So heavy," I said while bowled over.

"Don't drop him like that!" He picked "Rufus" up and turned it over. "Look, you scuffed him!" He went on to polish and buff the sword once more. "Sorry, Rufus, she meant no harm. She can't help it she's weak."

My right eyebrow twitched at his commentary. "Yeah, sorry for being weak." I moved back over to my own couch and sat down in a huff. *His ability to reason has improved, and I'm starting to fear he'll be smarter than me one day. Is it because of a past life, or because I have talked to him daily for the past two years? It's also possible he remembers his past life, like I do, though he's never talked about it. I'm sure he would've said something by now… right?*

Remembering Julilah's gaze when I was said to have no genesis number made me shiver. *She's scarier than I thought. When she thought I had no genesis number, she seemed pleased. Why would she want me to inherit nothing, anyway?*

"Oliver, did you get the impression that we're important at our party?"

"We are important," he said without even looking at me.

"Yes, but we were surrounded by kings and queens. Yet they showed us deference. Isn't that odd?"

He smiled. "Then we must be *really* important."

Yes, I guess so. Returning my eyes to Rufus, I noticed the sword was in fact quite well made. A golden pommel fixed with a chain and a tassel without a single thread out of place. A red ruby on the guard was especially striking as it was the size of my thumb. Admittedly, my fingers were small.

Though Oliver said I'd scuffed the blade, it only took a simple wipe on its surface and it was pristine again. The edge was scary sharp on both sides; it was closer to a medieval Europe weapon than a katana or Asian-styled sword. *I'm silly, always comparing everything to Earth. There isn't even an Asia here. Or a Europe, for that matter.*

Returning to the breathing technique, I skimmed through it. The book itself was leather-bound, and barely thirty pages in length. The pages were some kind of velvety parchment, thick and soft animal skins treated carefully to make this exquisite book. It definitely drove home that books were far more expensive than the mass-market paperbacks of my past life.

This had to take forever to make. The binding itself was done in some kind of thick string. There wasn't any gold or silver in the binding; however, the letters on the front were gilded. The spine was too thin to have letter work on it, or that was my guess, as it was blank.

I've been so spoiled, in how easy things were in the past, as well as how cozy things are on Anfang. I can't imagine what it would be like to live the life of a commoner. The family crest Oliver wore earlier was reminiscent of a baronet. Are we from an imperial baronet? That doesn't really make sense, though. The Imperial Baronet, or Cherry Kingdom's Royal Family has a very well-known crest, known for its unusual depiction of two cherries. Perhaps it's just my Earthen sensibilities that make me think its a bit... perverse?

Realizing there was nothing I could do about it, I dug into the breathing technique for real. It was short, but densely packed with information. Essence apparently enters the body through tiny pores, smaller than your sweat glands. This made it seem more like some kind of physical element than a magical energy.

One's nexus is an organ that influences essence directly. The more in tune you are to a given aspect, the more readily your nexus can pull in that element.

The book presented a man who is a fire elemental user. When he pulled in fire essence, he also dragged along in every other kind of essence. To bolster his fire reserves, he had to purge the other elements from his system.

Someone without a specific affinity is less likely to manipulate the elements and would need to purge *all* non-neutral essence, which is a challenging task. He's shown struggling with the task as a black tar-like substance leaves his body. These are the impurities that he is unable to affect. Being unable to properly harness them causes them to congeal into a physical form.

A warning is presented at the bottom of the page, that reads: "Those who do not cleanse the impurities properly once they are expelled may find themselves with an outbreak of miasma."

Whoa, so miasma comes from cultivators?

Another note is beneath this one, penned in a different handwriting, "The high goddess of craft has seen to it miasma is no longer."

High goddess of craft? Wasn't Eloria called that once?

The front of the book showed it was published in 7622 CL. *I'm not sure what CL means. Our calendars don't have any suffix on the dates. Does that mean this book is nearly ten-thousand-Anfang-years-old?!* I ran my finger along the spine and noticed it was pristine. *Surely it's a reprint.* I didn't know much about old books, but I was pretty sure that on Earth, anything even a few centuries old would look a lot more worn than this.

"Crap," I said aloud after reading further.

"What?" Oliver asked and raised a brow.

"I can't use this book yet."

He looked at it. "Is it," he poked the book's edge, "broken?"

His odd comment made me chuckle. "No. I need to have dantians to use these techniques." I pointed to the depiction of the prior man who had a dantian in his midsection. "This note here," I traced a line from his dantian, "says that you need to have a dantian to make use of a breathing technique."

Oliver nodded. "That sounds right. Daddy said I have really good essence retention. I can only access wind, fire and nootral essence, though."

"Neutral."

"What?"

Smiling I repeated, "Neutral, not nootral."

"Whatever." He waved his hand. "My wind is better than my fire. Daddy's upset that sunsor guy missed it."

I started to correct him and say, "sensor," but I decided against it. Oliver didn't mind me helping him with pronunciation every now and then, but if I made a habit of it he'd blast me in the face, gently, with wind and walk off.

"I'm just glad that Mama-Krissi is allowing me to know about cultivation now. Before she wouldn't even talk about it."

"It's so confusing though," Oliver said and hung his arms. "All this talk of the Steps you have to go through for each Realm." He held his head. "It makes my head hurt. I didn't need to do any of that, it just sort of happened."

Giving him a light growl I said, "Don't rub it in."

"Sorry sissy. It's just difficult." He smiled. "I'm starting to make some progress though."

"Yeah, congratulations on entering the Sky Realm."

He stood and stomped his foot playfully. "Hey! Who told you?"

"No one."

"So what, you noticed on your own?" He crossed his arms. "I don't believe you. Daddy has been trying to teach me how to sense others, and I still can't do it. How could you?"

Tilting my head I asked, "What are you talking about? It was your fight with Wyn."

"I didn't do anything that should have given it away!"

"He ran into you and you didn't move, at all. Then your feet glided across the ground, and you didn't make any footprints."

Oliver picked me up and spun me around, totally catching me by surprise. "I'm so excited!"

"About what?" He'd spun me at least eight times and it was making me a bit nauseous. "Put me down."

He obliged. "It's just that if you figured it out from that little information, you're going to be a good cultivator in the future. Maybe even better than me!" He furrowed his brows. "Not that I really know why people keep telling me that I'll be a good cultivator."

"Oliver," I said, sitting down to help my balance.

"Yeah?"

"Mama-Krissi said that most people don't enter the Sky Realm until they're a hundred-Anfang-years-old. That's *two hundred* Standard years. You're only one-Anfang-year-old. You're advancing a hundred times faster than normal."

"Oh." He beamed at me. "I'm pretty awesome then, huh?"

His lack of modesty was amusing, but his smile was infectious.

"Still think I'll be a better cultivator than you?"

"Oh, I didn't mean as strong." He waved his hand dismissively.

The bluntness of his words hit me hard and I closed my eyes a moment to avoid getting annoyed with him. I reluctantly laughed at myself.

He continued, "But daddy says that sometimes you don't need to be strong to be good. He said his master is an entire Realm below him, but he still can't beat him."

That is interesting.

Oliver's attention focused elsewhere. "I'm going to go outside and chop some wood with Rufus."

"Have fun." I would've told him it's not a good idea to chop wood with a sword, but I figured his brute strength would overcome that issue, and I was willing to bet that Rufus was up for the challenge. "Thanks, Oliver."

"For what?"

"Talking, I don't feel so bad about the gifts now."

"Yeah they were kind of lame."

Ouch.

CHAPTER SIXTEEN

THE WEIGHT OF REMEMBRANCE

A FEW DAYS later I dreamed of Earth. My prom night. I'd been stood up by the guy I was dating at the time, so Trish agreed to go with me and we planned to make a night of it. We joked that we'd end up watching a sappy movie and griping about... whatever his name was.

On the dance floor, I remember the music went to a slow dance. Trish took my hand and said, "I'll lead."

"You know I'm not good with this sort of thing," I warned her. "Remember last year when I fell down on my face in front of everyone?"

She put her arm around my back and said, "That's okay. These are steel-toed heels."

I looked down to check and she snickered in my ear.

"You actually believed me." The humor in her voice, hints of musk and spicy notes made her perfume intoxicating.

It forced me to pull away a bit. *Trish is always here for you; it's not like that.*

She pushed my bangs out of my eyes. "You're so much taller than I am. If either of us were the guy here, it's you."

"I'm no guy, I can tell you that."

The music slowed further and she put her head on my shoulder making me blush a little. Looking around, I saw that no one was really looking at us and they were enjoying their own private moments. *Get with it Anessa, it's only awkward if you make it that way.*

She pulled away from me and I looked into her magical brown eyes, shining in the low lights above. Her lips, usually painted in goth black, were a glistening soft peach tonight. My hand cupped her cheek and she closed her eyes. I pulled in and…

Shooting up in bed my hand went to my mouth. *What the hell was that!* I remembered our dance that night perfectly well; we never kissed and I never put my hand against her cheek. *Why would I romanticize her like that?*

My tiny fingertips played over my lips and my face heated up. *Gods, that was too real. Did I want that to happen?*

An image of a knife's edge streaked through my mind's eye and I held my head. *This makes no sense. What am I doing? The memory of what happened after I was put in the van is so vivid, yet… I miss her.*

I fell back into my crib. Seeing the bars around me made me laugh and cry. *Am I a prisoner to those thoughts?* Pushing it out of my mind, I turned to the side and cried quietly. *I know I didn't kiss Trish, just as I'm certain that in my final moments she didn't do that to me.*

As I fell asleep, my dream, somewhat unusually, repeated itself. This time I didn't fight it, desperately curious as to where it would go after. When our lips separated, the "me" in my dream longed for more. Then she spoke.

"You know I would never hurt you, right?"

I nodded to the woman I knew I'd never meet again.

"I just want you to remember that, I won't and would never hurt you."

Stopping to let my head touch hers, I said, "I know."

She faded from my view, as did everyone else. It was a reminder that the dream wasn't real. My mind shifted to a concert Trish told me she'd attended, except the thump of the bass, the jostling of the crowd around me, and the mesmerizing rhythmic beat weren't that of an experience told second hand. It was as though I was really there.

This was odd. My nails were painted as Trish usually did them and her skull necklace was around my neck, but I was at least a head taller than all the other girls, so I was definitely myself. I wasn't sure what was going on in this dream, but I lost myself in the experience.

After the song finished and the band spoke about the next song, their voices faded away.

"Are you listening?!" an angry voice said.

It was a jarring shift and my eyes went to the source. Trish's mother, though I couldn't remember her name.

"What were you thinking smoking this shit?" She presented a glass pipe with a blackened bottom and some residue in it.

"It's none of your business!" I said, completely out of my control. *This never happened to me, though I think I remember this – Trish said she covered for one of her friends once who had gotten in with the wrong crowd. But the voice is mine. This is strange.*

"It sometimes only takes one hit of ice to kill you if they lace it with something stronger."

"Look, it won't happen again," I said sternly.

Trish's mom said, "You're damn right it won't. You're grounded, effective immediately." She took "my" purse and rummaged through it, taking my phone. "You're not allowed to talk to any of your damn friends."

Moments passed in awkward silence. A banging came at the door, a voice said it was the police.

"Fuck," she said. "They better not find this. If I go to jail because of your screw up, so help me." I tried to leave and she grabbed my wrist. "Later I expect you to tell me their name."

"Whose?" I stared blankly.

She said angrily, "The person who gave you this shit."

That night, I relived no fewer than ten different things that Trish had told me. Except I was her and me at the same time. Waking up the next day as myself again was surreal.

Sitting in my crib I said to Oliver, who was smiling at me. "I have some things to work through, from before I met you."

Family wasn't something I was big on before. Mostly because I'd been alone for as long as I could remember. There was Julie, the minder assigned to me by the state AI, but she saw me more as a paycheck than a person – she wasn't someone I could rely on in an emotional crisis. Lacking a family was something I wanted to change.

"Mommy," I said as she was walking with me to our bedroom. "I had a weird dream last night. Can we talk about it?"

She knitted her brows and picked me up. "Sure. Hang on a moment, though." Calling across the room she said, "Kristine." The concern must've shown on my face because she said, "It's fine, she knows. But it's just her, daddy and me."

Kristine followed us toward our room. "What is wrong, Lily?"

"Can we talk about…" Mom paused and looked around. "*That* real quick? She has a few questions and I'm afraid I won't have any answers for her."

Kristine nodded in understanding. "Of course. Let me get one of the devices from my room so we have some privacy."

We waited in the hall for a minute or so, and she returned with an odd yellow cube in her hand. "I have it." When we entered our room she sat it on the small table in the middle of the room, then pressed down on its center. A line of white lit up around its perimeter. "Done. No one will be able to hear us." Her eyes went to me. "What happened?"

After explaining the odd dream, although I may have left out kissing my best friend, I asked, "Is it possible that what I remember, and what actually happened, are wrong?"

"I am not really following your dream of your friend with your final moments. Do you mind sharing what you remember?"

Nodding, I recounted what I remembered. The words came surprisingly easily.

After getting about half-way, I found Kristine was shaking me gently. "Anessa."

"What?"

"Stop honey. You do not have to say anymore. I am so sorry to have asked that of you."

Looking at Mom, I saw she had her hand over her mouth and was trying not to cry.

"That's weird," I said. "I told you everything as I remember it, but I don't really recall what exactly I said."

Kristine sighed and hugged me. "Child. Death and rebirth are complicated." She shook her head. "Do not try and recall that again for a while." Her eyes darted to the side, as though she was recalling something. "Sometimes what happened to you is imprinted and is so strong, that those you long for get all jumbled up with your memories."

"So it's possible that Trish didn't hurt me?"

Giving me a weak smile she said, "Does it feel right?"

"What?"

"Do you really feel that your friend hurt you?" She tapped my chest over my heart, and added, "Here?"

Shaking my head I said, "Absolutely not. I miss her terribly."

"Then you have your answer. I believe that it is exactly what it seems: a bad dream. When you feel the time is right, talk about those final moments with others. Those you care about. And remember."

I'd looked down while thinking about her words. She paused and I met her gaze.

"You are Anessa Carlyle now. That girl, the one who met that terrible fate?" She put her finger underneath my chin and smiled. "That is not you. Always remember that you have people here who love you and will care for you. Who will be there for you."

She kissed the top of my head. "And it is okay to cry."

"I'm not crying," I protested. Deflecting a little I added, "You're crying."

"We're all crying right now," Mom agreed and sat next to me. She pulled me into her lap and hugged me from behind. "I'll always be your mommy, remember that. If you have nightmares, or question the meaning behind something, you can come to me."

It was embarrassing, but I kept affirming her words and hugged her arms. Knowing that, for even a moment, I had believed Trish could have done that to me, hurt deeply.

Mom's necklace hit my cheek and I saw a charm in the shape of a hammer.

"What's that?" I asked.

"It's the hierogram of the goddess I cherish," she said quietly.

"Which goddess?"

She tightened her grip on me, and Kristine stood to leave.

Mom whispered into my ear, "Eloria."

There was something about the name that always tugged at my interest. Knowing that she was the goddess of death made me a little worried, though. "Wasn't she the goddess of craft at one point?" I asked.

Mom took off her necklace and held it in front of me. "That's right. This amulet is from that time period. It's been passed down through our family." She turned her hand over as though she wanted to put it in my hand.

I held my hand out.

"One day I'll pass this down to you." She paused and tickled my sides, eliciting a laugh. "Probably on your first wedding day."

"I look forward to it," I said, looking up at her. "Though I cannot guarantee there'll be a second wedding. It's still weird to me."

"That's okay." She lifted me and sat me on my own chair. "You'll have a long life. It's possible your views will change over the years. Just make sure you live your life well and are satisfied with the decisions you make." She tapped my nose. "That's what's important."

CHAPTER SEVENTEEN

FAMILY TIES / HIDDEN TRUTHS

MY TALK WITH Mom and Kristine made me more hopeful for the future. Though I wasn't keen on having more than one husband, or as my mom teased before I left her, a wife, I briefly wondered what it might have been like to have Trish by my side, forever.

"Let's see," I said aloud. I stood in the hallway outside my room and tried to visualize where Veronica's room was. Usually I had a maid with me everywhere I went as a guide, but I thought I'd try to find it myself today.

It took me two hours.

I'd finally entered her room and almost spoken before I saw her diligently applying that odd blue makeup. No, I was wrong, the blue stuff had already dried. She was applying the next layer on top of that, the twin five-point stars on each cheek.

Her eyes caught me in the mirror. She smiled. "Oh, hello." Turning to me, she asked, "What brings you here?"

"I just wanted to talk to you and see how you were doing."

Her words were hesitant. "I'm fine. Just getting used to applying this makeup. It's complicated and annoying."

"Who are you to marry, anyway?" I asked.

She sat down her brush. "You're too observant." She shot a look at the door, and I got the hint. Once it was closed she said, "The Emperor of Redwater."

"Emperor?!" I shouted.

She held her finger over her mouth. "Shh!"

"Sorry."

"It's okay, but since it isn't 'official,'" she rolled her eyes on that final word. "I'm not supposed to talk about it."

"Have you even met him?" I wondered.

Veronica had picked up her brush again and sat it immediately back down. "No." She began to fidget with her hands while facing me. "I'm worried about it. What if he's mean? I've heard some rumors."

"Then don't marry him," I said flatly.

She gave a half-hearted chuckle. "It isn't that simple. Mama-Lily helped us set it up before…" Placing her hand over her mouth she said, "Never mind. Needless to say, my opinion isn't a consideration. And it won't be unless I awaken next year."

My mind naturally filled in "Anfang year." It was odd; whenever talking about age, people were clear to specify which calendar they were referring to, but when it came to saying next or prior year, they always meant the Anfang calendar.

"You will." I hopped off her bed and placed my hand on hers. "I know it."

She looked at me without saying a word and brought me into a hug. "Though I know it's just wishful thinking, thank you." After letting me go she turned back to her task. Once she'd completed her simple outline, she started to fill it in and thicken it.

"That Genesis Number stuff is weird," I said.

"You're probably the only person who would think that."

Her words made me worry that Kristine had let it slip to her that I'd been reborn.

"Not having one, and all."

I released the breath I was holding.

"What're you doing?" Oliver's voice came from outside the room, and he opened the door.

My response may have been a bit curt, "We're talking."

"Okay. I was going to ask if you wanted to practice with Rufus." When he saw me not move from my seat he continued, "I guess not." He started to close the door behind him and he paused. "Will I have to wear that makeup when I get married?"

I waited for Veronica to respond.

"No, it's a girls only thing. Although maybe for you…" She shook her head at his obvious alarm. "Just kidding, you won't have to wear it."

Oliver left us, obvious relief on his face, and Veronica asked, "You two have a fight?"

"No, why?"

"No reason." She turned to me having finished the two stars. "You know you will have to wear this makeup, right?"

"Really?" I said. "There don't seem to be strong gender roles on Anfang."

She raised an eyebrow. "That is an odd way to put it. 'On Anfang.' I mean."

"So tell me about the makeup," I said, changing the subject away from my slip of the tongue.

"There's not much to say, that I'm aware of. When I was told that I'm to marry His Imperial Majesty, On-pa gave me a basic rundown of what was expected of the makeup."

"Didn't you ask her any questions?"

Veronica grinned. "Tell me. How well does questioning my on-pa usually go?"

An image of Julilah's scowl entered my head, and I held up my hands in defeat. "Good point."

Actually I might be wrong. Dad hasn't ever worn a dress, at least as far as I am aware. I guess there are gender roles here, I just haven't noticed them as much given how different relationships are. Something to look into later, I guess.

"So…" Veronica said, drawing it out. "Would you like to try on the makeup yourself?"

Hmm… What the hell. I said, "Sure!"

She sat me on her stool and spun me around.

In front of me there were no fewer than fifteen jars of who knew what. Some were unopened. The largest of them was the blue goop that she had put all over her face.

Veronica took what looked like a spatula and scooped a lot of it out, then she paused, putting half of it back. "Your face is a bit smaller than mine."

It was cool, but not cold, as she placed it against my skin. In one stroke she covered my entire left cheek; then she lifted the spreader up and moved to the other side of my face. It took her no more than three minutes to cover it in full. Once she was satisfied with it, she moved to my chin and neck, stopping at my collar bone.

Seeing the mask of a bride in the mirror, I wondered, *Will I find someone in the future?* Trish's image came to mind. *Will it be a girl or a boy?*

Veronica stopped and picked up a small brush, dabbing it with the tiniest amount of gold fleck. She tapped it against my forehead and the deep blue changed before my eyes, like it had done for her.

Gripping my dress I held as still as I could. I'll be honest: it itched like hell. Something about the rapid drying made it lighten a few shades, but that same process was nigh-unbearable to handle.

"Nice. The first five times Lana put it on me I scratched it off immediately."

"It sucked!" I seethed. "It felt like my skin was trying to peel off."

She sighed. "I know, it's irritating."

"Yet we all bear it," a deeper woman's voice noted, making me seize up.

"Hi Mama-J," I said. *Please be nice to me. I'm not even sure what I did to you.* Our first encounter reminded me she had a nicer side sometimes.

"You haven't added her resonant paint yet." Julilah sat next to me on a stool, displacing Veronica, who immediately gave way. "How many elements do you have at your disposal?"

"S—" I stopped myself. "Ten."

I knew that was a very unusual number, but Julilah did little more than raise an eyebrow and she moved on. "With no Genesis Number, you aren't limited to a symmetric pattern, like Veronica is."

She picked up a thin brush and started to paint in black. It was a complicated pattern I'd have to study for an hour just to appreciate. "Turn." I complied and she continued on my other cheek. The patterns were similar, but were not exactly mirrors of one another.

Once she was done with the black, she opened a can of emerald green and traced the exterior of the pattern on both sides. She continued with the remaining nine colors.

Julilah didn't trace every single bit of black in every color. I couldn't be sure, but it seemed as though she let her instincts guide her. From the corner of my eye, I was relieved to see that she wasn't doing anything rude on my face. Finally setting down the brush, she turned me toward the mirror.

I was reluctant to admit it, but she had done a beautiful job. She may be gruff toward me and not want me to inherit anything from the family, but she was an artist.

"Wow," Veronica said in a whisper. "That's so pretty."

"A woman's bridal mask is her message to the world what kind of woman she is," Julilah started. "If you do have access to all ten elements, the message you send should be powerful. "Choose a pattern that speaks to you. What I've done here isn't much; it's just an example. It took me six months to decide on my own mask. Since I am not a cultivator, it was much less vibrant." She smiled, as if remembering. "Roland said none of that mattered."

Her smile vanished and she once again glared at me. Then, without saying another word, she abruptly left the room.

When I couldn't hear her footsteps anymore, I asked Veronica plaintively, "Why doesn't she like me?"

"I have no idea," Veronica said. "You're adorable, and like Oliver, your future is bright."

Hopping off the stool I asked her, "As long as I awaken as a cultivator, you mean?"

She nodded. "Exactly." Resuming her efforts she tapped the black makeup with the same tiny golden brush. "That applies to both of us. If I am not so lucky," she sighed, and tapped an unopened tin the size of the blue mask container. "I'll be using a white-colored base, instead of the blue."

"Can I call you big sis?" I asked.

Her reply was swift and succinct. "No."

"Why?" I asked, startled.

Veronica had started to remove the makeup after penciling a copy of the star on her cheek in a book in front of her. My question made her stop.

"Tell me, if we were told to marry tomorrow, what would you do?"

Her question baffled me. "That is a weird question. Why would you ask that?"

"Exactly."

"That doesn't help me understand you."

"If you view me as a sister, it will make such a future impossible. We don't always have a choice about who we marry. If, for instance, you were to join my family as my wife, or as my future husband's wife or concubine, it could be awkward."

Her words were baffling. "It's already awkward!"

"Sorry. But since I'm not related to you by blood, you shouldn't think of me as a sister." She put her finger to her bottom lip. "If we were a commoner family, your views might be more normal, but things get complicated with noble families." She turned back toward the mirror and I caught a brief frown flicker across her face.

I eyed Veronica and she looked away. "Is there something you aren't telling me?"

"N-no." She coughed. "Nothing I can tell you."

Waving her off, I said, "Fine, fine. I'm used to not being told stuff by now."

She smiled. "Thanks for not pushing."

A brief image of me kissing Trish flashed in my head, followed by an awkward as hell image of me kissing Veronica, though I was a little kid now, so it was really cringe. I tried to wave away the image, leading her to look at me oddly.

Better you don't know, I thought.

CHAPTER EIGHTEEN

SCRIPTURES OF AWAKENINGS

Finday, Mankae 23rd, 1734
[November 12th, 2026]

CHURCH IS OFTEN a loathsome affair for nonbelievers. For the rest, though, it's a place to connect with the divine.

"Ugh, this stinks," Oliver said while picking at his two-layer jabot. It was a large neckpiece with an inordinate number of frills. He wore an equally frilly navy jacket over his pleated shirt. "Daddy said I have to sit still for a long time."

I said, "I'm excited."

"Why?" He tugged at the hems of his shorts.

I remembered my time on Earth when I was forced to go to church by Julie. "If gods and goddesses are real, then there might be something to church."

"Of course gods and goddesses are real," he said with a snort. "Right?"

His trusting nature made me smile. "We'll see, I guess. Aren't you curious about the church itself? I just hope it isn't stuffy."

"These clothes are stuffy!" he scowled.

"Please try to behave." I helped straighten his silken cravat, which was tied in a bow, then affixed the crested button in its center once it was in place. "Remember if you're bad, I get in trouble too."

He groaned. "Yeah, yeah."

"Let us go, you two," Kristine said.

We both bolted in front of her and down the hall. Thankfully we didn't meet Yllia along the way, because she would've griped at us for running indoors.

Our carriage was the Anfang equivalent of a Rolls-Royce. Adorned much like many parts of our house, with gilded accents over a glossy black sheen. Each of the matte white wheels was carved with horses or other animals, with a rounded red spike in the center for its axle. How they kept the wheels clean was beyond me.

"Settle down, you are not going to run ahead of the carriage." She hoisted me into the carriage, while Oliver had already jumped inside and was eagerly kicking his feet back and forth.

Julilah sat opposite us, looking out the window. Marcus and Lom were on her side. Each of them was strapped into a car seat, of sorts. Neither one knew how to say a single word. A stark contrast to Oliver and me, at their age of fourteen months.

The carriage lurched forward. Unfortunately for me, I was forced to sit in a blasted car seat like my two younger siblings. Oliver was exempt because he was big enough. Never mind that he was sturdier than even Julilah.

It was an entire hour to ride to the church. I'd nodded off on the way there, and Kristine woke me by removing my harness. Oliver and the other two kids were already out of the carriage and on their way into the massive building that sat outside our carriage.

It was easily four stories tall, eight if you counted the bell tower. It was reminiscent of Gothic architecture on Earth.

Two massive doors, each roughly twenty feet tall and eight feet wide, were open and letting people in. We didn't enter there however. The cobblestone path directly in front of the church was a muddied mess. There were stanchions leading up to the doors.

We approached the church from the other side, crossing a nice clean flagstone path to a bold red door that led straight to stairs.

Julilah was carrying the two younger boys in her arms, one on either side of her hips.

All the while Oliver was running around her, though she didn't say a word.

Kristine didn't let me down on the ground, and carried me up the stairs.

I didn't mind it so much due to my vantage point.

She stopped after the second flight of stairs. I noticed the queen of Rhinebur and a little girl to our immediate left as we entered. We continued on until we came to a third set of stairs that we did not ascend. Looking below, I could see the nave was populated with what I assumed was commoners.

Their garb was simple, some barely better than a sack with holes in it. Across from us were a handful of people on the same level. The first level balcony was mostly full. Based on the crests painted in front of them on the balcony face, I recognized that the first balcony was nobility and the second was Imperial nobility.

Based on the far side level with us being a duchy, and above that was an Imperial Duchy. *Something doesn't add up. We're supposed to be from the Cherry Kingdom as a baronet, based on Oliver's family crest the other day. Julilah mentioned that Mom's family was influential. Exactly how influential are they!?*

My eyes followed up the third set of stairs. They led to an area directly above the nave. The crest hung around it was for the Imperial royal family. *If this church is structured around the caste system, there's something I don't understand. I should ask Mom later.* I snorted. *Assuming she doesn't stonewall me, citing the scriptures again.*

During the fifteen minutes leading up to the start of service, I looked around. The nave was well lit because of lead stained glass windows above it, save for the box for Imperial royalty, whose box was equally well lit. We were fairly close to the edge, so I was unable to see the pulpit.

As others bowed in prayer, Kristine coughed and gestured for us to follow suit. Though I didn't really have anyone I wanted to pray to, I complied, keeping my eyes open enough to see around me. Oliver was just sitting in his chair fiddling his thumbs, until she tapped him on the shoulder and whispered something in his ear.

Once the prayer was over, a voice that sounded like tumbling rocks said, "We would now invite the children to join us for their service, starting with the honored laity."

Hearing this, Oliver tried to stand, but Julilah put her hand on his shoulder, urging him to stay seated.

To help him, I whispered while pretending to still be in prayer, "We're nobles Oliver, he wasn't talking to us."

We waited for another twenty minutes before the same voice informed those children of the highest noble blood to come forth. Kristine took Oliver's hand, then motioned for me to take her other hand.

I did so.

Julilah followed. She hadn't talked to me since the day she helped me with my bridal makeup.

We didn't go down into the nave, as I thought we would. There was another set of stairs beyond those leading up. There was a hallway with three doors. It was easy to deduce by the doors which one we'd enter.

The doors were colored white, then black, and finally another red door. There was little adornment on any of them, though I'd guess the room we entered was the smallest, even it was sectioned off into two halves.

Inside, Julilah, Lom and Marcus went to one side of the room while Oliver, Kristine and I went to the other. I spied a large cube hanging from the ceiling that was awful reminiscent of the one Kristine had used a month ago, only much larger.

A robed middle-aged man greeted us. His garment was royal blue with flourishes of silver along the hems. Around his neck was a thin golden necklace. "Gods be with us. Have these two little ones been in a class before?" He eyed Oliver and me. "And are you certain they are both cultivators?"

Kristine replied, "It is their first time. Oliver here has already awakened on his own. Anessa was able to see cultivator light, and sees static when she meditates."

"Good, good." He smiled. "Please take a seat at the table with Daughter Hy and she'll get you started."

"Thank you Son Mal." Kristine dipped her head lightly to him.

We joined a table with a total of one other child.

Daughter Hy was all smiles and her outfit was identical to Son Mal's. "It's great to meet you all. May I have your names?"

My brother held up his hand excitedly. "Oliver!"

"Anessa."

"Cav," a girl that looked to be five said in the quietest voice.

"Now then. None of you have ever had service before?"

We all nodded.

Kristine stood with Julilah at the edge of the room.

"Good. First, we must start with the basics." She looked to the ceiling and clasped her hands together. "Cultivation is a gift from the gods. Only a select few are given such a gift." She eyed me. "Not everyone here has fully awakened yet, but that's okay. If you're here, you're meant to be, as the gods have given you what you need.

"Essence is everywhere. Contained within everything, is at least some form of it. Once you've awakened…" She placed her hand on her stomach, and said, "…you will be granted the ability to store essence within your dantians, and make it your own." She went on about the gods, and the day of reckoning when they first descended on Anfang.

There were three major gods that brought the gift, a hundred thousand Anfang years ago. Their names are lost to time, though many others are known to Anfang. Today, the gods help children come into their power to avoid upsetting the balance of the world. She surprised me by saying that their efforts are also to help prevent the birth of magicians.

"They're an evil brought upon this world. Eons ago, a mighty goddess sealed them all away, taking their false awakenings from them, and restoring a balance to the world." She dropped her face to the ground. "Sadly, none of the magicians survived the sealing. They upset the balance, and to restore it, a sacrifice was needed."

Whoa. The goddess killed every magician?

"Her magnanimity was great and she saved the world from many calamities, though for each saving grace, yet another sacrifice was needed. But it's thanks to her efforts, and the lives of those who helped it be so, that Anfang is far safer than it was."

Daughter Hy went on to explain the goddess's graces and the sacrifices that were made to complete them.

It's scary to think that this goddess "saved" people through ending the lives of others. I'm sure it's no different than some religious crusades on Earth that believed they were in the right. Were all these due to the same goddess, or was it several merged into one over the years?

Oliver raised his hand.

"Yes?"

He asked, "What's her name?"

She shook her head. "Alas, her name was also lost to the countless march of time."

Round-about way to say "I don't know."

With Child Scripture Study over, we joined back up with Kristine. Julilah had her usual glare pointed at me; it vanished when I looked her way, though she most certainly didn't smile.

We returned to the stairs, and I thought it was a good time to ask, "Mama-Krissi, are we sitting with Imperial Nobles?"

She didn't chastise me, which was a good sign. "Yes. Though I will not tell you why quite yet. Right beneath us is the noble's gallery." We entered the balcony where we sat and she motioned toward the stairs on our left. "Above us is the Monarch's Aerie, used by Imperial Royalty, should they be in attendance. Our floor is called the Imperial Perch."

My eyes were drawn to the many reliefs carved into the railing leading up to the Monarch's Aerie. Some of them were downright sinister, while others were relatively serene.

Though I wanted to look further, we arrived at our seats, and to my pleasant surprise the rest of our family had joined us. Mom sat next to Dad, and on Mom's other side was Nicole. They were holding hands, which struck me as a little odd, since I knew they weren't related.

Looking across the way I noticed the Imperial Perch was sparsely populated. Beneath them, in the noble's gallery, it was quite the opposite. Those in attendance were packed like sardines.

Kristine and Julilah took to Dad's other side, while Oliver and I sat in front of everyone else, as we had before. Veronica sat to my right, followed by Lom and Marcus. Those two were remarkably well-behaved for their age, though they peered down in wonder as any child their age would.

Before I turned forward, I noticed Kristine and Julilah also held hands.

Families are complicated here. The Sister Wives would have trouble keeping track!

"How was your first time in your studies?" Veronica leaned in to ask.

"They were okay. There were a lot of things I didn't know." Given their staunch habit to limit information, I whispered, "Are you also part of the cultivator classes?"

She nodded. "I can see On-ma's cultivator light, as you can." A sigh left her. "Though I have failed three times to awaken." Holding her hand over a symbol on her necklace, she said, "I have just one more chance."

"You'll succeed," I said with a smile.

Giving me a light smile she turned forward as the ancient voice from earlier spoke up. "Today we will focus on the Malevolence of the Vile." There was a collective sound of shuffling as people got out what I'd assumed were bibles or the equivalent and began to flip through them.

In front of us were our own copies, in a little cubby hole, and I hadn't the slightest idea what page to look up. *Yay, this will be fun.*

Veronica prodded me and flashed the page number on her book to help me along which read, "Malevolence of the Vile" at the top. I did the same for Oliver once I found the right place.

The speaker began to drone on about the text that was right in front of us. It was exactly like the worst sermons I'd endured in my past life. Sometimes, visiting pastors on Earth kept things more interesting by livening the scripture up, giving us anecdotal tales from their own lives. Sadly that wasn't the case here.

My attention waned, and I looked back to see Nicole was resting her head against Mom's shoulder. Deciding I didn't want to think about that, I looked for other things to occupy my mind. The columns that held up the ceiling were painted in vivid detail. One showed angels beating back demons leading to the nave below. On the other side, the demons were winning.

A constant struggle, I guess?

Above us were the same windows, but they were far more massive than what I recalled seeing in churches prior. The detail level and colors they managed to pull out of the glass were breathtaking.

It gave the people and floor below us an interesting hue. Though it did make it a bit difficult to tell what color their clothes were.

After a few dozen excruciating minutes, I locked eyes with a little girl who was doing the same as I, looking around at others in pure boredom. Though the windows above made it hard to distinguish colors, I was pretty sure that her eyes shone a brilliant amber.

Before I knew it I was smiling, and I didn't even know why. Shaking my head, I scolded myself. *What's wrong with me? Smiling at a little girl.* Then I realized she was probably my age, and it was a little less awkward. Only a little.

"Did a boy catch your eye?" Veronica said making me nearly jump out of my skin.

"N-no." Her sudden interruption made my face burn red, and I looked toward the girl. "There's a girl who was looking at me."

Veronica looked down at her and said, "She's super cute!"

Her commentary made me want to shrivel up and die. *Don't say something like that about a child.* My blush redoubled. *She's talking about a little girl. Children are cute. Why is my head going stupid.*

Veronica started, "Would you like me to find out her—"

"Veronica, eyes on the scripture," Julilah said sternly.

Though Julilah was being a bit rude, I was secretly thankful that she had intervened. I didn't know if my heart could take much more of Veronica's attention toward some random girl I was staring at.

My eyes turned to the nave and I noticed she was gone, leaving me with an odd yearning I did not understand.

CHAPTER NINETEEN
AWAKENING / GIFT BURST

ONCE WE'D FINISHED our interminable bible study, the service ended. We began to depart and as we reached the grass outside, Oliver shouted, "It's over!"

Dad facepalmed and picked him up by his ruff. Oliver struggled a moment before he saw dad's stern face and went limp in his grip.

"Sorry daddy," Oliver said.

"It's fine," he said with a bemused chuckle. "I'll tell you what." He looked everyone with us over, his gaze lingering on the nobles milling about in the crowd. "Why don't we have a little exhibition match to burn off some of your extra energy?"

The boy perked up and practically jumped out of dad's grip, tearing the ruffles away from his neck altogether.

Dad tossed the cloth to Kristine who folded it neatly.

My brother was in the process of running circles around everyone present. His energy levels were like a rabbit jacked on a twelve pack of Red Bull.

"Calm down a little, son." Dad chided.

Oliver stopped on a dime and was almost bouncing in place. "Yes daddy."

Dad searched around the church's courtyard and when he was happy we all moved with him over to the clearing. "This should do nicely. Every one take thirty paces back." Julilah hadn't moved yet and Dad added, "For your safety." She complied without comment.

Before they did anything else she motioned for the boy to come to her. They spoke for a moment, and I swore Oliver glanced in my direction.

He rejoined Dad in the area he had chosen. One of the church clergy approached Dad and asked him a few questions. Afterwards I swear the clergyman pulled out a can of paint and began to mark the ground. Though I didn't see anything in his hands that would indicate he had paint.

A few other members from the church brought us out some chairs, and it reminded me of the level of attention we received at home, a strange experience, to be sure.

Goodness, this is becoming a regular event, the way everyone's acting.

A few stragglers from church, none of them commoners, decided to check out what was going on. Looking back I realized that the non-nobility were all being ushered away by some of the guards from home. This was an exclusive event, it seemed.

Mom was holding me in her lap on the chair she was provided. It was little more than a lawn chair, but it was better than standing, I guess.

"Have you seen them spar before, Mommy?" I asked.

"Not yet. Though I've heard Veronica talk about how Oliver 'disappeared' before her eyes."

Strange, he didn't vanish for me. Though he was very fast.

Most of this time Dad was talking with Oliver and pointing to the ground where the man had marked out their area. If I were to guess, Dad was making sure the boy knew what was expected of him.

Neither one of them had a weapon, but that wasn't uncommon for their skirmishes. Sometimes they used knives, but they mostly used bare hands.

With their talk over, they stood at opposite ends of the circle painted on the ground. Dad took a coin out of his pocket and flipped it into the air.

I tracked it to the ground and the instant it hit, Oliver vanished and a thump resounded in my chest. My eyes were like saucers, goggling at the difference in my brother's speed between now and almost a year ago. Were Wyn here to see this, he'd probably pee himself.

He's so fast. What kind of force do they have to put out for me to feel it in my chest? Moments after each of their strikes, I would also feel a light vibration in my posterior through Mom's legs.

She uttered one word: "Wow." Her grip on my midsection tightened.

As insane as it was, they weren't slowing down. In fact, it was the opposite. Their flourishes were coming faster, and faster. Their efforts were like a rhythmic drum pounding before an army marched into war.

Though when they started, I couldn't follow them at all, the pristine ground beneath Oliver's feet would occasionally explode in a spray of dirt and grass. Since he was able to fly, albeit low to the ground, it wasn't a frequent thing.

As impressive as my brother was, Dad was standing stock still with a smile plastered on his face. He hadn't used but one hand in the entire exchange.

On occasion I would catch a flicker of color right before Oliver struck. The streaks came quicker and quicker, and before long he was visible during every move he made.

Am I getting used to their speed? That's impossible — maybe Oliver is tiring? Remembering why they were doing this, I thought, *Dad did say he needed to burn off some of his energy.*

Though I thought Oliver must be running out of steam, in a surprise, Dad eventually switched to his other hand, his dominant right hand. "Good!" He shouted above the concussive bursts.

"I still can't hit you!" Oliver cried.

"The fact that you've done this much makes me proud," Dad yelled.

Veronica was standing next to me looking pensive. Each of their hits made her ears flinch and I wanted to reach out to her to console her, but Kristine came to her side and hugged her.

While I was paying attention to them, my ears caught Dad's panicked voice, "Oliver, no!"

Turning my head toward him, I pulled back in shock when I saw his small fist was less than an inch from my nose.

It was so sudden. Oliver's tiny, yet mighty, fist was so close I could almost feel it. Yet as striking as it was, he was stock still.

Everyone was. It was like someone had hit the pause button on reality.

Dad had finally moved from his place and was mere feet behind Oliver, but given how close my brother was, Dad wouldn't make it before Oliver's fist hit me. His hand was blurred, surrounded by an optical distortion as though it was moving very fast. Though everything was frozen, unnaturally still. *What the heck is going on?*

"Hello child," came an unfamiliar voice, as soft and fleeting as a rainbow.

Beside me was a startling woman. Not because she was a woman, of course, but because she had the pure white wings of an angel, and a golden halo to boot.

"H-hello," I said, thoroughly unnerved.

"Sorry to startle you young one. But you're in a dangerous situation right now." She walked over to where Oliver was and put her face close to his fist and me. "If his fist hits you, do you know what will happen?"

"It'll hurt a lot?"

She shook her head. "You'll die." Standing and placing her hand on my mother's shoulder she added, "And your mother will *also* die."

"Shit," I said, before I caught myself. I'd covered my mouth in recognizing what I'd said, or more accurately who I'd said it in front of.

Her response was a laugh that would've made me smile in any other situation. "No worries. I'm not going to scold you." She moved her hand to the top of my head. "You have the strength to protect yourself, did you know that?"

I blinked. "How?"

"You can either kill the boy…" she said and pointed to his head, making a fist as though she were going to strike him.

Before she could say anything else I rejected that notion, "No way! I'm not going to kill my brother." Though I wanted to protest more vocally, my legs and hips were rooted to the spot. Mom's arms were like a vice grip with everything stuck in place as it were.

She shook her head and only smiled. "…or you can redirect him." Her hand moved to his arm and she gestured up.

Oh, so I just Judo him, or something.

The angel tilted her head. "An odd word, Judo."

"You can," I started, and then finished my sentence in my head, *read my mind?*

Without saying a word she nodded.

Crap. This is so weird. At least I found out she could read my thoughts before I had a weird one. The brilliance of her voice played through my head and I blushed.

A laugh accompanied my thought.

Fighting through my embarrassment of soft crushing on someone who could read my thoughts, I asked, "Do I need to do anything special?"

"No, though you may want to hurry. Time isn't actually stopped. Just slowed."

At her prompting I turned back to my brother and noticed his fist was now so close as to be touching my nose.

Shit! The speed he was moving at was comparatively slow, but it meant I didn't really have time to think about my next moves. What happened next was surreal, and I moved with intent. My ears caught the angel gasping as my hands neared Oliver. She may have repeated my earlier expletive.

In this slowed state Oliver's skin was cold to the touch. I guessed because thermal transfer was affected by whatever the angel lady was using to slow time. Motioning up with his arm in my grip, and my other hand on his chest, he vanished in an instant.

The grass and dirt before us erupted in a spray several feet in every direction, and the ground in a hundred meter radius shifted up a full foot, causing everyone, including Dad to tumble over. It affected everyone, even those in their chairs.

Everyone panicked at the outcome and I was looking at the sky. *What the hell just happened!?*

Mom stood with me in her arms and looked around, shakily wondering what was going on. She sat me down and looked to the sky as Dad shot off into the air.

Several people around us were asking those nearest themselves if they were okay. At least I assumed that's what they were asking, as I couldn't actually hear a blasted thing because of an incessant ringing in my ears. Based on how everyone else was acting, they were in the same boat, because their body language said they were shouting.

A glance over at Julilah showed Kristine, Nicole and Veronica were huddled around her. My gut sank as I caught her menacing glare. It was far more severe than any I'd spied before.

Then, to my shock, I noticed the Angel was still here, sprawled out on the ground. She wasn't awake, though she seemed to be breathing at least.

When Mom noticed her, she dropped to her knees to pray. Minutes later, I saw dad touch down with Oliver in his arms.

Oliver was pale and covered in *ice*.

Oh gods, I didn't just kill my brother did I?

I ran to Dad, who stooped down to pick me up. Before he did so he put Oliver over his shoulder; to my enormous relief I saw his chest rise and fall.

Dad noticed the angel and sat me down. He handed my brother to Mom who rushed off with him toward the church.

Resting his hand on my head, my slowly recovering ears caught, "I think you just had a Gift Burst."

I wasn't sure what he meant. When I'd nudged Oliver up, an electric surge passed through me for far less than the time it takes you to blink. When Oliver disappeared, all I was left with was a twinge of numbness.

Kicking the ground proved I was no stronger now than I was before. Whatever he meant, it wasn't permanent.

CHAPTER TWENTY

SEARCH WITHIN / TOWARDS SELF-REALIZATION

GIFT BURSTS ARE a unique state children enter when their lives are in danger. Not every child is lucky enough to have one. Only those with sufficient future power, divine connections, or destiny are said to receive them.

I learned that they are called Gift Bursts for two reasons. First, because they represent their future potential. The second reason is the burst itself is a gift.

Oliver was in a different room than normal. Sitting in a bed, instead of a crib. He had a few bandages around his arm, but otherwise looked fine.

"I have no idea why I was trying to attack you," Oliver admitted. "The last thing I remember was daddy using his right hand to block me and then it went blank." His voice became eager. "Did he finally attack back?"

Shaking my head, I said, "No, but he did switch hands. Then I looked away for a second." Holding my fist out I said, "Then daddy shouted at you, to not do something, and your fist was right next to my face."

The color drained from his face. "I'm sorry." He looked down. "Daddy said my talents should never be used against someone I care about." Looking at me he added, "You're my sissy, I wouldn't hurt you on purpose."

Giving him a hug, since I knew he wouldn't hurt me of his own volition, I said, "I know you wouldn't. I'm just glad you are okay." Rubbing my arms as though I was cold I said, "You were covered in ice when daddy brought you back to the ground, you know!"

"Weird." He shook his head. "I don't remember any of it."

Before I could inquire about what Julilah had asked him before his bout with Dad, Kristine coughed. "Anessa. I know you wanted to visit when he woke up, but he really should rest."

Hopping off the stool next to his bed I said, "Okay." Turning back to my brother I said, "I'll stop by again later."

Minutes later I found myself outside the room they were housing *her* in. The angel. She still didn't wake up after everything settled down, so Dad had them take her back with us. He said it was only right, given that she was an agent of the gods.

Entering the room, I found him standing in the corner, as though he were waiting for something.

Is he protecting her?

Seeing me made him smile. "Come to see the angel again?"

It's something I'd done in between checking on Oliver and Mom. "Yeah. Any change?"

He shook his head. "She hasn't so much as flinched."

"What can you tell me about Gift Bursts?" I asked him.

"Not much is known about them, other than they are rare. Your Burst does indicate something a little unsettling though."

His words made me tense up.

"What?" I asked.

"You might be more powerful than Oliver in the future."

I tilted my head to the side. "Surely you are kidding."

Closing his eyes he tapped the back of his head against the wall. "Not even I could do what you did to Oliver." Dad paused and looked at me with a straight face. "And the truth is that Oliver shouldn't have survived what you did, Anessa." Nodding toward our guest he said, "I'm going to guess her continued presence is why he lived. Why we all were okay."

Turning to her, I said, "You think she protected us?"

"I know she did." He made a fist. "You get a feeling for these sorts of things as you advance as a cultivator. A blanket of…" He snorted, "something, covered me, and I would imagine everyone else. If she hadn't helped, you would've probably found yourself with a much smaller family."

His words made my breath catch in my throat. The thought of losing any member of my family wasn't something I wanted to imagine. I was still trying to come to terms with losing my last family.

Dad's voice came in a much more concerned tone, "Sorry." He came to me and squatted in front of me. "I didn't mean to scare you." He sighed. "That was careless of me."

"It's fine," I said halfheartedly. "It is scary though, to think of anyone getting hurt because of me. What caused the ground to explode and everyone to fall over?"

"You did," Dad looked back at the sleeping angel. He didn't say anything for a minute. "Though you almost did a lot more than that. She prevented the worst case scenario, and allowed for everyone to just fall over, instead of getting hurt."

"What did I do that was so damaging, though?" Looking at my hand made me recall Oliver's cold skin, and the thought of losing him resurfaced. "All I did was push up."

"When Oliver or I lift a carriage," he placed his hand on my shoulder. "that's all we do, too. It's as simple as breathing. There's not much thought behind it. The hard part is making sure we don't hurt those around us. That's why I've been teaching Oliver personally from such a young age."

The Angel stirred making Dad stand.

He made it one step toward her before he growled, "Griblin's giblets."

"What?" His odd phrase made me almost laugh.

"She's gone," he said simply with a huff.

Looking at the bed, I realized that she had indeed vanished on the spot.

Curious to how she might have done it, I climbed onto the bed and noticed it was no warmer where she was lying than the rest of the bed.

Dad looked at me curiously when he caught me sniffing the bed. "Need I ask?"

Realizing what I was doing my face heated up, and I protested, "It's not what it looks like!"

He smiled. "Should I explain what it looks like?"

I launched a pillow at him, which he deftly dodged. "The bed wasn't warm from her lying in it, so I wondered if she left any traces behind." Hiding my face in the remaining pillow I decided then that I'd chuck it at him too.

"Looking for clues is not a terrible idea, though explaining what you're going to do goes a long way." Dad chuckled.

"You're just teasing me because you know I had a past life. You wouldn't tease me like this if I were a normal kid, would you?"

His smile faded, and his tone firmed. "If your future potential is higher than Oliver's…"

"Alright then," Kristine said. "Based on your entry level text for breathing techniques, your first step is to close your eyes." She twitched her nose and sat across from me.

I complied.

"Then try to measure your breathing in equal breaths. Hold. Then release." Her voice became distant. "Once you have…"

They'd changed my teacher from the dicey grump queen to her wife, the whiskered academic. She was a more suitable choice given I'd shown promise as a potential cultivator.

Recalling my meditation lessons with Trish, and the basic nature of the manual, I started to push myself into a trance. The biggest differences between being in a meditative state on Earth compared to Anfang, were the ease with which I could enter a trance, and the odd static I would see with my eyes closed.

Once I entered the trance state; however, it got trickier. My aim was to move the essence around me in a regular manner. This was difficult because the entire point of a trance was to not think. Kristine had called it directed thinking, though she admitted it had been difficult for her at first.

Trish's voice overtook Kristine's.

"You're supposed to filter the qi through yourself," Trish had said. "You next guide it toward your qi centers and let it flow from your head on down."

Her next words almost caught me off guard. "With seventeen types of energy to manage, ordering them might be difficult, but try lining them up as separate threads and weaving them into strands, so all of them are taken in at a consistent rate." Her "hand" touched my stomach. "Feel inside yourself for your chi centers."

I'd opened my eyes, almost expecting to see her standing in front of me, but instead I found the room was empty. *Weird how she was using Earthen terminology.*

Not even Kristine was around. It seemed she'd left me once I'd entered my trance.

Closing my eyes, I tried again. It was a while before I was back to where I was. *Stupid imagination. Making me think Trish was here with me.*

Recalling her words, I tried to look within and after a few dozen attempts, I was shocked to suddenly "see" without my eyes. A bit different than visualizing an object, because the place around me was entirely unlike anything I'd seen, and I entered this place while emptying my mind of thoughts.

Noticing the outline around me, I realized it was indeed within myself, though I was more like an empty shell with a fiber optic network strung throughout. Moving to my stomach, where one of my dantians should be, several of the cables terminated at a nebulous void that had nothing in it.

Is this what they mean by a bud? It's as though there is nothing there. Moving throughout the rest of my "body" the results were much the same. *Voids, every single place.* The oddest part about it was the connections leading to them. Perhaps it was the presence of those cables that was indicative of a bud.

I wish Trish was here, so I could thank her. Shaking my "head" I realized the futility of that desire. Trying to keep my mind *blank* while having these thoughts seemed counter intuitive, but I supposed the point was to not think of anything too complicated. As soon as I thought about Earth, the area around me simply popped like a bubble, shaking me awake.

That's disorienting.

Kristine reentered the room. "Have any luck?"

Giving her a half-baked smile I said, "A little, though I'm not sure what they mean by dantian bud."

"Right. They are not literal buds like a flower; they represent potential. For a dantian to manifest, a connection of sorts must be formed." She held her hand over her right eye. "For me, before I awakened, there were countless threads that all went to the dantian behind here." Pointing to her other eye she added, "Over here was a complete blank. There was not one meridian."

"So those weird [fiber optic] cables were meridians?"

"Fibre optik?" she repeated uncertainly, then shook her head. "They are not cables, of that I am certain. Once you have mastered the ability to enter your Personal Space, and can do so at will, your next task will be to push essence through your meridians while remaining in that mental state."

She held up a finger. "It is one thing to grab at the essence around you with your nexus," holding up a finger on her other hand she said, "Quite another to do so with intent, and visualize it at the same time."

"What is the point of visualizing the essence in my Personal Space, as you called it?"

"The point is to familiarize yourself with how the essence affects your meridians. Identify your limits, and start to push the essence toward your dantians." Holding her hand to her eye again she said, "Even without a dantian, some have caused a blooming to occur by doing so. It is a way to possibly awaken early, if it is meant to be."

She shook her head. "Do not be afraid if you cannot, though. For some are forbidden from awakening early. In particular, should you experience any pain in pushing essence through to your dantians..." She leaned toward me.

"Stop."

CHAPTER TWENTY-ONE

TREANT TWINSPEDITION

AS OLIVER AND I turned three, we exited our home and dashed toward the forest. It seems when you have a super-powered brother, the concern over your well-being is assured in your parent's mind, even as a toddler.

Though I walked a little better than a child my age, I was still nowhere near where Oliver was in competence. We resolved our speed issue with a small wagon that was little more than a raft with wheels and a handle.

"Please slow down!" I shouted over the rattling of the blasted thing.

"What? I can't hear you!" Oliver said with a laugh. Then he looked back at me and winked, which told me he could hear me just fine.

"Slow down I said!" I knew that bopping him on the top of the head was a bad idea, so I fought the urge.

He sped up. "Go faster? Sure!" I'm sure the maids in the house were watching this with equal measures of concern and humor since my screams were punctuated with peals of laughter.

By the time we reached the forest, and he'd slowed down, I was glaring daggers.

"What?"

"I should stop coming with you," I grumbled.

"You like our twinspeditions!"

What he called our foray made me groan. It was a term conjured by the maids that Oliver enjoyed using immensely.

"I enjoy getting out of the house," I growled the next bit through clenched teeth, "and your presence is unfortunately mandatory."

He grinned and started to walk backwards into the forest along the small pathway we made six months ago. Though "small" is a relative term. It was twice as wide as Rufus and as tall as Oliver.

The forest floor was littered with tree roots, making our little trolly unable to follow us. We were on foot from here.

"This part takes forever though," he said, almost bored about saying it.

"We could jog or run," I sighed, "but I'm not nearly as fast as you are."

"I could get us there faster, if you'd like."

Our goal was a small clearing we'd found in our seventh or eighth excursion. It had a tiny spring-fed lake in it that had clear water, despite the mud that surrounded it.

"And how would we do that?"

Hiking his thumb behind himself he said, "Piggy back."

My arms went up in an "X," and I said, "No way. The last time we tried that you almost dropped me." Stamping my foot I added, "On purpose!"

He scratched his head. "I said I was sorry. It was only meant to be a joke."

"I almost peed myself!"

A mischievous grin spread across his face. "You *did*."

The moment he said that I ran toward him. "And *you* promised to never bring that up!"

Five minutes later, two minutes after I'd worn myself out giving chase, I gave in. "You win. Carry me."

"Okay!" he said, his enthusiasm giving me pause.

"Promise you'll go at a sane speed. One that won't kill me if you trip."

He chuckled nervously. "R-right."

He was planning on going full speed! I cautiously approached him and hugged him from behind.

"Ready?"

"Ye—aaaah!" I never finished that single word as it turned into an all out scream.

He was going so fast I was sure that he was breaking some vehicular speed limit.

"What the nether Oliver, you promised!" I shouted over the wind blasting past my ears.

"You won't die. In fact, I can still go faster, you know," He turned his head toward me, "if you want."

His brazen lack of concern made me shift my grip to his face in an effort to turn his face forward. "Keep your eyes forward, goof ball!"

"We're here," he said and decelerated at a break-neck speed making me feel as though I was smacking into a wall.

He let me down and I stumbled over to the nearest tree, where I unloaded lunch and possibly some of breakfast. Once I'd recovered enough to talk I said, "That wasn't nice."

"What?"

"You know what. I'm not like you. If you stop that fast," I tapped my sternum, "it *hurts* me, Oliver."

He winced a little. "Sorry, sissy."

Hoping to clear my mind of it, since he's strong but still trying to grasp how he should act, I decided to sit down to meditate.

An hour later Oliver asked, "Do you want to practice with Rufus?" He was holding his prized sword forward for me to take.

"I might read for a bit first, then I'll give it a try, okay?"

He nodded and moved a few dozen paces from me before starting to swing his sword. At the speeds he swung it, the danger zone was a bit larger than most might expect.

Facing a large boulder that intrigued him from the day we found this area, he reset himself and paused. After a while he thrust using his wind essence, producing a thin layer of wind that shot forward and gouged out some of the rock. Though it wasn't deep, he had made progress each week we came here.

Every so often he would stop and look my way. It was clear what he wanted. After the fourth time of giving me puppy dog eyes I shut my book.

"Alright, let me see this 'Rufus'."

He practically jumped forward toward me, luckily making sure to sheathe his sword first.

One thing Dad had driven home the day after Oliver got Rufus was to be very careful with it around other people as it could kill them. Dad spent more time describing what kill means than giving his warning.

Gripping the hilt, his sword nearly fell to the ground as Oliver released his hold, and I took the full weight.

"I can't believe this… is a light sword," I gasped out.

"He only weighs five pounds!"

Five!? The sword was barely two foot long, but for it to be that heavy it explained why it was difficult for my three-year-old frame.

"Rufus is happy," Oliver said.

His odd commentary made me roll my eyes. I could barely hold the sword, so I wasn't about to swing it full force.

"Okay, do you want to learn about proper form?" Oliver asked.

Holding the sword vertically, I said in a grunt, "Sure."

He went on to correct my form, moving my feet further apart, adjusting my shoulders. It was oddly fun, and by the end of it, I had to admit that Rufus was much easier to hold.

Swinging Rufus, I would occasionally get the feeling that it was trying to pull me forward, more than physics should suggest.

"Sissy, can you hear?" Oliver asked.

"Hear what?" I said while sitting on the ground, drenched in sweat. Rufus was lying across my legs in his sheath.

Oliver smiled. "Rufus is singing."

Arching an eyebrow at my brother I said, "Singing? What do you mean? I don't hear anything."

His shoulders fell and he said, "Oh. I guess you need to be awakened to hear him."

Looking at Rufus I wondered if I should get my own weapon. *The fact that there are swords indicates that people fight with them. Wyn didn't seem to even know that Oliver was far out of his league. If they would've been an equal match, how would the fight have been different?*

"I can't wait for you to awaken," he said.

"Hm? Why?"

"With your gift burst, and seeing how happy Rufus is acting, I think you'll be incredible."

His words made me sigh. "Hard to say. The gift burst apparently isn't a guarantee. If I don't awaken at all, I'll probably just be married off to someone."

"No way." He thumped his chest with his fist.

Thanks, I thought until he finished.

"I'll make sure no one ever marries you."

You don't have to go that—

Then a loud creak broke the air, sounding like a tree twisting wildly in the wind, except there was barely a breeze.

Oliver looked up only to be smacked and crash into his favorite boulder, doing far more damage to it than he'd done with any of his "Wind Strikes" as he'd called them.

"Oliver!"

It happened so fast. Turning my head toward the sound I saw something that absolutely shouldn't be here: a treant. A living tree that had uprooted itself and started to move on its own. In the center of its trunk was a vile face with gnarly bark teeth.

Seeing Oliver wasn't moving, immediately it moved between us and bellowed at me, "Food!"

I'd gripped Rufus tightly, backing away as fast as I could while keeping my eyes peeled on the monster. I knew all too well that anything I did with the sword would be flirting with death. But at the moment, having a sword seemed like a much better idea than not having a sword.

Then my brother shouted, "Sissy, throw me Rufus!"

"Y-you're too far away," I said, barely above a whimper.

"Just do it, it'll be fine." He smiled. "Trust me."

Doing as he asked I threw the weapon, which barely made it half a foot in front of me before dropping toward the ground.

But Oliver held out his hand and the sword shot forward toward his outstretched palm.

The treant was oddly motionless. It was looking back between Oliver and I, as though it were deciding whether it should go for me or him, though its focus was more on me, which was concerning.

"This way you overgrown stick!" he shouted and sliced at the beast.

To our mutual surprise, Rufus didn't cleave the monster in half, but stuck halfway.

A deep growl emanated from the tree-beast and the holes for its eyes shifted in a downward slant.

Now it was pissed.

Oliver used its anger over the sword in its side to move closer to me. "Hop on." With a flick of his hands, his sword disappeared out of the side of the barked brute.

Without thinking about it, I did so and held on for dear life. To my surprise Oliver's pace was measured and far slower than our trip here.

He's being considerate. My initial relief faded when I realized that his consideration was putting us in danger. Looking behind us, I saw the treant was pursuing, running even faster than Oliver. It was thrashing its branches toward us, missing me by mere inches.

"Crap, speed up! It's right on our tail!" I said.

"Okay," he said, "hang on."

Closing my eyes I gripped him tightly and although he sped up, it was still far slower than before. Then I realized that each step he took his eye winced ever so slightly.

He's in pain. Maybe he wasn't going faster because he couldn't. *Double crap.*

Our speed was now barely above the monster's. On occasion Oliver would falter, and the beast would make up the ground my brother had managed to make between us. Though it seemed to be getting even faster.

It was then that my family went through my mind, and I worried *we* wouldn't make it home. "Oliver," I said with a shaky voice, "Leave me behind."

"What!?" he said, and almost tripped. "No way."

"At least one of us needs to get away! You're the strongest, and the oldest," I said. *Though only by a few minutes.* A light tugging on my dress told me it was scary close. "I'm sure you're already next in line, anyway."

"Don't say that," he said and made an effort to push ahead. "I told daddy I would protect you. A man doesn't go back on his word."

"But—"

"No buts!" he said fiercely.

It's not like I can stop you. I smiled despite the situation. *Though you're not quite a man.* The path before us brightened and I realized we were almost out of the woods. *Thank the gods.*

"I'm sorry, but it might get bumpy again once we get to the cart."

I hugged him tighter from behind. "That's okay."

But once we left the wooded area we decided to forgo the "cart" altogether, as the monster was almost upon us.

"It's too close, sorry. I'll have to carry you like this."

Though we said that, the treant hadn't followed us. After we'd been given enough room to breathe, Oliver sat me down and we walked the rest of the way. There wasn't a single minute that he didn't turn to look behind us.

He's the one who will be a great cultivator some day.

Once we'd returned home, we found Dad. He was outside and was going over his own bare-fisted forms. You'd think he'd practice them at a blazing speed, but his drills were at a pace that even I could follow.

Noticing us he took one look at Oliver and asked, "What happened?"

Oliver laid down on a bench and didn't say anything, so I filled Dad in.

He got Oliver a washcloth and then placed it over the boy's forehead. Then he stood with a deadly gleam in his eyes. His movements were perfectly controlled and calm, but in that moment, I realized that he was furious.

"Let's go slay us a treant," Dad said and hoisted me onto his shoulders.

CHAPTER TWENTY-TWO
WEAPONS AND HEIRSHIPS

ASKING YOUR MOTHER to buy you a knife is generally a bad idea. At least, it is when you're three-years-old.

"Absolutely not," Mom said, and tapped her spoon against the side of her teacup. She sat it onto a cloth napkin next to her saucer. We were sitting in her study. A gaudy pink chandelier hovered above the table we sat at. My request seemed even more out of place in the excessive refinement of the room.

I complained, "But I don't want to be defenseless if I end up in a situation like that again."

Her attention focused on me. "About that. There won't be an 'again.'"

"What do you mean?"

"You and Oliver won't be going on any more jaunts in the forest, I can tell you that much." Her hands went to her hips and she glared at me.

"That's not fair!"

"Okay," Mom said. "Do you know how to use a knife properly?"

Her words stung and I knew where this was going. "N-no."

"Can you hold a sword without it throwing you off balance?"

"No," I growled.

A small smile crossed her lips. "Do you know how to care for a weapon?"

"Fine!" I shouted. "I get it, I wouldn't know how to use it and I'd probably get myself hurt."

She nodded. "Good. As long as you understand."

"If I do learn all of that, can I get one then?" I said, thinking I was being sly.

"No. You'll hurt yourself." She tried to pick me up, but I dodged her. "What's that about?"

"What do you mean?" I said, pretending not to understand.

"You're avoiding me." She patted her lap. "I wanted to give you a hug and talk to you more."

Whining, I said, "I don't wanna."

"Act your ag—" Mom stopped realizing what she was saying. "You're more mature than this, and you know it. You don't need a weapon. Oliver will be around to protect you."

"And if he isn't?"

"He will be." She once again patted her legs. "Now come here."

Grumbling, I complied and allowed her to pick me up.

"You know I'm just worried about you. Swords and knives are dangerous." She hugged me and her voice softened, "I only have one Anessa."

Hugging her back I looked to the floor. "I'm scared."

"About what?"

"Oliver actually got hurt by that treant. If he didn't get up, because he was knocked out, or something like that, what would've happened?"

Mom pursed her lips. "We'll figure something out for you, okay?"

I nodded.

"No one told me Oliver was hurt," she admitted.

Crap. I hope I don't get Dad in trouble.

"How could you tell he was injured?"

When I explained what I'd seen during our desperate flight from the treant, Mom held me tighter.

"I'm sorry you had to go through that." Mom brushed my bangs behind my ear. "It makes me even more certain that you two shouldn't go back to the forest."

"We like to go, though." Remembering the sense of freedom I get in the clearing, I said, "It's quiet, and it's a chance to get out of the house."

"Is the house so bad?"

"We're waited on hand and foot. Whenever I leave my room, there's almost always a maid following me around, like a minder. I'm never alone." Thinking to myself, *well, except when I sneak around at night. Though I imagine that'd stop if they ever caught me.*

Mom sat me on the ground. "You know young lady, you can tell anyone who is bothering you to go about their business."

"I can?"

"As a young lady of the house, they should listen to you."

Ah. Fan did tell me that I could even tell Yllia what to do.

Mom picked up a bell that sat on the table in front of us and gave it a ring.

The maid who heard it was Yllia.

"You called, mistress?"

Why does she show up whenever I think of her? Shaking my head I realized, It's pure *coincidence. Not everything has a deeper meaning.*

"Okay Anessa," Mom said. "Tell Yllia to stand on one foot."

Tilting my head to the side I asked, "Why would I do that?"

"I'm trying to show you something."

"But it's degrading," I protested. "Besides, I like Yllia."

"Ma'am," Yllia said to Mom. "May I?"

Mom nodded.

"It's fine Anessa. Please go ahead. We are here to attend to your every need." She smiled. "It wouldn't bother me a bit, as long as you're not mean-spirited about it."

Sighing, I realized they had me beat here. "Okay Yllia, please spin around and then stand on one foot."

She obliged, though it seemed her balance wasn't the best, which I found odd for a head maid.

REBORN IN THE PERFECT FANTASY WORLD

"Stand on both feet, jump, clap, and bark like a seal twice."

Mom raised a brow at that one and covered her mouth when Yllia started to move.

After she returned to two feet, I heard the door open and Fan stood there watching Yllia.

Once the head maid was finished, she realized Fan was watching, and Yllia's face and neck started to glow red.

"Sorry Yllia," I whispered.

"Fan," her commanding voice came.

"Y-yes Yllia?"

"What business do you have here."

Fan was fidgeting with her fingers and looking between Yllia and Mom. "I heard the bell, but had to finish my task before I could answer. I didn't m—"

Mom cut her off, saying simply, "You are dismissed Fan."

Fan gave a bow and exited the room as quickly as she could.

Mom turned to Yllia, "Don't give her a hard time about that."

With a nod Yllia said, "As you wish."

Curious to try it again, though I realized it was a little childish, I said, "You are dismissed, Yllia."

She gave me a sly grin, and bowed before leaving without a word.

Once the door had closed Mom finally broke out in a quiet laughter.

Then we heard the door click, which made us both giggle, though Mom giggled a little harder.

"I feel silly," I said, "I hope Yllia isn't mad at me."

"It'll be fine." Mom wiped away a tear. "The timing was poor on Fan's part, but I don't expect you'll make the maids bark too often."

Opening my mouth, appalled, I said, "I won't do it at all!"

Our focus turned away from making the maids bark, into something more serious.

"You know my concern is with your future. Either you or Oliver must assume the Carlyle Mantle when your daddy retires." She returned to her seat. "It's not clear yet who it will be."

Taking a seat across from her I said, "It's obviously going to be Oliver. You've seen what he can do yourself!"

She took her tea into her hand and swirled its contents. "Perhaps it will be him, but you know you are far more level-headed. Strength isn't the only thing a leader needs."

Our talk reminded me that I'd been meaning to ask her, "Speaking of which… on our first Anfang birthday, Oliver wore a patch on his jacket that was for Cherry Kingdom, a baronet level crest." Remembering the inside of the church I said, "And we sat next to the Monarch's Aerie, along with the other Imperial Nobles. Why is that?"

Mom had just lifted her teacup to take a drink when she froze. She sat it down on the saucer. "I'm afraid I can't talk about that right now."

"Why not?"

"It's complicated."

Julilah's commentary about Mom giving up her family's right to inherit came to mind. "Is it because of your family?"

She frowned. "What do you mean?"

"Julilah said that you gave up a lot to marry daddy."

Before I could add more Mom jumped in, her tone cross, "And just what else did she tell you about my family?"

Flinching at her tone, I said, "Not much, other than they are powerful and influential and to find out more, to ask you." I'd never had an opportunity to ask about what Oliver and Julilah talked about when my brother all but attacked me. It seemed the animosity between Mom and Julilah had only increased since then. It told me they were likely aware of something, and had talked about it. Since they hadn't talked to me, I knew for sure they wouldn't tell me if I'd asked.

Mom closed her eyes and sighed. "She didn't say anything else?"

I shook my head.

She continued, "I'll discuss it with your daddy. If he thinks you should know, he'll come talk to you later." She sat her tea down. "Will that work?"

"Yeah."

"Speaking of the future," I tried to ease into what I knew might be an even more contentious topic. "What happens if I'm not a cultivator?"

"That would simplify the matter of succession. Oliver would be announced as the heir to the Carlyle Mantle."

Pushing her I asked, "Is that all?"

"What else is there?"

Focusing on her teacup, and avoiding her eyes, I said, "Would I be forced to marry someone?"

"There's…" Her voice trailed off. "A strong possibility." She crossed her arms. It seemed body language that meant the same on Anfang as it did on Earth.

She doesn't want to talk about this. But my future is important to me! Given how difficult it'd been to get her to talk about anything I decided it was best to push a little, since she was being unusually open. "Do you already have someone in mind?"

Her eyes darted around the room as though she wanted to look at anything but me.

"Mommy?"

She sighed. "It's been discussed, yes, though your daddy is certain you will be a cultivator and it won't matter."

Whoa. That they'd thought this far ahead blew my mind. Picking my jaw off the floor, I asked, "Who?"

"The Emperor of Redwater," she said, gripping her arm.

"Wait. Isn't that who Veronica is marrying?"

With a nod she said, "Yes. He has a consortium of wives."

Why is he collecting wives? Then my stomach sunk, and I asked, "Won't that make things awkward with Veronica."

Exhaling slowly she said, "It could." She shook her head and added, "This isn't really a proper topic for someone your age, though. If you must marry him, it won't happen until you're an adult, *and* we're certain you won't become a cultivator."

"There's still a possibility though?"

She nodded, though the frown on her face said she wanted to be done with this topic.

"Last question. I wouldn't have to… marry Veronica, would I?" I thought, *Veronica did bring up this very possibility.*

"Where did you hear that?" Mom asked, clearly cross.

I tried to push myself further into the cushion of the plump chair I was in, to no avail. Difficult to do when your feet barely reach over the edge of the chair. "That doesn't matter, does it? Would I have to?"

Turning her head away from me, her voice dropped an octave and she said, "There is a very good chance of that, yes."

Leaning forward, I said, "That's weird!"

Mom closed her eyes. "The Emperor of Redwater has a few strange tastes." Before I could raise a hand to protest, or ask additional questions, she said, "Leave it there. You *are* far too young for me to tell you more." Her tone said firmly that line of discussion was dead.

"Okay," I said. *Given I'd have to marry Veronica…* Again I waved my hands in the air to clear it of my thoughts, granting me an odd look of both annoyance and bemusement from Mom.

I will not marry my sister, yuck. Veronica's voice popped into my head to remind me that she is *not* my sister. *This planet is weird.*

CHAPTER TWENTY-THREE

ROLAND'S EVENING CONVERSATION

MINDFULNESS IS THE act of being open to new ideas, promoting empathy toward your common man. You gain an awareness of others' feelings and ideations without being judgmental, and the willingness to compromise where needed. It encourages presence of mind and moment. Meditation is often used to help foster mindfulness, and I was using it to do so now.

"Anessa," Dad said, breaking me from my meditative trance.

"Yeah?"

"Are you trying to cultivate?" he asked with a chuckle. He was wearing his military dress garb – a navy button-up vest atop a white shirt, over which a darker jacket sat. The oddest part of it, to my eyes, was the silky cape that he wore. It seemed old-fashioned and impractical.

His presence wasn't welcome at this time and I griped, "I know that this isn't cultivating. I'm trying to get used to how this feels. I don't know how to influence essence yet, so I'm mostly familiarizing myself with my meridians."

"Without dantians, meditating with the purpose of cultivation is more of a mindfulness exercise," he said.

I realized he wasn't going to let me continue, so I stood and threw the pillow I was sitting on at his face. "Are you just here to tease me? I was given this task by Mama-Krissi."

"No," He easily dodged the pillow and plucked it out of the air. "I'm not here to tease you. Sorry for upsetting you. It's been far too long and I'd forgotten the early pre-cultivator steps. Lily wanted me to come see you, because you had some questions?" He handed the pillow back to me.

Instead of asking questions, I unloaded my frustrations on him. "She won't let me have a weapon!" I stomped. "Of any kind. Not a sword, a dagger, nothing." Relaxing the fist at my side, that I didn't know I had made, I said, "I'm worried about how I'm going to protect myself, if you or Oliver aren't there."

He held up his fists. "How about I teach you to use your fists, would that work?"

Remembering Oliver's prowess in fisticuffs instantly made me bounce in place. "Yes please!"

He smiled at me while chuckling. "You can be a lot like Oliver sometimes, you know?"

Turning my head away from him I harrumphed. "Of course. We're twins after all." His comment made me think, *I don't mind being compared to Oliver.* A mirror on the far wall showed that my dress was lightly wrinkled. I took a moment to smooth it out. Then I noticed the leggings I wore underneath weren't even, so I corrected that, as well.

"You know I'm a strict teacher, right?"

"Oliver tells me all the time," I said. A light queasiness hit me, making me almost afraid at what I'd agreed to.

"You'll be fine. Oliver's okay, isn't he?"

"I suppose so." Of course, he could literally glide over the ground and could move faster than sound, and I could not. My unease redoubled.

My eyes drifted over the crest on his shoulder and it reminded me of the one Oliver had worn on our first Anfang birthday.

"Daddy, we're from Cherry Kingdom, right? What kind of nobility are we?"

"I'm not really able to tell you about that quite yet. There's a bit of…" his hand went to his stubbly chin. "Paperwork that's been tied up."

Paperwork? I tilted my head. *For talking about what kind of nobility we are?* Curious to know more, I told him that I'd noticed we sat with the Imperial Nobility in church.

"You would notice that," Dad said ruefully. "It's hard to remember how mature your mind is sometimes. We should be able to tell you something soon. I can't share anything openly right now."

Openly, I scoffed in my head and resisted the urge to roll my eyes. I asked, "We're in private, right now, aren't we?"

He waved his hand. "Even with the knowledge of a past life, unless you were a ruler, sometimes the less you know about nobility and politics is better." With furrowed eyebrows he added, "We will tell you when we're able to, though. Okay?"

His tone was remorseful, so I didn't press him further. "What about Cherry Kingdom? Oliver wore a crest or something on our first birthday. Was it from your home kingdom?"

"That's right. He chose a bad day to wear it though." As if expecting me to ask another question, he held up one hand. "No, I can't say more about why it was a bad day. Nobility can be troublesome sometimes."

"What's our hometown like?"

"What? Oh, our baronetcy was small, but it's mostly populated by beast-kin. I think there were about four full humans there. We oversaw a small town named Pitts. Every able-bodied serf used to work in the mines. We encouraged the commoners to work too, but it wasn't mandatory." He coughed. "Nobility was excluded."

I chuckled at the name of the town, and reflected on his words. *"Was" small. Either the town has grown, we no longer oversee it, or something happened to the mine. If the ore dried up, the town likely did too. Also, that's a* lot *of beast-kin, isn't it?* Seeing as Dad didn't seem to show any signs of being a beast-kin, I thought, *He must be one of the full humans.* I asked, "What's a serf? And was the town nice?"

"Serfs are in the caste below commoners. They are bound to the land, but they are not actually slaves. Yes our town was nice. Though, it's not a very big town. Barely above a village." His eyes went distant. "The cherry blossom trees were *divine* in the spring." He scratched his cheek. "It's sort of how Lily fell for me. A story for another day I suppose."

Seeing as he wouldn't give more details about our noble heritage, my focus shifted to my upcoming fisticuff lessons. I asked, "So when do we start training?"

Dad looked at me and smiled. "I envy your enthusiasm. It reminds me of myself, when I was around twelve-Standard-years-old."

Doesn't answer my question, though.

"I was always worried about how weak I was," he continued.

Looking at him I said, "*You* were weak?"

He nodded. "Of course. I was a mortal once. When I awoke as a cultivator, I wasn't even a thousandth the strength Oliver is now." He sat down and ushered me to sit next to him. "I was so far behind everyone else." His eyes had a look of a distant memory. "There's a big pressure to advance early and often." He shrugged. "It's unfair, but that's the world we live in."

"Did you have many friends?" I wondered.

"As a kid? Sure." Shaking his head he said, "Though once you become a cultivator there's a shift in priorities. No longer are you solely thinking about your own future, but your family's future."

"What's it like?" I leaned toward him. "Being responsible for the Carlyle family?"

A sharp laugh erupted from his chest. "Today? It's not so bad. When I was a young lad; though, it wasn't easy. Awakening late made me feel as though I had a responsibility to catch up, or our lands would suffer for it."

"Why would they suffer?"

Pointing to his head, he said, "It was in my head. While being a cultivator changes things, I wasn't smart enough at the time to recognize what I should have been doing." He shrugged. "How could I? I was only twelve."

"Was it difficult?" I asked.

He tilted his head quizzically.

"To catch up, I mean?" I clarified.

"In a manner, yes. I focused too much time on trivial things." He went silent for a while, then said, "Like Vir. He was kind of a bully, taking his frustrations out on me. After my final awakening, I learned that my efforts to one-up the boy were misguided." A smile crept across his face before he wiped it off with his hand. "When I finally came into my Earth element, everything fell into place."

"Did it make you stronger?"

"Vir said that I had become too smug after my final awakening." Dad playfully put his fist on his jaw. "So he broke his hand on my face the day after. It didn't even hurt." He coughed. "To be clear, his efforts didn't harm me. Vir ran away, tripping over himself."

I can imagine it would be a big shock breaking your hand in such a way.

"Before that, my urge to improve at any cost was tremendous." With a sigh he continued, "Kind of like Veronica's situation."

"About that," I said. "If she doesn't awaken, will she really," I paused to consider my wording. "…be married off to the Emperor of the Redwater Empire?"

Dad nodded. "She would." He shuffled as though he was uncomfortable. "As you would… if you do not awaken by the time you are sixteen-Standard-years-old."

I said, "It's weird to me, that Veronica and I would both end up marrying the same man."

He cleared his throat. "And one another."

That's another person who is clear about that. That is so freaking strange.

"Yes, and that," I said and rolled my eyes. "What's so special about that Emperor?"

Dad avoided my eyes. "Well. We have a few connections with Redwater's Imperial Majesty. You'd be guaranteed a good, and more importantly safe, life."

Thinking about how gender roles seemed similar to those on Earth, I asked, "Is it because I'm a girl?"

His eyes shot to me and widened. "Heavens above. No. It's because you would be a mortal. This is a dangerous world. The life expectancy of a mortal is short in the grand scheme of things." He placed his hand on my head. "I would want to ensure you live it peacefully. With an emperor as a partner, your safety is almost assured."

"Okay," I said. *That makes some sense.* My mind went to his other words. "Why would I marry Veronica, though? That's weird."

He once again avoided my gaze. "That's complicated. I might tell you when you're older."

"Is it because I'm a toddler?" I asked in a flat voice.

With a smile he said, "Yes."

"I'm a child in body only, remember? What's the deal there?"

Dad clicked his tongue. "The Emperor of Redwater has a few odd…" He seemed to be grasping for the right word. "…proclivities."

"Got it," I intoned. "He's a fellow pervert."

"Hey!" he protested. "I am not a pervert. My preferences are—" His face turned red. "—perfectly normal."

If I take Dad's word, that means that… My mind once again drifted to kissing Veronica and I shook my head. "Not going to happen," I muttered.

"What isn't?"

This planet is making my *head weird.* I sighed. "Nothing." Thinking on it further I realized, *No, my head feels weird because I died and was dropped into a completely different world. Culture shock sucks.*

Dad seemed to sense my discomfort. "Though you did experience a gift burst, there's a chance you will be deemed not worthy."

With a sigh I slumped in defeat.

"But," his tone lightened. "You are Oliver's sister. By virtue of being his twin, I'm certain you will awaken."

Let's hope you're right, Dad.

CHAPTER TWENTY-FOUR

UNDERSTANDING THE POWERLESS WITH VERONICA

FAMILY CRESTS, OR coats of arms, were devised in a period when the common man's literacy was basically nonexistent. On Anfang, just like on Earth they help identify someone as friend or foe from a distance.

After my meeting with Dad, I decided to find Veronica to ask her about Redwater's Emperor. It only took me ten minutes to find her room this time. *Progress!* I thought.

Her door was mostly shut, though through the crack, I could see her sitting at her small vanity. In each of her hands was a strip of cloth with something embroidered on it.

"Veronica?" I said, and pushed her door open a little further.

She wiped her eyes and said, "Yeah? Come on in."

Moving over to her I saw the cloths were embroidered with crests, though they weren't any I recognized. They both had a light blue base color, trimmed with an even brighter colored hem. They were obviously crests, but the overall design was quite different from what is seen in Westwood.

"What are those?"

She handed one to me. "Crests from Redwater."

"Huh. You'd think they'd be red?"

She laughed, though the timbre of her voice said she was melancholic. "I thought the same thing."

"What's the Emperor of Redwater like?"

Veronica had a half smile before I asked that, which melted in an instant. "Demanding. And—" She shook her head. "No, never mind."

"Tell me," I put my hand on her wrist. "I might need to know, too."

She pursed her lips. "Let's put it this way: I might have all ten of my kids by the time I'm twenty-four-Standard-years-old."

Oh shit. So he's a horn-dog? Worried I might push too far, I said, "Is there *anything* good about him?"

Looking down and thinking she said, "Well, he is rich." Her smile was a bit off kilter. "Not that I care about money, that much."

"How many kids does he have so far?" I asked.

"Sixteen and counting."

"Wow. Does he have a sky-high genesis number or something?"

With a nod she said, "His number is sixty, though there's a chance my final engagement won't actually be with the Emperor."

Oh this is new.

"His Imperial Majesty is old, and there's a chance his eldest son, Evan will take his place before I turn sixteen."

I smiled. "Isn't that good?"

She shook her head. "Evan has no genesis number, like you, but although he's had several wives, he has no heirs of his own."

"I guess that might be concerning for him," I admitted.

Taking a sip of her tea she said, "He has had children, but each and every one of them has been female." Her tea was strong and it almost punched me in the nose. Alcohol, mint, and some other flavors that I couldn't quite place.

"I thought you said—"

Veronica said, "Here's the bad part: every time he has a girl, both the baby and mother are put to death."

What the hell?!

"I'm scared." She squeezed her own arm. "I don't want to suffer a similar fate."

"No kidding!" I said, "Tell your on-ma and on-pa that you want to call it off."

"It's not that simple!" she said.

The intensity in her voice made me step back.

"Sorry. It's only thanks to your mommy, Mama-Lily, that I was even able to have this opportunity. If it weren't for her, I'd be lucky to be a concubine, let alone a wife."

"Oh," I said and my voice trailed off. Although, I thought perhaps being a live concubine would be preferable to a dead wife, I didn't pursue it. *Given he executes his wives, I can imagine how he treats his concubines. I wish there was something I could do.* Changing the subject, I held up the crest she had handed me. "Where is this crest from?"

A smile crept across her face and she put her hand on my cheek. "Thank you." She took the cloth and said, "This is the Imperial Royal Family's crest." Pointing to the dragons dancing around its edge she said, "Most Imperial Royalty integrates a dragon of some form." She paused. "At least that's what On-pa says."

"I hope you Awaken on your next ceremony," I said softly, "you know?"

"I know." She gave me a sad smile. "I hope you do, too."

"Why's he able to get away with putting his wives to death, anyway? Don't they have any say?"

Veronica had started to move toward another crest and her hand froze. "They do not have a say. He's the Imperial Prince, and his word is law. If someone so much as looks at him wrong, their head could roll."

Ah. Dad did warn me about calling Westwood's Imperial Majesty, Jorin Q'Tar improperly.

Giving her a hug I said, "Here's hoping that neither of us have to go through that."

"You're such a smart child," Veronica said, then pulled away from my hug. "If the worst comes to pass, I'll be sure to protect you."

Holding my arms up in an "X" I said, "Don't think like that. Let's hope we won't be there in the first place." Recalling my conversation with Dad I asked, "How was my mom able to help, even?"

She shook her head. "I don't know much, but Papa-Rolli recently got a promotion." Holding her arms out she added, "A massive one." She looked toward her door and then back to me. "All I know is that it had something to do with you, Oliver, and Mama-Lily."

Our birthday seemed like it was a really big deal. What happened? My eyes drifted to her bed in my rumination, and I noticed a book titled, "The Noble Matron: On Motherhood and Marital Duties." *She's really thinking about being a Mom this young? That's so sad.* Curious to know more, I pointed and asked, "What's that book about?"

Instead of answering me, she stood and promptly covered the book with her pillow. "That's not a book for children."

Her comment made me tilt my head to the side. "Aren't *you* a child?"

"I won't be in a Standard year," her face dropped to the floor. "Since I'm a mortal right now, I have to prepare myself for the possibility—"

"Stop!" I said and waved my arms. "Enough of that. I'm sure you will awaken. What if it's one of those self-fulfilling prophecies?"

It was her turn to be confused and she raised an eyebrow. "What?"

"It's a concept where your efforts help bring about the outcome, because you're already sure it will happen. If the gods, or whatever powers allows us to awaken can read our minds, they might not be pleased at your view on things. That would in turn make you not awaken as a cultivator."

Veronica's eyes became distant as though she was lost in thought. After what seemed like far too long, she said, "Maybe you're right." She exhaled. "I'll still have to prepare for the worst, but I should also plan for the best."

I gave her a bright smile. "Exactly. Your on-ma is a cultivator and a cat-kin, just like you. Have faith in that and believe."

"Huh," she said, then picked me up and squeezed me tight. "Thank you."

Tapping her shoulder I squeaked out, "I give! I give!"

She released me and asked, "What?"

Gasping for air I said, "Nothing. I'm good now."

Which was the wrong thing to say, because she continued to hug me after that.

Ow.

Once I was free, I bid Veronica farewell and thought about the promotion Dad got. Then I realized, *Dad never told me about our background, and why I might inherit the Carlyle mantle instead of Oliver!* I'd been so focused on getting a weapon for protection, the question had slipped my mind.

I was determined to fix that and went on a search for him. Though I was unsuccessful, I did find Oliver practicing by himself.

He saw me approach and sheathed his sword. "Sissy!"

With my best unamused face on display I said, "How's training?"

"Trying to get better at wind blades. Daddy said once I master them, they will be even better than trying to cut things with the sword itself." His attention went to his side. "But don't worry, Rufus. I'm not going to stop using you. We'll be together for a while."

He's actually talking to his sword as though it's alive. Weird.

"Oh yeah?" he said while looking to his side. His eyes returned to me. "Rufus says hi."

"Hi… Rufus?" I said disbelievingly.

The sword at his side seemed to vibrate all on its own and Oliver clasped his hand over it. "No, you can't go to her," he said with a sharp tone. "She can't even lift you right."

"Uh huh. Should I leave you two… alone?"

His face snapped to me. "What do you mean?"

"You seem to be having a disagreement."

"Oh, no." He waved his hand. "Rufus says he can't wait to be by your side. Once I no longer need him, he says he'll be your partner."

Looking to "Rufus," I then said with a hint of confusion, "I look forward to that, I guess?"

It shook again, I guess in response to my words.

CHAPTER TWENTY-FIVE

TRUTH AND TITLE

SINCE MY PARENTS had a penchant for being evasive. I decided to revisit the library in hopes I could find a book or two about Mom's lineage. Unfortunately for me, when I arrived at the door it read, "Keep Out, cleaning."

The door was ever so slightly ajar, so I decided to peek inside. Only for a maid to rush over to me and squat to my eye level, blocking my entrance. "I'm sorry little lady. We've been tasked with cleaning the library and its books today. Was there a specific book you were looking for?"

Behind her, I could see several stacks of books all over the main table. At least seven maids were lined up and checking the spines and flipping through the pages, for what I guessed was wear and tear. One of them was even *dusting* the inside of each page.

That seems stupid.

"I was hoping to find a book on my mommy's family," I said, trying the honest approach.

The maid looked behind me and around to see if anyone else was available to speak to. Seeing no one, she said, "I'm sorry, but I don't think we have that here." Her eyes shifted to the side as she spoke, which gave me the impression that she was lying.

"Are you sure?"

"I am sure."

Crossing my arms, I said, "And I can't come in here?"

With a deep bow of her head she said, "I'm sorry, but no. We're moving a lot of the books in and out, and it would be terrible if someone were to trip over you, or drop something on you. The books are quite heavy, you know?"

A light fire burned in my chest, but I realized she was just doing her job. Sighing, I let go of my frustration, and dropped my head to the floor. *Well their timing sucks.* Seeing that she was not about to move from my path and a few other pairs of eyes were now on me as well, I decided to go elsewhere. *Maybe Dad will have a change of heart and answer my questions.* Recalling how he speaks about cultivation made me smile. *He doesn't seem as strict about things as Mom.*

My smile seemed to concern the maid and she gave me a nervous grin.

When I walked off, I heard her sigh behind the door as she closed it.

Thinking about the time of day, I realized Oliver was likely having his morning training with Dad, and I headed toward the courtyard where they usually practiced.

Before I could see them, I could hear them. An occasional loud cry would come before a loud crash.

Must be swordplay. I'm surprised Rufus is still in one piece. Upon rounding the corner, I saw them dance around one another. I realized that Oliver's speed had more than doubled since his bout at church.

Goodness me, I thought as a flurry of loud cracks rang out. Each hit me in the chest and gut. As they moved, I saw elements of Dad's fisticuff training in Oliver's movements.

Dad had decided I needed a lot more strength training before he could even take me on directly as a pupil, so while I couldn't train with him quite yet, he did teach me basic forms. Most surprising was Dad finally needed to use two hands to defend himself against Oliver.

I know Dad said I might be better than Oliver one day, but seeing them as they are now, I can't see that happening. Shaking my head, I sent up a prayer that I'd at least not embarrass my brother.

Every few strikes Oliver would take a dirt nap. It seemed Dad had started fighting back. While Oliver's footwork didn't leave a mark on the ground, his frequent introductions to the ground would leave pock marks. I swear one was shaped like his face, though most were palm shaped.

Their session went on for another three minutes before Oliver planted his sword in the ground and leaned against it. Huffing, puffing and coughing as though his lungs were on fire. His outfit was ruffled and dirty, and mud covered half of his face.

Seeing the lull, I approached Dad. "Daddy, can I ask you a few questions?"

With a small twisting flash of light, his sword disappeared into his ring. I'd recently learned about storage artifacts like this, which cultivators could use to pack items away in some extra-dimensional pocket. They often took the shape of jewelry or other clothing items. I'd first seen one in action when Oliver tucked Rufus away while we started to run from a living tree.

"Sure sweetie, what would you like to know?" He flicked his wrist and the ground they were training on rippled and reformed, erasing the imprints of Oliver's hands and face, leaving a perfectly flat surface in its wake.

No wonder the place always looked so pristine, even after one of their destructive training sessions. His choice of words, "sweetie," was new, and it earned him a raised eyebrow. I asked, "You mentioned before about our family and how discussions on it were tied up in paperwork. Can you tell me more about it now?"

He hit his palm with his fist, and I realized he'd forgotten.

"Right. I was supposed to talk to you about that." He turned to my brother. "We're done for the day, buddy. Would you like to take a seat next to your sister?"

He'd finally recovered some and had managed to stop coughing, but Oliver was still huffing a bit. "Sh… sure." Collapsing onto the chair Dad brought out he put Rufus away.

Taking my seat, I asked, "I'd heard you had a massive promotion, and mommy's family helped make it happen."

Dad rubbed his chin. He said under his breath, "Now that's something I don't remember telling anyone." He shrugged. "It's something like that. Your Mommy's family is kind of a big deal. I'd love to give you more specific details about them, but that's something she needs to explain."

I sighed inwardly – *More secrets!* – but settled in to hear whatever he was ready to share.

"Over the years," he started, "I'd turned down several offers for promotion. I wasn't in the military, and our family lived peacefully in Cherry Kingdom in the town of Pitts." Pulling out a chair for himself he sat and leaned toward us, giving our impromptu chat a campfire vibe, without the fire.

"Our town has a mine in it, as I've already told Anessa. It's main product is copper, the town's primary export. However, what I didn't tell anyone, was it also contained a rich vein of essence stones. Some of the best in the world." He smirked. "We never exported any of that."

Oliver tilted his head to the side. "What's that have to do with your promotion?"

Dad chuckled at his impatience. "I'm getting there. It was this vein that allowed me to become who I am today." He shook his head. "Not everyone is a greedy genius of essence like you, Oliver. Most people have to find resources to grow their power."

"Is the ore packed with essence, or something?" I asked, unsure if I was correct or not.

"Exactly right. My aim was to advance in power over time," he looked to his right, toward the south, "and leave Anfang behind."

I could scarcely believe what I was hearing. I raised my hand and felt instantly silly when he said with exaggerated formality, "Yes, student Anessa?"

Heat touched my cheeks and fled just as quickly. "Leave the planet? Why would you leave Anfang? Where else would you go?"

"Well. Once you move past the Sky Realm, Anfang's struggles start to lose meaning. The very next step, is naturally, to seek new challenges, and go further." His smile was replaced by a brief grimace. "That won't happen for me, though, without the emperor's help."

Dad's horrible at explaining things. What the heck does the emperor have to do with this! The Emperor was so far up the totem pole that it was akin to the heaven and the earth. A Baronet was lucky to have a town to oversee.

"Our mine dried up, or at least it did for me." He looked over our shoulders and smiled. "At least until your mother and I fell for one another. She changed everything, and opened new doors of opportunity."

We heard Mom sighing behind us. "Roland, you're being so indirect *I* am having trouble following you."

Praise the gods! Save us from this nonsense. Then I remembered she usually wouldn't tell me much about anything.

Dad placed another seat next to himself and Mom joined him.

"Perhaps it's time to tell you about my family." She pulled a crest from her front pocket, like she was flashing an ID badge. I recognized the dragon motif right away. It was an Imperial Royal crest.

Holy shit! Mom's royalty, Imperial, at that. I'd read up on crests of our region as part of familiarizing myself with Anfang. I kept it to Westwood because the planet is gigantic. Like, twice the diameter of Jupiter gigantic. It wasn't clear to me why we weren't all squashed flat by the gravity, but I'd long since come to suspect that the laws of physics didn't exactly work the same way here.

"My maiden name is Lily Q'Tar. I am the Imperial Princess of the Westwood Empire. While I am no longer in line for the Imperial throne, I haven't lost all my pull. A spot opened up for our family to be promoted, and since we have two Imperial heirs of our own," she motioned toward us, "our request was granted."

"Wait," I said disbelievingly, "You mean our family was promoted because of Oliver and me?"

Mom nodded. "You lived past the age of general mortality. As such, when an Imperial slot came available, I put in a request to my brother, Jorin Q'Tar."

Dad coughed and looked around us. "Lily is the only one who is able to get away with calling His Imperial Majesty by name, without honorifics." He sternly said, "Don't ever omit them yourselves, okay? Not even in private."

We both agreed.

"What kind of Imperial nobility are we?" Oliver asked. He looked at the family crest on his chest. "Did our crest change?"

"We replaced the old Greensbaro Imperial Dukedom."

Dukedom?!

I stammered out, "That places our family right below the Emperor, doesn't it?"

Mom nodded, "That's correct. It made a few people a little upset to be overlooked, but when they heard who asked—" Mom shrugged. "They backed down."

Yeah, of course they did! I wanted to shout, but realized it would be of little use. My mind was reeling from this revelation.

"Do you have any other brothers or sisters?" Oliver asked.

"No, none that I'm aware of." She turned her eyes to the sky as if she were thinking. "If they were born off-world, they wouldn't be eligible for the throne anyway."

"What's off-world mean?" he asked innocently.

"That means they weren't born on Anfang," I said and turned to mom for confirmation. "I'm guessing being a native of the planet is relevant somehow?"

Nodding along she added, "Those born off-world are generally given different opportunities."

Mom stood and hugged Dad from behind. "The resources your daddy gets from the empire are great, but he doesn't get them for free."

Dad exhaled. "No kidding. I had to become Westwood's main striker." He put his hand on Mom's and held a finger up on his other hand. "That means, if we ever go to war, I'm on the front lines." He grumbled, "For *every* battle."

"Isn't that fun?" Oliver asked an excited smile creeping over his face, clearly not understanding Dad's frustration.

"It's exhausting. Imagine going out and training our soldiers in fake skirmishes, every day, but without breaks. Then speeding off to the next group. While we aren't at war right now, I still have to practice constantly to keep sharp."

"How often do you practice?" I asked.

"Daily." His tone soured, "That old bat Eugene is a slave driver."

Dad trains Oliver every single day, while also running drills to maintain constant battle-readiness. He must get practically no rest. The amount of energy that would require boggled my mind. *And he can* fly *on top of it all.*

CHAPTER TWENTY-SIX
ROYAL REVELATIONS

THE REVELATIONS UNLOADED on us shattered my worldview, military efforts aside.

"Is that why our first birthday was so much of a spectacle?" I asked.

"Yes," Dad said. "The local kings wanted to kiss as—"

Mom bopped him on the head mid-sentence. "Language! They simply wanted to… show their appreciation for our family."

Dad rolled his eyes.

Oliver pulled Rufus into his lap. "Well, I thought it was great. They gave me a great friend." His grin stretched ear to ear. "I won't forget it!"

Shaking his head Dad said, "That was their goal, Oliver."

Clearly not understanding, my brother tilted his head to the side in befuddlement. "What's wrong with giving me neat things?"

"Nothing is wrong with it," Mom chimed in and squeezed Dad's shoulder. "When you're older I'll explain it to you better. To put it simply, sometimes people do nice things, but they don't do it to be nice."

Rufus vanished into Oliver's storage ring with a twisting pop. "I don't understand. But I believe you."

"That—" I started, but held my tongue. I wanted to say that you can't believe something you don't understand, but the blank look on his face said I'd only confuse him further.

To help the conversation along, I asked, "Is there anything we need to know after these changes? Do we act differently, have our own title, or so on?"

Mom responded to my question with a smile. "All you need to know is that, for now, nothing changes. You will both have titles in the near future. Things are still in the works. There has been no clear determination on your *order*; however, in the right of succession, so you're both currently more or less in sixth place."

Dad said, "And the odds of either one of you being selected are slim to none. His Imperial Majesty's family is well-guarded. Enemies would be a fool to try anything directly, since the personal Imperial guards can counter even me.

"As for the Carlyle Mantle, you're both first in line at this time."

That means one of us will inherit an Imperial Dukedom. A figurative weight settled on my shoulders. *I am not ready for anything like that.* Realizing it was mostly in my head, I asked, "How large is our family's domain now, anyway?"

"About twenty kingdoms," Dad said simply.

"T-twenty!?" I shouted, leaping to my feet in surprise. It then reminded me there were about twenty kings and queens at our birthday party. *Those sneaky*—

"Don't let it startle you." Mom said, "There's several years before either of you have to think about that."

Oliver's next question was on the tip of my tongue. "Why aren't you in line for the throne mommy?" He looked back to Dad. "And why couldn't daddy take the throne?"

Dad went rigid at Oliver's question, but he answered the boy. "Buddy, it's dangerous to even suggest that I might 'take' the throne. Someone might get the wrong idea, okay?"

"Okay...?" Oliver looked like he didn't understand but he agreed.

"As to your other question," Mom said, "Your daddy, as a baronet, was far beneath my station." She looked down at a line of ants that was marching between us, then pointed to them. "Oliver, imagine you were to marry one of those ants."

Ouch that stings. To compare your status as though people beneath you are bugs.

Dad turned his head a bit and briefly made a fist before relaxing it. I didn't imagine he cared for the analogy either.

Oliver got onto the ground and looked at them. "That would be weird, they're bugs."

"Some people are big headed," Mom said. "They compared our marriage in the same way.

Oh, she's making this analogy for Oliver's sake.

Dad seemed to relax a bit at hearing her words.

"The short version of what you're saying is," Oliver said "they punished you because you married beneath yourself?"

Mom said sharply, "Yep."

"You still have sway though. The punishment was simply that you can't be an empress, under any circumstances?"

She sighed. "That's mostly right. But to be honest my chances were slim to begin with, just as yours are." Her fingers dug into Dad's shoulders, which didn't seem to bother him. "However, I also lost the funds that come along with being an Imperial Princess."

Ah, that explains why we're broke. Dad didn't get anything other than permission to marry Mom.

Another incongruity clicked in my head. I asked, "If we're basically living on a Baronet's budget, how come we have so many maids and such a large home?"

Mom gasped and looked down at Dad. "Did you ever tell Anessa where we are right now?"

"Nope," he said with a rueful laugh. "But you didn't either."

"This isn't *our* home," Mom explained, as I stared agog. "We're currently guests of the Queen of Rhinebur, Her Majesty Fleure. Remember Anessa, you were given that gemstone on your birthday? That was Fleure. This is her home, not ours."

For a moment the color drained from my face, remembering Queen Fleure's reaction when I inadvertently disintegrated her very valuable gift. Mom simply smiled broadly. *I hope I don't owe Fleure anything for that.*

As if reading my mind Mom said, "That was a gift, don't worry about losing it. In fact, it broke doing exactly what it was intended to do."

"What's that?" I asked.

"It was a Greater Essence Stone. When you touched it, you absorbed every drop of its energy." Mom shrugged. "I don't know how or why, though. That's a question for your daddy. The existence of essence stones is fairly common knowledge, even among us mortals, but you need to be a cultivator to use or understand them."

Dad added, "That stone looked like a rainbow because it held essence of every element in it. Only someone with every affinity could absorb it. To anyone else, even me, it's just a pretty rock."

"I didn't do anything, though," I protested. "When you startled me I tried everything I could to grab it after I threw it in the air."

Dad pointed at me. "That. Your determination likely manifested a teeny bit of Will."

Mom covered her ears. "I'm going to go before I hear something I shouldn't." She kissed Dad's cheek and walked away.

She's really a stickler about those scriptures. Very weird.

"Will is how cultivators influence the world around them. Even though you aren't an awakened cultivator yet, the fact that you absorbed the essence from the stone is another positive sign that you are likely to awaken later. That's because no mortal can manifest Will. No matter how hard they try."

"The other day you called my meditation a mindfulness exercise," I said.

"Yeah?" Dad said.

"How do you use it to access your dantians or connect with them for that matter? They store essence, don't they?"

He nodded. "That's right, they do store it. However, as for accessing it. I don't know what to tell you. It's like breathing. Do you think about breathing?"

"Not exactly, no." I said. "But if I try, I can control my breathing. Is it the same for your dantians?"

"I…" He rubbed his chin. "Don't know. I have never tried. I'm not really sure what it would do for me, though." He raised his left hand. "If I control my breathing, it's useful for holding my breath." Raising his right hand he said, "I don't need to hold my essence; even the thought is rather silly."

So there's no time when you'd need to "hold your essence," huh?

"But, I'll think about it. Maybe there's a good reason for it." Shaking his head he continued, "Though I don't think it'll help your situation any."

At the edge of the courtyard was a roll of gauze. It was what we used to wrap our fists when we practiced.

"Daddy, would you mind if we tried to spar?" I said, and put my fists together.

"Sure. Though don't be upset if you end up practicing on your own."

I sighed. "Fine."

After I'd wrapped my knuckles I saw Oliver watching me with a grin as though he were excited.

"What?"

"Nothing! I'm just happy you're finally joining us."

"Oliver," Dad said sternly. "She isn't joining *'us'*. Anessa will be training against me, and then practicing on her own. You two will not spar for a while."

I nodded emphatically. "At least wait until I awaken, or whatever. You'd knock my block off."

Oliver's enthusiasm deflated along with his posture. "Yeah, yeah."

"Practice your forms while I give your sister some pointers." His eyes turned to me. With his hands behind his back and his imposing form before me, he said simply, "Are you ready?"

Moving to a point ten feet from him, I said, "I guess?"

Dad cleared his throat. "Posture, Anessa."

Taking his words to heart, I turned my side toward him, making my attack surface smaller than it would otherwise be. Not that there was a lot of me to attack anyway.

"Here I go," I said, and rushed toward him. When I was three feet from him, my world spun and I found myself on my back. There wasn't even an impact. "What happened?"

"You're very green," Dad said and looked down at me. "Why did you close your eyes?"

"I did?" I blinked.

"You did. Are you afraid of throwing a punch?"

"N-no," I lied. "I'm afraid to hit you."

He laughed. "You will *not* hurt me."

"I know, but I still have qualms about hitting someone I care about."

"Hmm." Holding out his hand, he said, "What if you imagine I'm someone you don't like?"

Standing with his help I said, "There's no one I don't like. I'm only three-Standard-years-old. I'm too young to have enemies."

"True," he chuckled. "Let's try again. Since you don't have any enemies, maybe imagine I'm someone who is trying to hurt Oliver."

Someone trying to hurt my brother? Laughing internally I thought, *Their funeral.* Then I realized, Dad could easily hurt Oliver, and Dad probably wasn't even the strongest person on Anfang.

"Ready?" he asked.

"Yes." Doing my best to visualize my dad as a dark and imposing stranger intent on causing my brother harm, I shifted my weight and moved forward. Last time, I'd yelled when I started off. This time I was focused on the task in front of me.

Dad smiled. "Much better."

My first ten attempts met nothing but air. His smile was lightly mocking me, and I was getting frustrated. When he trained with Oliver, he would at least block his attacks with his palm. He wasn't even bothering to do that with me. "Stop dodging!" I yelled.

"Okay," Dad said and held his hand out like an umpire ready to catch a ball.

This prompting just irritated me further. He'd found a way to irritate me. On my next strike he caught my fist and immediately let it go, making me face-plant.

"That's enough for now," he said with a smile.

Picking myself up off the ground I said, "Yeah. Do you have any pointers?"

"For starters, I appreciate that you don't want to hit anyone that's not your enemy." He teasingly shook the hand I'd punched. "But when you get riled up, you forget all the basics I taught you. For the next hour, practice your forms." He waved his hand and a steel dummy appeared from his storage ring. "Use this as your target." With a smile he added, "Don't worry about breaking it, I have more."

His casual comment made my brow twitch, and I halfheartedly said, "*Okay.*" *Why do I feel like he's mocking me?*

Oliver said, "Can we resume our training?" He eyed me. "If that's okay?"

"Of course it's okay." His silly question made me laugh. "You don't need my permission."

The boy smiled and held Rufus in a defensive posture.

"We're switching to fisticuffs," Dad said, playfully adding, "My hand's still numb from your sister's attack."

"Oh please," I growled. "Laying it on a bit thick, aren't you?"

He shook it again with a smile.

Oliver started to wrap his knuckles.

Over the next ten minutes the two sparred while I was off to the side practicing my forms – an irritating, though necessary, endeavor. Every so often, while sparring with Oliver, Dad would shoot me a glance and call out something I was doing wrong.

It showed what a wide gap there was between the two of them. Defending himself against Oliver took up so little of his attention that he could multitask by training me at the same time.

My brother could K.O. any fighter on Earth without any trouble, yet in this match-up he was still definitely the student.

Dad would occasionally tease me by shaking his hand. Motivation to do better, I guess.

Thanks, Dad.

CHAPTER TWENTY-SEVEN

OBSERVATIONS / JULILAH'S GAZE

Quattoroday, Totharae 18th, 1735
[March 6th, 2028]

IT HAD BEEN two months since Dad joked about *"holding your essence"* and he hadn't spoken of it since. I was tired of waiting for him to say more.

It was the dead of night, far past my usual bedtime, but I was restless. It wasn't clear if it was my training with Dad earlier in the day, or if it bothered me that he had refused to spar with me for the past two months.

I knew I was bad at fighting, but it hurts my pride a little to be put off in the corner to practice alone. He'd even forbidden Oliver from showing me any pointers, unless he was just directing my efforts towards the dummy Dad had put out.

He told me not to worry about damaging the practice dummy, but the look on his face when that one disappeared said otherwise. Not even I was exactly sure what happened.

Sitting on my bed I committed myself to figuring out my dantians, or the "dantian buds" as they were. *The book Kristine lent me talked about a nexus. But every time I've looked for one, I've come up empty.* However, I had developed some skills over time.

My Personal Space, the place I enter when I meditate with intent, had changed over the past few months.

No longer was it a hollow void. I could even visualize my bones, and organs. It goes without saying that the first time I started seeing them it made me a bit squeamish.

Bringing up a mental image of the book reminded me the nexus should be next to the heart, behind the sternum. Yet again, when I looked there it was absent. *Maybe I'm thinking about this all wrong? Maybe it's not behind my breastbone, but inside it?*

Going on this hunch, I tried to peek my "head" inside and broke out into a smile. *Found you.* Imagine a pure white sea urchin whose quills connected to the bone, which were also twisted in a spiral.   The strands spinning out of it were whisper thin. *Weird. Wouldn't something like this make my ribcage weaker?*

Curiosity won its battle against common sense, and I tapped one of the multitude of lines. Doing so caused it to emit a faint light along with a soothing humming sound.

Cool. Then I realized I didn't actually have hands in this area and I wondered how I'd "touched" it. Moving "myself" forward toward the center, I decided to retry my efforts only to find my entire world exploding into a colorful static.

A few seconds passed before the light show dissipated enough to make sense of it all. *What was that? The nexus controls essence. Was every single speck of light essence?!* Since I knew "I" wasn't actually sitting in front of it and wouldn't dissolve in a burst of energy, I nudged it mentally and a similar, yet weaker effect flashed before me.

It's very chaotic. Over the next few hours, I tried again, and again. Each time I worked with it, I started to see a pattern. Every point of light was every kind of essence, overlaid on top of one another in a polychromatic jumble. With a bit of concentration, I was able to single out individual colors.

Then they turned into patterns with even more effort. Until finally I worked into making them individual strands of the same color like Trish had suggested I do. Once I'd done so, I realized there were seventeen. Wait a minute. *Sir Orris said there were* sixteen *elements.*

Going back to my meditation book, I found information about "non-elemental essence" which made me realize the odd one out was likely neutral. The gray color. *Strange, I have never influenced essence directly until this, but I still* know *that's different than the others. Is that why Dad equated dantians to breathing? This is just a natural thing everyone knows?*

Thinking too hard about it hurt my head, so I decided not to. *A question for Dad later.* My inner world fell apart when I heard a click and I looked back at my door, my senses aligning with the external world again. The moons on Anfang gave the house an odd atmosphere on some nights. Fandar bathed me and my room in a peaceful blue, yet the hallway was lit by Lokar, a particularly sinister red this evening, from some window beyond my room.

It's nothing, Anessa. Pushing down the creeping sense that something was wrong, I thought, *I must've just forgotten to shut the door all the way.*

Oliver's bed was empty. That's because being in the Sky Realm meant he didn't need to sleep. Ever. He practiced his forms at night behind the main stables, though he was required to have a sound barrier in place at all times. The first night that he didn't use one made the animals go mad with fear.

When you can punch at Mach three, you sound like a thunderstorm.

My eyes lingered on the open door. I'd half a mind to get up and close it, but I figured it wasn't hurting anyone. So I turned back around and refocused myself inwards to refining my attempts at creating strings of essence. Weaving the sixteen elements together as though they were a cord wrapped around the gray neutral. The cord was impossibly thin.

I could stack a million of these side by side and it'd still be thinner than a hair. Eying my meridians I realized just how much essence they could carry, though I didn't actually know how much energy was in essence of any variety, so what I could do with it *now* was irrelevant.

Pain would lance through my body every time I'd push the essence strands toward my "dantian buds". This would instantly break me out of my concentration. Without my focus, or a properly functioning container to hold the essence, it would rapidly leave me like a leaky bottle cap.

Yay, I can move invisible threads around but not do anything useful with them. I was realizing that cultivation was quite difficult, and every day I envied Oliver more and more.

Something itched inside my nose, and I sneezed. When you sneeze, it amplifies the scents you'd usually ignore. Except this time it was ten times worse.

This was really unpleasant; it was like my sense of smell was attacked by a rabid wet dog. Were anyone to be watching me, they'd see me pawing at and rubbing my nose. A most unusual sight, I'm sure.

Gods, what the nether. Garlic, mint, and a pungent mix of other unique smells assaulted me. *Am I allergic to one of them? This is horrible.*

Walking over to my dresser, I blew my nose. As quickly as the onslaught started, it passed. *Was it something I did?* When the flash of agony went through my body, I let go of the essence around me. At the time I had been trying to push essence toward the main dantian in my head. There were three total in the head, one for each eye, and one for I guessed the brain itself.

It was shortly after I was hit with the pain that I sneezed, and my sense of smell went haywire. The dantian in question was awfully close to my nose, so I wondered if the essence itself was affecting my sense of smell.

Curiosity energized me and the lingering fear that I was being watched vanished. Moving back to my bed I closed my eyes and built up the essence once again.

Moving the essence to the tips of my fingers on my dominant hand, I released it. With my eyes open I touched the surface of my bedding and was surprised to find every nook and cranny was obvious. The tiny divots between the woven surface, even a minuscule piece of dirt I flicked to the side.

Is it a placebo effect? I wondered, and used my off hand to repeat my efforts, and it felt as smooth as the silk it was. *Huh, neat.*

Through the next ten minutes I tried this approach on my other senses and found that I could enhance all of them, except for my vision. When I got to my final sense, hearing, the onslaught made my world spin and I nearly lost my dinner.

Repeating it a few times, to acclimate myself, I realized that I could hear the crickets outside clear as a bell. The shuffling of feet in the hall. To avoid hearing my own breath, I held it. That's when I realized that a measured breathing was constant among the sounds in the night. It was the kind that made the hairs on my neck stand up. Whoever it was, was furious. And close.

Taking a few moments to identify the location of what I could hear, in front of me, the tick-tock of the clock on my dresser, the occasional pat of the cloth shades hitting the wall on my left – the windows weren't air tight – and finally the stranger's breath. Coming from behind me.

From the crack in my door.

Goosebumps formed on my skin and I turned quicker than I thought the person could move. It was Julilah. The tip of her nose lit blue by Fandar. Lokar gave her eyes a menacing look. Before I could say anything, she closed the door.

Seeing it was just Julilah sent a wave of relief through me. *Maybe I was imagining her anger? Who knows how long she was really there, she could've just been closing my door.* That's what I told myself, at least.

After that, no matter what I did, I wasn't able to reenter my Personal Space. Being unable to do much of anything without dantians dampened my enthusiasm, and since I'd just experienced a bit of a scare, I knew I wouldn't be able to sleep.

The library isn't that far away. They'd finished cleaning the books in the library, and then moved straight on to renovating part of it, leaving it inaccessible for some time. This trek down the hall was uneventful, but the sense that I was being watched never left me.

Among the sea of books, I found what I thought I was looking for. "Precursors to Cultivation" Right as I was about to remove it from the shelf, a voice called, "Who's there?"

I froze on the spot and slowly turned toward the voice. It was the same cat-kin maid that I'd evaded months ago. She was staring right at me, and was holding a lantern.

Crap.

"Anessa," I squeaked.

"I see," she said. Her voice measured and unamused. "Please wait here for a moment."

Double crap.

In less than ten seconds someone had taken her place. They held the light forward on me the entire time as the cat-girl ran off to fetch *someone*.

When she returned, with Mom in tow, I knew my duck was cooked.

Shit.

"Thank you," she said to the two maids. Crossing her arms, she added, "You are both dismissed."

"Hi mommy!" I said to break the ice.

"What are you doing here, in the middle of the night," her voice dropped an octave, "young lady?"

"Um…" In my fear of what they might do if I moved, I realized I was still in the off-limits area of the library. I admitted, "Looking for a book."

"Mhmm." Mom nodded. "You know you're not supposed to be in that part of the library, right?"

Thinking myself clever, I said, "But it's not the adult–"

"I know very well what is in that area." Her tone sharpened. "Due to the scriptures, not even I am allowed to browse that section. I know you're permitted to learn in the cultivator scripture studies, but that's because it's under supervision."

"S-sorry mommy."

She held out her hand. "Come on then."

Taking her hand she led me out of the library. As we approached the maid's area, a few pairs of eyes ducked out of sight behind the mostly-closed door as we walked by.

It wasn't so much that I'd gotten caught, as the look on Mom's face. My stomach roiled and my face and chest grew hotter as we went. Clearing the final hall, I spotted Julilah.

Before I could be sure about what I thought was a smile on her face, she flicked her fan open, hiding her mouth, while she fanned herself.

Surely she didn't…

CHAPTER TWENTY-EIGHT

FAMILY DINNER / NOBLESSE

Quattoroday, Evantaiae 18th, 1735
[May 7th, 2028]

ALMOST A MONTH after I was caught sneaking into the library, my ban was still in effect. I also had to write an apology letter to Her Majesty Fleure for my transgression.

Before us was the largest meal we'd had since our first Anfang birthday. Nearly every inch of the table was covered with some delectable dish or other. In the center of the table was an entire boar. I'd nearly freaked the first time they did this, though I'd gotten used to it. This was almost business as usual, save for the sheer quantity.

"Everyone," Dad started and raised his glass. He tapped its side with a fork. "I'd like to announce that we're departing for the Redwood Kingdom tomorrow."

This was news to me.

"Daddy, why so soon?" Though I'm regularly left out of "adult" conversations, I still generally thought I knew more or less what was going on, and this departure seemed pretty abrupt to me.

"We've stayed in Rhinebur long enough," he motioned toward the end of the table. "Our host has been more than accommodating over these few years."

Following his gesture, I noticed the same overdressed woman from our birthday party. Instead of gold, today she was adorned in a silver dress drenched in jewels of several colors.

Trying to be discreet, I whispered, "Why were we here in the first place, and why Redwood instead of Pitts?"

Dad coughed. "Well, that's complicated. Put simply, Pitts is our hometown, but our new estates are in Redwood."

His comment made me chuckle inside. *Our hometown is the Pitts.*

He shook his head, seemingly reading my mind. For all I knew, he could, though I doubted it.

"As for why our host lent us her manor, Lily went into labor in Rhinebur when we were discussing…" He paused as though searching for the right words. "Politics. Her Majesty instantly offered her estate up for our use." Shaking his head he looked at Oliver and me. "The road is difficult on newborns. And until recently, the railways were experiencing issues with beasts tearing up the tracks."

Fleure spoke up, "It has been my pleasure to host you," her eyes were decidedly fixed on Mom. Then she waved over the table with her glass. "–and your family. You are welcome back anytime."

Ah, brownie points.

Mom smiled in response holding up her glass.

"Speaking of," Fleure said smoothly, "My steward says everything is on track. They've arranged a walk-through if your family is up for it."

Mom replied. "That's perfect, thank you. Were they able to secure our suite?"

Their conversation drifted into details of our trip and I tuned it out since some of it didn't make any sense to me. I *was* curious to see a triple-decker train car, though.

Since they were having their own talk, I decided to ask Dad, "Why weren't Oliver and I told sooner that this isn't our home?"

My question got a collective chuckle out of the adults.

"Anessa, we figured it was obvious," Dad said.

"Obvious? How?" I asked disbelievingly.

He gestured to the side and Fan stepped forward. "Look at the symbol on her arm."

Fan showed off the insignia and moved closer to me, so I could get a good look. It was reminiscent of Cherry Kingdom's emblem, but was decidedly simpler.

"Okay, that sort of looks like Cherry Kingdom's crest, how is that supposed to be obvious?"

Dad smiled. "Rea."

One of Fleure's maids stepped forward. Now that I knew the overdressed staff were under her employ, it was obvious, but I still wasn't seeing the part that should have screamed "not our house."

The maid named Rea, presented her back and hiked her thumbs toward the design.

It was of a silver river running through a forest.

Very enlightening… seriously? How's that obvious.

Dad saw that I'd furrowed my brows. "It's a forest river. Bordering the Redwater Empire. Their symbol is well-known throughout both Empires for its imagery."

"I mean," I started, "I get it *now* because mommy told us whose house we're in. But how was it 'obvious'? The pattern is abstract and blends in with their outfit." With a shrug I added, "I figured it was just a pretty motif. The shoulders on the uniforms of the staff have a flared look to them. When paired with the white rim of her collar makes me think of clouds. It breaks the cohesion and brings it closer to the Cloud Forest, which later became the current Obsidian Forest–"

Fleure slammed her hand down onto the table, making me flinch. Staring at Mom with a flinty gaze, she said, "Is that what you were trying to tell me?!"

"Well…" Mom began and the two started in on the fact that the house staffs' outfit was a *recent* change. Or at least recent compared to my age. At one point she moved to talk to Fleure in a quieter voice. I had no idea how this discussion of uniform decoration and embroidered crests had turned so serious.

As I tuned out this conversation as well, I realized how much of a child I had become in my time on Anfang. *When Mom and Dad talk to me, they keep their topics to what they think I know, even if the words they use are not necessarily simple. There's so much about Anfang I still have no clue about.*

Realizing there wasn't more I could do to fix this than read, and sadly, grow up, I turned back to Dad. Recalling the first conversation that went over my head, I asked, "What's a walk-through?"

"Our security will cordon off the train, and we'll walk through the commoner cars." He shrugged. "That's pretty much it."

"Why does it feel like you're leaving something out?" I asked, suspiciously.

"It's supposed to be something about us," his voice took on a pompous air, "'being closer to the common man.'"

His words seemed to run counter to his perspective the other day when Mom said she had effectively married an ant. "Weren't you barely above a commoner yourself?" I asked.

With a nod Dad said, "Yes. That's why this whole thing doesn't make sense."

Ah, he hasn't mentally reframed his mindset to being a higher-class nobleman.

Mom, having finished her conversation with Fleure, piped in, "Roland, you need to get used to it. Meeting commoners was easier for you before because of your status. Expect your ability to effectively showcase your noblesse oblige in person to vanish after this trip."

Dad looked at Mom as though *he* was lost, so she continued, "You'll oversee twenty kingdoms. Your peers will be people such as Lady Fleure, and not the foreman of your mine in Pitts. If you even see him again in the next ten Anfang years, I'd be surprised."

Her words seemed to strike a chord, and his expression grew distant. After a few seconds he said, "Then if I am going to meet him again, it should be tonight." He rose from the table and nodded to Queen Fleure. "Your Majesty."

Mom corrected him, "Roland. Her title to you is Lady."

He sighed. "Lady Rhinebur."

Seeing his reaction, Mom gave a weak smile.

Does Mom not like correcting him, or is it that she knows this will be difficult for him?

"Isn't Pitts over fifteen thou–" I'd started to say, then I heard a tell-tale sign that "normal" doesn't apply to Dad: a sonic boom followed by a faint rumbling. "Never mind." Seconds later a much louder boom shook the dishes on the table and made my ears *pop*. What seemed like shouting from the sky, took over the prior noise. It took a minute before the cacophony faded enough for conversation to resume.

Mom put her face into her hand and grumbled, "Roland."

"Was that horrific sound daddy?" I asked, afraid that I knew the answer.

She sighed. "Yes, and he's going to hear about that racket later." With a smile she held up her hands and said, "But not from me."

Who exactly would want *to tell him off?* I wondered, "How fast can he go even?"

My answer came from Oliver. "A hundred thirty thousand miles an hour." He shook his head. "Though when he goes that fast, he's usually a lot higher up in the air." He held his hands over his ears. "That was so loud! I've only seen him go that fast when I've been inside his bubble. Inside it is quiet."

A few seconds passed as those at the table seemed to forget how to speak, and stared at the boy as though he'd grown another head.

Mom's tone firmed, and she stared Oliver down. "You mean that ruckus was a choice?"

Oliver's smile faded and he looked down. "Y-yes, I guess so."

Her eyes weren't on me, and I made my own gaze scarce.

A few maids clustered around Queen Fleure and she started giving them terse instructions. Seems dad's dramatic departure had spooked all of the animals.

In the entire town.

It had also spooked some of the people at the table. The look on Kristine's face was mirrored on her daughter Veronica's. They both had their ears down and the tails were puffed out behind them.

I imagine the sound was worse for them.

Mom's voice took on an unexpectedly false and cheery tone. "The other reason we're moving is you're both going to start school when you both turn five-Standard-years-old."

"What's school?" Oliver asked innocently.

Moving forward in my chair I asked eagerly, "Do they have a big library?"

Looking at Oliver, she said, "School is a place of learning." Her attention turned to me, and she gave me a sly look. "Yes, it has a library." She paused and a simple grin managed to peek out. "Though the same scripture rules will apply."

Making a small fist I balled up the anger at her words into my fist and released it. *She's not doing it out of malice,* I reminded myself.

"Will I still get to spar with daddy?" Oliver asked.

The clamor outside had finally quieted down, leaving an odd silence in the air. My ears caught Kristine quietly cursing Dad's decision to leave in such a hurry.

Mom put her elbows on the table and placed her chin over her folded hands. "I'm not sure about that, but there might be someone you can spar with at the school."

"Will they be as strong as daddy?"

She smiled. "Maybe."

He stood and shoved his chair behind him. "Really!" It skittered across the tiles in a high-pitched screech.

The noise earned him more than a few glares. It seemed more than a few people were still on edge.

Oliver dipped his head to everyone. "Sorry." He pulled his chair back up to the table, finished off his tenth plate of food, and then yawned.

"All right you two, get ready for bed. Tomorrow morning you'll have a big day ahead of you." Mom's smile broadened. "You might even have something waiting for you in the morning."

CHAPTER TWENTY-NINE
TRAIN RIDE TO THE FUTURE

Midday, Evantaiae 19th, 1735
[May 9th, 2028]

THE FOLLOWING MORNING Fan woke me up early. She had clothes laid out and ready for me. They were unlike anything I'd worn before.

A peach-colored shift that was basically a medieval equivalent of a short slip. Embroidered with filigree along the collar and chest.

Next to that was a silk taffeta petticoat, a lacy charmeuse underskirt and an apron. If that weren't enough, the "dress" that went over all of this was comprised of several parts, including a bodice, a doublet, and an outer skirt. The doublet and outer skirt were a teal brocade material with light gray accents, and the rest was an off-white. On the shoulders was a gold and silver embroidered crest, which I guessed was our new family crest, and a fleur-de-lis.

Finally there was a belt, which I assumed brought the two halves together.

Most concerning for me was something I'd largely ignored since I was reborn. There were no undergarments beyond the shift. I'd generally compensated for this by wearing leggings, which around here were typically used by boys, to preserve my modesty.

"Fan," I said evenly. "Where are the leggings?"

"What leggings?"

Holding the shift up to my body I showed her how high it was. "This barely covers anything at all!"

"Right," she said, with no concern whatsoever. "Would you like Oliver to leave the room while you get dressed?"

Going over to my dresser I pulled out the hosiery I usually wore, and threw it onto the bed.

"Yes, that's a first step. I usually change in the bathroom." Looking over the ensemble, I added, "But *this* might require some help."

Fan unceremoniously plucked what I'd thrown onto the bed and put it back. "You won't be wearing that, I'm afraid." She held up a finger and pointed toward me. "Your mommy already told me so." She deflated, and said pleadingly, "Please don't cause me any trouble."

Oliver, in a rare occurrence, was asleep on his bed. Although he didn't *need* sleep, he had eaten half the entire boar last night and presumably needed some time to digest it. There had to be something otherworldly about cultivators, because my brother had eaten literally twice his weight in boar meat! That was a real magic trick, to me.

Fan must've been watching me because she picked him up and called for someone at our door. After they took him, she told them about his equally ornate outfit.

They called in two people to help take his outfit to wherever he was getting dressed. The second person only carried the dummy that held his belt. Which made me wonder, *Just how expensive are these clothes!?*

Noting their care, I saw the clothes laid out neatly onto my bed, but the belt was to the side on a dummy. *I'm going to guess that's the most expensive part.* It was also the simplest looking, save for the maroon, jewel-encrusted brooch-like ornament at its center.

"Can you turn around while I put this shift on?"

Fan put her hands on her hips. "Anessa, I've given you baths, why are you being strange?"

Giving her my best puppy-dog eyes, I asked, "Please?"

With a sigh she said, "As you wish."

I'd never worn a petticoat before in my past life, not even at prom. When you're six feet, finding nice clothes in a world built for the average is a challenge. So back on Earth, my clothes had been relatively simple. Unlike Anfang's more elaborate fashions. And this outfit seemed even more ornate and complicated by those standards. My inexperience met me head-first when I tried to put on my petticoat.

Fan watched for a minute or two before asking, "Would you like some help?"

Sighing, I said, "Yes, please."

She made quick work of it, wrapping my waist and fastening it in place. Then she moved on to the underskirt, which went over the petticoat. It snapped into place much the same.

The sleeveless bodice was more like a vest. While I put it on, Fan busied herself with adjusting the underskirt and making everything sit nicely. Much like the prior layer, the apron needed finessing so it was centered properly.

"Ugh," I said, as she tightened the lace on the doublet. "Does it need to be so tight?"

She smiled. "I was actually being gentle."

Great.

Without her, I would've never got the outer skirt in place since it was open in the front and seemed to be more to show off the apron, which I found odd. Once it was roughly in place, she secured it around my waist by lacing it into the doublet in five spots around me.

This is so unnecessarily complicated. Though it did remind me of when I helped Trish get ready for a renaissance fair. She had me tie up her corset in the back. I had a final that day, so I was unable to actually go with her.

Fan put the belt around my waist and said, "I was told to inform you of this, above all else: wear the belt. Even if you're in a hurry and put the simplest outfit on." She secured it around my waist. "Make sure you put this on."

Feeling like an over-stuffed turkey, I asked, "Is it special?"

"Something like that. I don't know *why*, only what I was to say."

Finally, she handed me a teal beret made from the same material as the over skirt. I just looked at it for a moment.

"Really?"

She nodded. "Really."

Grumbling I sat it on my head and she went to "fixing" it. Then she used a hairpin of sorts to secure it in place. Although I was so laced-in and wrapped-up in this complicated get-up that I doubted I'd be doing anything active enough to risk losing my hat.

Fan held out her hand and smiled. She said, "Look at yourself in the mirror."

Following her lead, I stood before the full-length mirror in our room and gasped. I looked like an honest-to-god princess. The clothes were tight, heavy, and to my eyes, wildly impractical. Though I'd simply gotten dressed, the look reminded me our lives were about to get more interesting.

"Good morning Lady Anessa," Dad said. Today he wasn't wearing his usual military attire; his outfit was a multi-layered affair as well. It was mostly black with flourishes of white. The mantle on his shoulders was finished with a much larger version of our new family crest on his back.

"Morning daddy. These clothes are stifling," I said.

He pulled at his collar. "You're telling me." With a sigh he said, "We'll just have to get used to it."

I'd been following alongside him and stopped in my tracks. "For how long?"

He turned to me and wiggled his fingers. "Forever!"

Knowing he was trying to tickle me, I gave a squeal that was more piercing than I wanted and evaded his grasp.

He caught me, of course.

During his efforts to torment me, a cough stopped us in our tracks. It was Julilah. "We need to get moving." Her outfit was much the same as it usually was, though it had even *more* detail and I think her dress billowed out more.

Dad smirked and put his arm around her. "Yes, my dear."

In a rare exchange, I saw her smile broadly. Though I tried to follow after them I was again stopped by Fan.

"Anessa, please stand still. I need to fix your dress."

Her interruption made me cross my arms. "Fine."

It took her five minutes to undo the chaos caused by mere seconds of tomfoolery.

Finally, we took a carriage to the train station; however, a few people were absent.

"Daddy, where's mommy and Oliver?" I asked.

"Oliver was a little slow to get around, so we went ahead."

"Oh, okay."

When I caught sight of the train I did a double take. Triple-decker cars that were three to three and a half times wider than I was used to on Earth. They were a sight to behold, though they were somewhat shorter than what I was used to. I might have been the only one gawking at it.

As I made a motion to exit the cabin, Dad stopped me. "Hold on, sweetie. We need to wait for our security detail."

"Can't you protect us?" I asked.

"Of course he can," Julilah said flatly. "But there's a proper way to do things. While he could most certainly protect us, it's not his place to do so. There will also be times when he isn't around." She leaned back and looked out the window. "What would you do then?"

As usual, Julilah was right. Though her way of putting it always rubbed me the wrong way.

Shortly after, a knock came at our door. Whoever was on the other side opened it without waiting for a reply. It was a dapper gentleman with a villain's curly mustache. "Good morning Your Imperial Grace," he said and bowed. "We have completed the security check, and have found…" he paused. "No issues."

"Very good," Dad replied and stood. "Let's go girls."

Exiting our carriage, the "big deal" factor went up. On either side of us was a guard, and there were two more on standby. When we moved, they moved.

Moving closer to the train, the walkway was stanchioned off almost all the way to our carriage. The passengers yet to board were standing outside with their luggage curiously looking at us. We were new, so there was little chance they knew who we were. The fact that the area was secured so well definitely left an impression. On both sides of the aisle.

When we reached the train entrance, our escorts took to either side and stood there like statues. Inside it looked much like you'd expect a train to be, but far wider. There was plenty of space to walk down the aisle, and each individual passenger had their own cabin.

The last train ride I went on, you were allotted a seat and that was basically it. Here there were only eight cabins, per car, per level. Some space was used by the stairs and the entrance.

The corridors were of pure steel, though people who had boarded before security did its thing were roped off from exiting. Once again there were several looky-loos who seemed more confused or inquisitive to our walk-through.

After we entered the fourth train car, Dad stopped. "Jean!"

Jean had a complicated expression. Along with us was a single senior guard, Mr. Mustache, I called him in my head. Jean's eyes kept flickering between Dad and Mustache.

"Go ahead," Mr. M. said.

"H-How have you been Roland?"

"Great, it's nice to see you again."

Julilah stopped a few feet in front of me and had turned toward us.

Dad's conversation seemed to drag, and she said, "Roland. I'm going ahead."

He nodded. "Go on. I'll catch up."

Julilah did so and I was left in an odd spot. His demeanor said he would be a few minutes still, so I decided I'd try and catch up to Julilah, who had raced two cars ahead of me already.

I'd nearly made it to the end of the car when Dad shouted, "Anessa!"

Freezing in place I put my hands over my head, caught completely off guard. Hearing him say nothing else, I turned back toward him.

Instead of talking to Jean, Dad was holding up someone I didn't know, supporting the man with his arm over his shoulders.

"Sorry for yelling," Dad said. "This gentleman simply had too much to drink," he handed off the stranger to Jean who took him inside the cabin to his side. "I just didn't want you to get too far ahead of me."

I'd been afraid to move since he shouted, and when he reached me he swooped down and picked me up.

I protested, "Hey, I can walk."

"I know, I just want to carry you." He looked me in the eyes. "Is that so bad?"

With a huff, I said, "I suppose not." I heard a few voices behind us, talking in hushed tones. "Can I stand on your arm daddy?"

"Um," he arched his brow. "I guess?"

Using my higher vantage point I looked over Dad's shoulder.

Jean had something covered with a cloth.

Based on the outline I could see, I asked quietly, "Daddy. Why is Jean holding a knife?"

Dad stammered at my question. "O-oh, Jean was simply showing me a present he got from his grandfather. I told him to cover it so it wouldn't alarm the passengers."

Narrowing my eyes at him I asked, "Really?"

He nodded. "Really."

Being carried, even while standing on his arm, made me more self-conscious of our unusual situation. I hadn't been this tall in quite a while, not since the days of my lofty Earthen body. It was kind of nice, though at the same time, it probably looked like he was carrying a doll around. *I hope this doesn't start any weird rumors.*

When we exited the final car into the suite we reserved I gaped at the sight. The entire car was a single giant room. Sure, it was divided off with furniture, but it was about a thousand square feet by itself. Instead of three levels, it was all one chamber. The walls were likely still steel, but you couldn't tell with the elegant veneer and decor that surrounded us. The window on either side spanned almost the entire length of the car. "Wow."

Dad sat me on the floor.

Sitting on a couch opposing Veronica I saw Julilah reading a book to our side. She lowered it enough to see me and clicked her tongue. After that she stood and walked off.

"Did I say something wrong?" I asked Veronica.

"I don't know." Her nose twitched and she turned around, watching as Julilah left the lounge car. "On-pa seems tense today."

For the first time, Veronica was wearing a dress. Problem is, when she turned around she put her knees on the couch. She had also forgotten to slot her tail through the garment's layers. I guessed she didn't have the same kind of help that I did when she got dressed this morning.

Her lack of familiarity with the gown meant she was currently raising her skirt, petticoat and shift up, exposing her rear.

Dang this world and lack of proper undergarments.

Dad said, "Was that Julilah leaving?" He folded his arms and sighed. "She a had guard that led her to this car, but I told her we need to stay together once we're here."

Without thinking, I ran over to Veronica and pushed down her dress and tail, while facing Dad.

He looked at me like I was a madwoman.

"What are you doing Anessa?" Veronica asked.

"Yes," Dad said. "Do tell."

"Daddy, can you um…" Looking around the lobby I realized it was just one open space. "Turn around?"

"Why?"

"Wardrobe malfunction?" I said nervously.

"Wardrobe what now?" he asked, perplexed.

Veronica jumped over the couch making me fall back onto the cushion.

From my new vantage point I saw Veronica's face was beet red.

"Please turn away!" she said.

"O–kay," he said and complied.

"You too," she said to me.

"Okay."

It took her a minute to correct the issue, and she said finally, "Okay, done."

"What was that about anyway?"

She stammered. "I wasn't fully awake when I got dressed, and I'm not used to dresses at all." Pulling her tail around in front of her, into her hands she played with the tip. She looked everywhere but at us.

"You'll get used to it," Dad said absently, his tone clearly saying he didn't grasp the gravity of what happened.

"Veronica, wanna go explore?"

Her tail perked up behind her, this time without taking her skirt with it. "Yes."

For thirty minutes we looked over the lounge. It included a bar, a small bathroom, a dining area, a piano, and a seating area facing the gigantic window.

"Sorry if I embarrassed you," I said finally.

Veronica replied, "It's okay."

"Are you mad at me?"

"No, why?"

"You asked me to turn around, too. I wondered if I'd done something wrong."

She sighed. "It's not that. Remember the whole emperor thing?"

I nodded.

"It's just awkward, thinking about the future." Once again she started to play with her tail. "If you were to be my–"

"Stop!" I held up my hands and did my best to push down the embarrassment. "Remember, we're not supposed to think about stuff like that. Positive thoughts."

Her ears flattened out and she let go of her tail. "They're not entirely bad thoughts," she said in a small voice.

"I'm not even four-Standard-years-old." I exhaled. "That's not something I want to think of… not for a while yet." At the time I had the thought, *I don't have the heart to tell her I'll never see her in that way.*

At the end of our exploration, the train car started to move. We took to the plush seating near Dad. Seeing no one else had joined us made me ask, "Daddy, where's mommy, Oliver and Kristine? Weren't they supposed to meet up with us?"

Dad had apparently grown bored watching us ramble about and was reading a book. Though I knew he was still perfectly capable of watching us while reading. He closed his book and patted the seat next to himself.

Once I'd taken my seat he said, "They're actually on a different train."

"What? Why?"

He shrugged. "It's just a safety thing."

His words put me on edge. *Should I be worried?*

"It's not that we expect any danger," Dad consoled. "We should just always plan for it."

Veronica had taken to licking her thumb and pawing at her ears.

Dad chastised her. "Stop that Veronica."

She froze mid-lick and eyes widened like a cat caught doing something wrong. "What?"

"Don't groom yourself like that." He turned to the side. "Fan."

She'd been silent as a mouse and stepped forward from the corner of the train car. Looking around, I saw a few familiar faces. Our head maid and two others were unobtrusively waiting in the other corners.

Did he call for Fan because she's the closest, or because he favors her, just like Mom does?

"Yes Your Imperial Grace?" she asked.

"Please assist Veronica." The playfulness in his voice vanished. "Make sure she knows not to groom herself, or at the very least, the *proper* way to do so."

She bowed. "Very good sir."

Why is Fan being so formal?

At each of the exits to the lounge were two soldiers standing on either side of the door. *Appearances?*

Fan helped brush Veronica's ears and fetched a mirror to help her do it herself.

Looking out the window, I realized that the train couldn't have been doing more than thirty miles an hour, making its stately way down the tracks in no particular hurry. When Dad told us about the trip last night, I had looked up our likely route. It was over eleven thousand miles. "Daddy, how long is this trip going to take?"

In response, he turned back to his book.

"Settle in, Anessa," he said. "We're going to be here a while."

CHAPTER THIRTY
NEW HOME / CONNECTIONS

Triday, Lokandae 8th, 1735
[June 14th, 2028]

OUR TRIP TOOK sixteen days. Anfang days, that is. In Earth days, it was over thirty-six. I was very glad by the end of it we had luxurious accommodations, and was equally glad to be out of them.

As I stepped out of the train car I stretched, and said, "Thank the gods we're finally here!"

Today's outfit was much like on my first day, but it was a rich-purple with flowers along the hem of the outer skirt. My hat was one of those tiny hats with feathers sticking out of it that had little use other than being "stylish" I guessed.

To my dismay, our freedom was short-lived. We were ushered onto yet another carriage and made to wait until our security detail had checked ahead.

"This waiting stinks," I grumbled.

Julilah surprised me and replied, "I am inclined to agree."

"Maybe I should just fly us there and be done with it," Dad complained.

She glared at him and said, "You've been grounded, remember?"

"Griblin's giblets," he said. "Eugene and his–"

"Eugene didn't blast across the sky loud enough to scare half of Westwood." Her tone soured, "It ruined Kristine's mood that night, too."

What does she mean by that?

Dad mumbled, "Sorry."

Veronica covered her now crimson face.

Kristine and Julilah are Veronica's parents, which means... My thoughts were interrupted by a rather impure mental image, so I looked out the window.

He whispered, "I'll make it up to you, both of you."

"Daddy," I said crossly. "I can still hear you."

Our carriage began to move eliciting a sigh of relief from everyone.

"What's our home like?" I asked, changing the subject.

He laughed. "No clue."

Right, this is as new to him as the rest of us. Taking over a noble title that isn't ours is strange.

Twenty minutes of awkward silence led Veronica to finally say, "Wow." She was sitting opposite me and had a better view of what we were approaching.

Turning around and standing on my seat I saw a gigantic gate. It was so large that by the time we were next to it in our tiny carriage I couldn't even see the top from my window.

Holy crap. Wait, she could be getting ahead of herself. Maybe it's just one of the gates between sections in Redwood's capital.

"Anessa," Julilah said. "Turn around and sit down. That is not safe."

"What's going to–" I said and then the carriage stopped at the gate and I smacked my head against the seat. *Ow.* Following her suggestion I did as instructed.

She didn't say anything further, but when I looked at her she raised her eyebrows and nodded as if to tell me, "See, what'd I tell you?"

"Are you okay?" Veronica asked quietly.

Rubbing the side of my head I said, "Yeah." I whispered, "It mostly hurt my pride."

Dad, sitting next to me, hugged me from the side, rubbing my arm. It didn't help the pain, but I did feel better.

After we made it through the gate we stopped once more. Again we waited on "security."

Veronica's tail shot straight up beside her. I have wondered several times what having a tail might be like. But after her issue at the start of our trip, I was glad I didn't have to deal with it.

In the down-time Dad commented, "Oliver is going to get a kick out of Kile."

"Who's that?"

In answer he just shook his head. "You'll see."

When they finally knocked, we exited and saw a building in front of us that rivaled the Biltmore Estate. In the distance were several buildings nearly as big as the Florham.

"Welcome to the Carlyle Estates," Mom said. She had apparently arrived before us.

We followed her and I was bursting with curiosity. "Estates? You mean there's more than one?"

"Mhmm, everything within these walls is ours now." She stopped in place. "Though it's not like we get it for free."

Curious as to her meaning I said, "Oh?"

"Your daddy is the mantle of our family, the patriarch. Which means he's responsible for collecting taxes, attending meetings on improvement projects…" She went on for at least five minutes listing just his responsibilities.

Near the end of it, each new thing she listed made him sigh. His nodding implied that he knew about them, but was less and less pleased about it the more he heard.

"Now then. Lana is over there," she pointed to the north, at a vast estate anyone would be pleased with all on its own.

Dad said, "Sorry love, I have to go meet with the house butler. There are some things I need to get squared away."

Mom nodded, then turned her focus to Veronica and me. "Marcus is over there."

Julilah and Fan left with Dad, leaving just Veronica and me.

"You're giving each two-year-old an estate of their own?"

Mom nodded. "They'll have someone with them at all times. Julilah will visit him as needed." She turned to me. "You, and Oliver are in the main estate. As the heirs to our new domain, you two are best kept with us." she said to Veronica, "We'll have someone get you settled in to your own area later. If you'd rather stay in the main estate for a while, just let me know."

"So I don't get my very own [mansion]?" I said, a little jealously. The English slipped in unconsciously. I was surprised there wasn't a clear Estar equivalent.

"I'm not sure what a man-shin is, but if you mean your own estate, no. It's not that we're being mean. We just have something else in mind for you."

Dropping my arms I thought, *Yeah, more babysitting me. I mean I get that I'm not even four-years-old yet, but still.* Looking over at my not-brother's and my younger brother's places made a little burst of hot envy rise up in my chest.

"Lily-li," came a familiar voice.

Mom turned around with a broad smile, only to be glomped by Nicole.

Nicole furthered my surprise by giving Mom a kiss on the lips.

"Okay, so that's a thing," I said before I caught myself. *It isn't super surprising though, they're always holding hands at church, though this is the first overt sign I've seen.*

The two broke away from one another, and Mom said to me, "I guess you and I need to talk later?"

All I could do was nod.

"Sissy!" Oliver said and almost bowled me over. He grabbed my hands and was jumping up and down. "Mommy told me we have a new teacher!"

Mom held up a finger and said, "Actually. That only applies to you, Oliver."

"Oh," he said. Then he continued to jump. "I got a new teacher! It's the same one that trained daddy."

"Speaking of," Mom said. "Why don't we go meet him?"

Oliver's face brightened further and he let go of my hands. He started to run circles around Mom. "Let's go, let's go, let's go!"

Did being cooped up for a few weeks make him even more *hyper?*

Mom guided us into the main estate, through at least ten hallways, and finally out into a courtyard that was surrounded by the estate on all sides.

This is big enough for four football fields, in all directions!

In the center was a slightly raised platform. As we approached it a man standing on it moved through various martial arts forms of some kind. The smoothness of his movements put even Dad to shame, and they flowed like water from one motion to the next. Next to the platform was our half-brother Lom, who was standing and watching him.

"Is that Kile?" Oliver asked and jumped into the ring.

Up until that point the man ignored us. But the instant Oliver's foot touched the platform his form blurred and he held the tip of his training sword at Oliver's nose, making him fall over.

"Oliver," Mom said with a cheery voice. "Meet Kile."

The boy's initial reaction was to stop in his tracks. After he saw the man's movements, he started to smile. "Awesome!"

"If you enter the ring, be prepared to spar," Kile said in an aged voice. He tossed Oliver another training sword from his storage space.

"We didn't come here to spar," Mom protested.

"Oh, come on mommy. We'll only go a few rounds," Oliver said.

She sighed, it seemed his energy was infectious. "Fine. Best of three."

"Five?" Oliver countered.

"I don't know," she said. "We're all awful tired from the trip."

"I'm not!" he insisted.

I'd watched Oliver and Dad spar numerous times. Oliver was blindingly fast, superhuman even. But his movements were often wild, and chaotic. "That's okay, mommy," I said. "I don't think it'll take long."

Kile looked my direction and narrowed his eyes. "Why? Because he's in the Sky Realm?"

Interesting. Who told him that? I shook my head, and remembered how he moved. "No. Because you're skilled." Looking at my brother I added, "He can teach you a lot. You're really good Oliver, but I don't think you can beat him right now."

"All right," Mom exhaled again. "Best of five."

Kile took his position in the ring and said, "Position yourself opposite of me, and get ready."

"Okay!" Oliver said, and complied.

Kile looked at me. "Do you want to initiate each round?"

"I guess," I said. *What does he want as a sign to start?*

"There are stairs on that other edge," he said and pointed to the side. "Stand between us near the edge of the ring."

After I'd done so, I held up my hand. "Okay." Swiping my hand down in a chopping motion, I said, "Start!"

A blink later and Kile was behind Oliver. He tapped his shoulder with his wooden sword. "One." In the same time, he'd moved back to his starting position. He turned to me. "Ready."

I repeated my motion and Kile batted Oliver's sword out of his hand and placed the tip of his against his chest. "Two."

H-holy crap.

Kile moved back into position and nodded to me.

"S-Start."

"Three," he said, even quicker than before. This time Oliver was somehow on the ground with the tip of Kile's sword at his throat.

I'd expected Oliver to lose, but damn. No wonder Dad says he's never beat Kile. He's lightning fast… or faster.

To my surprise, he moved into position again, and waited for Oliver to stand. The old gentleman nodded.

My hand struck down a fourth time, and before I heard, Kile say "Four." A clack rang out. Oliver had managed to counter the first strike.

Before Kile could reset again, Mom interrupted. "Okay. You're done for now. Best of five already went to Kile."

"You're awesome!" Oliver said. "When do we start training?"

Kile put his sword away, as well as Oliver's. "We just did."

"Right," Mom said and rushed over to Lom. "Oliver, Lom is going to be your squire starting today. He will help you get dressed, maintain Rufus, and generally assist you with anything you might need."

Oliver smiled. "Will Lom and I be able to spar?"

"No," Kile snapped. "You would kill him, likely on accident." He put his hand to his chest. "I'll take care of his training."

Why is Lom being trained by Kile, but Mom said explicitly that he's not my teacher. Given it ran completely counter to what I remember squires doing, I asked, "Why does he have a squire he cannot train himself? That seems unusual."

"Oliver's strength is unusual, for his age at least." Kile sat on the edge of the ring, looking at me. "Until he has improved his control, it's better this way."

My brother was running around the littler boy, whose ears were plastered to the side of his head, his tail puffed up in agitation.

Yeah Kile's right. Little Lom wouldn't last a day. Pointing to myself, I said, "What about my training?"

Kile's eyes darted from me to Mom a few times before he said, "Ma'am?"

She came over to me and put her hands on my shoulders. "You… won't be training."

I pulled away, turning toward her and said, "What? Why not?"

"Well, girls–" she started.

"What does me being a girl have to do with it?" I said, cutting her off. "Lom's younger than me, and *also* not a cultivator yet." My hands went to my chest. "Does that mean I won't be training with daddy any more either?"

Mom pursed her lips and shook her head.

"That's [bull]shit!" I shouted and stormed off.

CHAPTER THIRTY-ONE

THE LADY'S MAID /
LESSONS ON PRIVILEGE

MOM CAUGHT UP with me, and picked me up by hugging me from behind, reminding me that I was still a child. She said in a soothing voice, "Calm down, honey."

"It's not fair!" I complained. "Daddy told me if I were to marry Redwater's Emperor, it would be because I was still a mortal." I wiggled in her grasp, hoping she'd let me down. "Now you're telling me that I'm not even being trained because I'm a girl?!"

Mom did set me down, but she turned me around and held me close. "It's complicated, honey. There is a very slight edge given to boys when they're your age on physical activities." Her voice was soft. "But Lom's in a similar situation, actually. If he never awakens, he'll trade his sword for a pen, and his privilege for *duty*. He would be the husband and consort of someone powerful."

Knowing Lom wasn't out of the woods oddly took some of the bite out of her refusal to let me train. "Sorry," I said, muffling my words against her chest.

She stroked the back of my head. "It's all right. Let's go find your new bedroom, okay?"

"Mhmm." I replied, but thought, *This is still unfair.*

"Oliver, Lom," she said, "let's go."

We entered the estate and went through another maze of halls. Mom knocked on a door made of deep brown wood which had a "kids shouldn't be here" vibe.

A tall slender man opened the door. His face had oddly forgettable features I had difficulty recalling. "Yes, madam?"

"Mr. Morris, are you done with Roland? If so, could you help me find the childrens' rooms?"

He bowed, "But of course."

Leaving the room filled with leather couches and chairs behind us, we wound through the house once again. It seemed like a maze to me. How Mom could navigate it was beyond me.

"Here we are," he said finally and opened the door. Everything inside looked like Oliver's portion of our old room, dialed up to eleven. He had a proper mantle for Rufus, an enormous array of clothes, and a second bed, which it turned out wasn't for me.

"Lom, you'll be sharing a room with Oliver." Mom put her hand on his back and ushered him inside. "Please try to get along."

He said, "Yes ma'am." His voice was high-pitched and almost sounded like a kitten mewing.

Gods he's so cute.

Mom sat me on the floor. "Anessa, your room is over... here?" She looked to Mr. Morris for confirmation, and he nodded. We moved across the hall and she opened another door. My room was, for lack of a better word, girly. There were hints of my prior decor, but thankfully the gaudy flourishes of Lady Fleure's home were absent.

Thinking myself clever, I asked Mom, "What's stopping me from practicing my forms in my room?"

Before she could reply, Mr. Morris said, "Sarah."

A girl with black hair stepped around the corner, startling me. I fell on my bottom and may have shouted in surprise.

"Were you just standing there, waiting?"

"Yes," she said flatly.

She had a similarly murky face as Mr. Morris did. *Weird. Is this odd feeling and difficulty remembering their faces on purpose, so that we don't become attached?*

"Anessa," Mom said. "Meet your new Lady's maid. She will help you with your day to day issues..." After pausing a bit she added, "Actually, let's let Sarah fill you in. I'm going to turn in for the evening. I know it's early, but I'm beat."

My door closed and Mom left me alone in a new room with a stranger. She was tall, and I would say pretty, but that was based on her hair, ears, and general outline.

"Hello," I said awkwardly, trying to break the ice.

"Hi."

"Where are you from?"

"Here."

That wasn't helpful, though I suppose if she lives here, she may have been born to another maid?

"Will you stop me from practicing my fisticuff forms if I were to do them?" I asked.

"No, but I would be obligated to tell your mother, mistress Lily."

"Do you know *anything* about me?" I asked. "You saw my mommy a minute ago, but would you even know where to find her?"

"Relevant staff received a dossier prior to your arrival. It contained a breakdown of your family hierarchy. It included who was in what room, or estate."

Convenient. So why didn't Mom know where my room was? I figured she had only arrived shortly before we did and only knew where Mr. Morris could be found. "How old are you?"

She turned her head away and didn't answer.

"Have you always been a maid?"

Silence.

"Do you actually want to be here?"

"I am–" She winced, I think. Then took a breath and smiled. "Very happy to be serving you."

Yeah, right. Not very convincing, I thought.

"Do my brothers Lom and Oliver have their own manservants?" I asked, wondering if that was a Lady's maid equivalent.

"Yes, they do."

"Mom said you'd fill me in on what you do. Though I have to say you seem to be answering my questions with the bare minimum needed."

"I apologize Lady Anessa." Sarah bowed to me, far deeper than I thought she should. "There are simply certain topics I cannot discuss."

I sighed. "Okay, no problem. What can you do for me?"

"I will plan your days, assist you with any letters you want sent. Act as a liaison for any tasks you need completed that require talking to craftsmen or otherwise. Your classes will either be taught by me, or I will attend them with you."

Okay, so she's like an assistant, I thought, until she continued.

"Change your clothes. Help bathe you. When you become a woman, I will assist you with any related concerns that arise."

Oh gods, I hadn't thought of what that *will be like given our lack of certain garments. Mom's done a good job of* never *talking about it, either.*

She went on to explain how she'd take care of getting my clothes cleaned, mended, and refitted. Her list of responsibilities made Dad's look short, but they were all focused on one thing: me.

"And me? What will I be *allowed* to do?"

Before she answered my question she changed focus. "How about we get you changed for bed?"

Backing away from her I said, "I can change myself."

"Lady Anessa," her voice firmed. "It is my duty to assist you. I will be by your side for your entire life. If you feel you don't trust me, I can ask madam Lily to provide you with someone else. But you must accept that either I, or someone like me, will be attending to you around the clock."

She hasn't done anything wrong. Looking at her face showed a brief moment of clarity. Her eyebrows were furrowed and turned down in a light frown. It was evident that she was worried.

"I-it's fine. What do you want me to do?" I asked.

"You needn't do anything." She pulled a stool from the side of the room and lifted me up onto it. One by one the layers of the stuffy garment I'd worn for the day were peeled away. Moving my hands above my head, she took off my shift and quickly put my night gown on.

Her eyes never drifted into uncomfortable territory, constantly focused on the task at hand.

Sarah started to button my outfit up. She said, "You don't need to keep your arms up anymore."

I was worried over nothing.

Once I was changed, she pulled back my covers and laid me down. That was more awkward than anything, since I was quite capable of doing so myself.

"Next time," I said making her pause. "Let me get in bed on my own, okay?"

She nodded, then proceeded to black out the room the best our old-school shutters could. Once she was finished, she offered a sleep mask, which I accepted.

After I put it on, she said, "Good night."

It made me realize that neither Mom nor Dad really made an effort to tuck me in at night after we were out of diapers. Sarah's words were reminiscent of the few times my prior Mom, Naia, had done so. Suddenly I felt unaccountably lonely.

Good night, Sarah.

When I woke up, or more accurately, was woken up, Sarah was busying herself unpacking the remainder of my things, which had finally caught up with me. The sun was barely up, based on the little light peeking through the blinds.

"Sorry to wake you Lady Anessa," she said. "Though, part of your daily routine includes waking up by first-ten."

Her comments earned her a groan as I flopped back down.

"Today, we have lessons on etiquette. Then table manners. Breakfast, followed by free time. First lunch, then horse riding, but only for an hour, since you're a beginner."

As she continued on with an ever-lengthening list of things I had no interest in, but would be doing anyway, I put my pillow over my head and screamed into it.

After I was done, I removed it and Sarah just stared at me, though I could tell she was fighting a smile.

"Once first dinner is over…" she continued, and I sat up and hung my head in frustration.

Finally finished with her monologue, I asked, "What's the difference between table manners and etiquette?"

Sarah smiled. "Good question, Lady Anessa." She held out both hands, and gestured with her right. "Manners are about controlling your emotions and behavior so you interact well with others." She wiggled her left hand's fingers. "And etiquette is how to act in social situations. What to say, what subjects to avoid, things like that."

"So they're similar, but have distinct purposes?"

She nodded. "Right."

"Can I ask you a favor?"

"Yes, Lady Anessa."

"Would you just call me Anessa?" I asked.

She paused for a moment before replying. "I am sorry. It's not really acceptable for me to do so."

"How about when it's just you and me? You can also avoid saying my name before most sentences. It is a bit stifling."

Sarah crossed her arms. My request seemed to run counter to what she was told, I'd guessed.

"I should be able to do that," she said eventually.

Giving her a bright smile I said, "Thank you."

"At breakfast this morning," Sarah said, "we will go over the utensils and when to use them. These lessons will cover every meal."

"Ugh," I said, "You mean I have to go through the same lessons whenever I eat?"

"Not quite." Sarah shook her head. "Different meals use different flatware, and you'll be expected to know when and how to use each. If you choose to do it yourself, I'll cover the proper way to spread butter on bread, how to toast and react to an offer to do one…"

She went on, and on.

When we got to the dining table everyone in our family was in attendance. *This is nice.* For a moment I was looking forward to actually sharing a meal with everyone.

My eagerness crumbled when Sarah sat down a yellow cube and tapped the top of it. The manservant with Oliver, Lom, and Marcus did the same. Even Veronica's new Lady's maid had prepared a small "cone of silence" so to speak.

This one seemed different than what I was used to. Unlike the one Kristine had used over a year ago, this one also blocked out external sounds.

Great. At least I'm not alone in this– It was difficult to keep a straight face. Dad had his manservant helping him. Looking over, Julilah's Lady's maid was assisting her with… something. Julilah seemed to be holding up one of the utensils and pointing at it.

"Anessa," Sarah said. "This is a butter knife." She pointed to the outermost knife with a rounded tip.

"I know what a butter knife is," I said with a groan.

"Hmm. Okay. If you decide to spread your own butter," she said and fetched the butter dish. "Your knife should be used once for your bread." She took off some butter from the dish and presented it in front of my face. "Don't take too much, it's greedy. Be sure not to take too little, because you will not be permitted to double-dip, as it were. This butter dish is used by at least four people."

She then went on to explain how to angle the knife on the bread so as not to tear it. I watched in mingled disbelief and horror as she very seriously demonstrated the process of correctly buttering my bread.

This sucks.

CHAPTER THIRTY-TWO

TRIBULATIONS, SISTERHOOD AND THE FUTURE

LOUD VOICES OUTSIDE my bedroom woke me from my slumber even earlier the following morning.

"What's going on?" I said in a bleary-eyed stupor, rubbing my eyes.

"Please go back to sleep," Sarah said, and sat on the edge of my bed.

The clock on my wall read first-eight. "Why are you even here this early?"

"I've been here since first-six," she said, and motioned to the edge of the room at a smaller desk that folded up onto the wall. A tiny lamp sat on it. Its light was so weak, that I wondered how she could even see using it. "I have your day mostly planned."

The voices continued outside my door. I got out of bed and moved toward the noise. My teddy bear on the dresser near the door had fallen over. I took a moment to right him. Sarah had made the odd choice to put clothes on him. *It's still weird they have these. Are there even bears on Anfang?*

"Anessa," Sarah chided, "Eavesdropping is hardly behavior becoming of a lady."

I narrowed my eyes at her. "Maybe so, but yesterday was thirty hours of etiquette, manners and the like. You haven't given me lessons on *this* yet. And this lady is curious. Plus, they're clearly standing right in front of my door. If they wanted to keep this private, they could easily have held this conversation somewhere else."

She exhaled, and I heard her move back to the corner and start writing.

Turning to watch her for a few seconds I thought, *Great, so she's actually going to lecture me on this!*

Even at my door, I wasn't able to tell who was arguing. The voices were muted by the solid wood, though they were very intense. One seemed calmer than the other, and was far quieter. Not knowing what they were talking about nagged at me. *Are some of our staff arguing with one another over who cleans what?*

Feeling a little reckless, I gently pulled the handle down, so I wouldn't make any noise, then eased it open a crack. The source of the voices became clear.

"Why are you defending them?" Julilah screamed. "You know what they've done." A stomp on the floor reverberated, vibrating my feet and eardrums. "This house, the money, and all of it is unnecessary!"

"Maybe so. But do you not want what is best for your son Marcus," Kristine countered, "and our daughter Veronica?"

"Of course I do!" The anger in Julilah's voice was palpable. "But *our*," I heard two thumps, I assume from hitting her own chest for emphasis, "status has fallen a great deal with Roland since that bitch Lily weaseled her way into his heart."

Holy crap. Her words sent a chill through me.

"Watch your tongue, Julilah." Kristine's voice was firm, but quieted, "You cannot talk about a member of Imperial Royalty like that. People have been executed for less."

"I don't care, Kristine." Julilah paused, a whine as though she were crying bit into her words. "She stole my status as head wife, and he fancies her over both of us lately. And because Oliver was born, neither Lom nor Marcus had a chance to inherit anything."

Another thud.

She continued, "Adding insult to injury, that bastard has *your* boy following him around like a damn puppy. Doesn't that piss you off at all?"

"I would be remiss if I said I was completely okay with it," admitted Kristine.

Oh shit. The chill I felt before vanished, leaving me numb. *Neither Kristine nor Julilah like Oliver?* Julilah and I hadn't seen eye to eye for a while, but knowing Kristine might feel the same way made my eyes sting.

A pause hung in the air, and Kristine added, "But not for the reasons you are bothered by it. Oliver is not yet capable of teaching Lom anything. Oliver is barely older than Lom. However, I will not disparage Roland's boy for decisions made beyond his purview. It is not fair to him."

Thank the gods. I was worried that they both hated him. Julilah's just upset about losing her status as head wife. Why would they make that decision?

"And what about Lily's little witch child?" Julilah said, venom evident in her voice.

What? Is she talking about me?

"Talking from day one. That's just not natural," Julilah spat. "When I taught her briefly, she would always give me a condescending look like she was better than me."

My stomach roiled at her words. *It's not my fault I could talk from day one. If anything, I looked at her with respect because she's scary.*

"Careful, wife," Kristine said sternly. "You have overstepped more than once with that child."

Julilah has overstepped? Was it actually her that tattled on me when I went into the library? What else is Kristine talking about? My mind went to the genesis test and the old woman, Gray, and when Oliver almost attacked me.

Kristine continued, "You seem to hate her simply to hate her. Perhaps you need to spend some time with Sir Blackwood."

"And then there's *that.* The respect he carried before all of this is gone. His proper title is His Majesty Bal Blackwood," Julilah's anger-turned-sobbing continued. "Maybe I should!" A clink broke up her words that sounded like someone dropped a coin. "This is all driving me crazy."

It got quiet. I suddenly felt very guilty. *This wasn't meant for me to hear.* Sarah's words, *"That is hardly behavior becoming of a lady"* gnawed at me. *I can't let Julilah's words hurt me too much. She's clearly working through some things. Should I talk to her about this someday? Or would it be better never to mention any of this?*

I turned to Sarah and asked, "Are you going to tell on me for listening in?"

"No," she said. "I would be pressed for details about their conversation, and that's tantamount to gossip among the members of the family. It would cause me more harm than good."

"Sorry," I said.

Her brow wrinkled in a slight frown. "For?"

"You were right. I shouldn't have listened in."

She nodded and turned back to my schedule. "Before, you said they should be careful where they are arguing, right?"

"Yeah?" I asked.

"Sometimes emotions boil over, and where you are doesn't matter. I know curiosity can make it tough, but eavesdropping is a bad pastime to have."

With a sigh I replied, "Yeah, you're right." I then tried to close my door, and found it hitched on something. When I looked down to see what was preventing it from closing, I saw a small white ring. *What's this?*

Sarah spoke up, spooking me. "What's wrong?"

"Nothing," I said, and palmed the ring before I could get a closer look at it.

Hexoday, Lokandae 20th, 1735
[July 12th, 2028]

"Okay," Sarah said, "Hold still."

"Is this necessary?" I complained. "I've been holding still for the last hour!"

"We're almost done," she said as another maid went around pinning pieces of cloth over me with needles.

She was lying, of course. It took another hour. My only solace was the fact that Oliver was forced to go through much of the same in his room. Since I wasn't permitted more than my shift during the process, Sarah had put up shade curtains around the work area, in the off chance someone entered the room.

"What's that outfit for, anyway?" I asked. The brief moment I caught a glimpse of it in a mirror, the outfit seemed plain compared to my usual clothes. Somewhat reminiscent of clothes worn by a girl who followed a time-crazed animal down a rabbit hole. The similarities made me chuckle.

Sarah smiled at my inward humor. "It's for tomorrow's church service. When you try for your–" She rolled her lips under her teeth and looked at me nervously. "Never mind."

"Yeah, yeah. You can't talk about the ceremony tomorrow. I know it exists, but not why or what it's about. Big secret. Hush hush."

Exhaling she said, "Thank you for not pressing me on it."

A loud yell came from the hallway, startling me. It was Oliver, "I'm done! This holding still is stupid."

"Young master," his manservant said frantically, "Please, put some clothes on at least!"

That's no surprise.

"Let's hope they can finish his outfit before tomorrow," Sarah teased.

I said, "If they do, it'll be a miracle."

Sarah and I locked eyes for a moment and shared a laugh.

The sound of footsteps filled our hallway, and had been all morning. It was our birthday tomorrow. This time there would apparently be no kings and queens in attendance, though that did little to dampen the energy clearly in the air.

"What have they been doing today that requires so much effort?" I asked Sarah.

"I know they hired a huntsman for wild game. The game will be dressed, bled and cooked by tomorrow," she said and helped the seamstress carefully remove the pins, marking each spot with a black stick before doing so. "They're preparing confectioneries, cakes, and testing various dishes in the kitchens to make sure it all comes together."

She paused and tapped my nose. "Usually we would have had this all figured out months in advance, but with everything else that needed to be handled regarding your family's arrival, it was pushed back."

I can imagine there's a lot to do when an entirely new family takes over a series *of estates.*

"Yllia put her foot down, and said there was no more time." She chuckled. "That was a week ago." Her smile vanished. "Mr. Morris pushed back on her until today."

Sarah clearly doesn't like Mr. Morris. Seeing her discomfort, I changed subjects. "How has Fan been adapting to the situation?"

Sarah tilted her head to the side. "Fan?"

"My mommy's Lady's maid?" I said.

"Ah," she avoided eye contact. "Her situation is complicated at present."

I took Sarah's hand and said, "They didn't fire her, did they?"

Before she could answer, a knock came at my door.

"Just a moment," Sarah said for me, apparently relieved for the interruption.

It took her two minutes to get me presentable, though she put me in a simpler dress.

"Please enter," I said.

Yllia entered and bowed. "Anessa, I'm here to fetch you for your parents."

Around the corner I could see Oliver and Lom. My twin was wearing clothes now, thankfully.

"Okay. What's it about?"

"I was only tasked with fetching you; I do not know the details."

Is it a big deal if Yllia herself is the one fetching us?

Sarah attempted to follow, but Yllia held up her hand and gave an apologetic smile. "I was instructed to bring only the affected parties."

When we entered the dining area we sat at a smaller table to the side. Dad, Mom, and a woman with olive-colored skin were present. She looked familiar. She wore a deep green robe with darker floral flourishes. Emerald earrings and a necklace complimented her appearance. The silky brown eri, hem guard and obi gave a good final bit of contrast.

The Japanese-style flourishes suddenly reminded me of my old home, and the time I went to a tea ceremony with Trish. I smiled sadly inside at the memory.

The extended family was there, including my non-siblings Veronica and Marcus.

Yllia herself passed out drinks to all of us, then bowed to leave.

"Thank you all for joining us," Mom said and turned on one of the sound barriers I'd learned were called an S-ROB, or a short-range obscuring barrier.

Dad was looking away and a bit standoffish.

She cleared her throat. "I was hoping to have this conversation later, because we're dealing with quite a lot right now, but a key part of Imperial nobility is the establishment of a harem."

No one said a word. A quick glance around showed everyone was as dumbfounded as I was. Though Oliver and the younger kids didn't seem to understand.

"Is she…" Nicole said, and pointed to the woman with them.

"Yes. She is the first member of Roland and my's harem. Fan Mul," Mom said, "Though I'm sure you're all pretty familiar with her."

"Hi Fan!" Oliver waved.

She smiled. "Hi Oliver."

Fan looks so different without her glasses and maid outfit.

"Wait, so what happened? My head's still spinning from this mess we're in," Lana said. "What does Mama think?"

Dad winced at her comment. "Julilah left to spend some time with Sir Blackwood a week ago."

"Daddy, why didn't anyone tell me?" she shouted.

Lana's outburst made my skin prickle. She could sometimes channel her mother's intensity.

"She didn't want to cause anyone undue concern," Mom said. "'This mess,' as you called it was a bit too much for her right now."

I remembered Julilah's argument with Kristine. *I'm definitely not telling Mom about anything Julilah said.*

"As for why we're bringing this up now," Mom started.

Fan looked down at the table.

Mom continued, "Miss Mul and Roland were involved in a little bit of impropriety." She held up her hands. "Nothing too serious, but since the dynamics of our situation are already complicated, we thought it best to formalize it."

She nudged Dad's side. "He didn't disagree, and I've always had a soft spot for Fan."

Nicole was now bunching up her dress anxiously, and avoiding eye contact.

"Nicole, baby, we'll talk after this, okay?" Mom said.

My eldest sister nodded, but said nothing.

The hourglass clock on the mantle nearby made me think, *I'm in a soap opera.*

Once we were released from that awkward get-together I caught up with Veronica, who had remained quiet the entire time.

"Are you okay?" I asked her.

"Not really," she said with a sigh.

"Want to talk about it?"

She held her hand out and I took it. "Sure," she said. For a few minutes we walked in silence, while she chewed her bottom lip. "You remember my birthday on the sixth?"

I nodded.

"I am officially an adult now." Veronica squeezed my hand. "On that same day, I got a letter from Evan, the eminent heir of Redwater."

"What'd it say?" I asked and wondered, *What is an eminent heir?*

"That he's looking forward to our official meeting," she looked at me. "And yours."

"W-why does he even know about me?"

She shook her head. "I have no idea. Neither On-pa nor On-ma knew either."

"If it's just meeting him, I suppose there's no harm, right?"

"He and I will be getting married," she said in a shaky voice.

I stopped. "What?"

"His expectation is that I will not awaken." She let go of my hand and held her hands to her chest. "But I'm afraid that even if I do, his presence," she pointed to the ground, "*here* will make it difficult to turn him down."

"Crap," I said.

"H-he even mentioned possibly taking you with us."

The hallway around us seemed to stretch as her words hit me, and I shook my head. "Double crap." I paused for a moment to clear my head. *I'll need to talk to Mom about that. Like hell I'm going with some stranger, even if he is an emperor.* I asked, "You don't want to go with him, right?"

"No, I don't." She began to fidget, then twirled her hair around her finger. "I want to find someone myself, not have them found for me." With a look of longing she said, "You know?"

I thought back to all those romance novels I used to see in her room, and got an inkling of what she was feeling. I asked, "Do you have anyone you're interested in?"

Veronica's finger stopped. "No. Not really. It's just not something I want decided for me."

So she's in love, with being in love?

"To be taken out on a stroll," she looked up at the ceiling and seemed to be far, far away. "Or be treated like a lady simply because they want to."

Veronica's always been a tomboy, so I never would have pegged her for these kinds of feelings. Maybe it's because she isn't being allowed to choose? Remembering one of her books was from the forbidden section of the library I amended my thought, *No, it's probably like I thought, love for love's sake.*

We both headed for the restroom, having been affected by the drinks they had offered us over and over again.

Hoping to move the topic away from a stranger who might basically abduct us, I asked, "I'm worried, too. You know who my mommy is, right?"

"Yes, she's the imperial princess, why?"

"Just the whole notion that we're in the running for the Imperial th–"

Veronica rushed forward and covered my mouth, then looked around before sighing. She said quietly but sternly, "Don't talk about that in the open."

Once she let me go I said, "Why not?"

"I don't think that's public knowledge." She sighed. "At least, I wasn't aware." Her voice dropped to a whisper. "You aren't a direct blood relative of the Emperor, you're just extended family." Motioning toward me she added, "Which means you're the backup line of succession. That's not public information, because if someone were trying to conduct a coup, it would put you in danger."

"You're awful knowledgeable about this. Are there classes on this, or something?"

Shaking her head she said, "No, it's not that. On-ma's grandparents had a similar issue come up. A coup failed in her tribe because the attackers weren't aware of the backup lineage."

Her cautionary example set a light chill to the air. "Noted."

Veronica paused for a few seconds then said, "If you are... selected." She smirked. "Maybe I can be one of your wives."

Rolling my eyes, "As if. I still see you as a sister."

"I know, but–" she made fists at her side. "–if I'm one of *that* emperor's wives, I could use seeing you to escape for a while."

Seeing her clear frustration on display made me want to say, "*If that dark situation were to pass, sure.*" But there was too much I didn't know about this world, and same-sex marriages, or if I was even able to go forward with such a thing, even if it would offer Veronica reprieve.

"Let's change the subject," I said firmly. "Fan looked so pretty!"

"I know, I hardly recognized her. The whole harem thing is weird, too."

"Yeah," I said, drawing the word out. *So much for that being a softball topic!*

Veronica asked, "Like, what even is a harem?"

Oh... she doesn't even know! My mind raced hoping to find a clean answer that wasn't awkward. "I think that's a question for your on-ma."

"So you don't know either?"

"N-nope, not at all," I lied.

"Hmm…" She leaned forward to get a closer look at me. "I don't believe you. So I'm going to guess it's something embarrassing?"

"Not exactly, but it is embarrassing to have to explain it to someone four times my age."

Fortunately, I was saved by Kristine's angry voice breaking through the air.

CHAPTER THIRTY-THREE

TANGLED TIES / CONFOUNDING RELATIONSHIPS

"I CANNOT BELIEVE you, Lily. Do you know what you have done?" Kristine said.

"Of course I know what I've done," Mom said. "I told Nicole we would resolve some issues after we talked to everyone about Fan."

Veronica and I were moving toward our bedrooms and we stopped around the corner. Mom, Kristine and Nicole were right in front of my bedroom.

Either it's a popular place for secret conversations, or they're not thinking their argument through.

"This way," Veronica said and we entered her room instead.

Instead of closing her door like I hoped she would, she instead kept it open by two feet.

"We *really* shouldn't be listening in," I said, remembering Julilah and Kristine's argument.

Veronica sat down next to her doorway and patted next to her. "Either sit, or go to your own room," she said with a smile.

It seemed Kristine had taken a moment to consider her next words, because she continued, "Fan is another bone I have to pick with you and Roland." Kristine growled. "Whose idea was it to start a harem?"

"Jorin's."

"With all due respect, it is none of his damn business."

"Kristine, you know that it's codified for any Imperial nobility to have a clear and present means to secure dynastic continuity."

An odd thump sounded out, making Veronica flatten her ears.

"Uh oh," she said.

"What?" I whispered.

"My on-ma is very mad. That was her tail hitting the floor."

Kristine's tone was seething. "That… may be true, Lily." She snarled, "But I do not have to like it. You recall I was opposed when it was suggested."

"I know," Mom said apologetically. "But please know that we'll be sure to keep you informed of any additions. You will also usually have veto rights. Fan was only added without your knowledge because–" her voice dropped to barely a whisper. "–Roland had already bedded her."

Veronica gasped, a little too loudly for my liking.

"That's a lot more than a kiss," I said, then realized that they were around the corner, and Mom was likely whispering. I poked Veronica. "Hey, how come I'm able to hear them?"

She flicked her ear. "It's probably because of Papa-Rolli."

Arching a brow at her I said, "What? You'll need to explain more than that."

She turned to me. "Well, Nicole has On-ma's whisker lines because Papa-Rolli has regressive–" My not-sister froze and her tail bristled. Slowly, she turned her head toward the door, and I peeked around her.

Kristine was standing there looking right at us. She pointed at us and said, "Follow."

Crap and double crap. My stomach dropped and churned. *Holy crap.*

Though she has always been someone I've looked up to, seeing the intensity in her glare and the resoluteness in her voice made me realize we'd *really* stepped in it this time.

When we rounded the corner and I saw Mom and Nicole, I did a double take. Their outfits were *not* what I was expecting. Whatever they had been doing before the argument was clearly more adult oriented as there was little left to the imagination.

I chose to look firmly at their faces.

Mom crossed her arms on seeing us and shifted her weight onto one of her legs. As we got closer, I saw she had furrowed eyebrows, completing the anger trifecta.

Who knew just overhearing something could be so bad.

"Were they listening to us?" Mom asked.

Kristine nodded.

Mom said, "What's the meaning of this?"

Veronica's tail wrapped around herself and her ears hadn't recovered from the first time they fell. "I'm sorry Mama-Lily. I shouldn't have, and I don't have a good excuse."

Mom's attention turned to me. "And you?"

Before I could say more than, "I–", Veronica cut in. "She told me we shouldn't be listening, but I told her to sit down next to me."

"Is that true?" Mom asked.

I said meekly, "Yes mommy."

"We may as well continue our conversation, since it's not exactly secret," she said.

"Wait," I said. "Mama-Krissi."

"Yes?"

Pointing to my bedroom door behind her, I said, "I don't know if you're aware, but that's my bedroom."

She cocked her head slightly. "And?"

"Well, I–" I started, but quickly froze up. *I need to tell her, since it's been eating at me.* Taking a breath I continued, "overheard you and Mama-J talking by here before she left."

She drew in a sharp breath. "Oh."

Mom's voice grew cross once again. "So this isn't the *first* time you've eavesdropped?"

Kristine held up her hand and shook her head. She turned back to me and crouched to my level. "I am sorry you had to hear that. Julilah is just having trouble adapting." She looked up at Mom. "We all are." Placing her hand on my head, she added, "Please do not take what she said to heart."

"Okay. I'm really sorry." Since she left without saying anything, I asked, "How long will she be gone?"

My peripheral vision saw Veronica's ears perk up.

"I do not know, sweetie. It might be a while before she can work some things out, but she will be back."

I smiled despite the tension. "I'm glad. If you send her a message, tell her I miss her." Though my comment was a little white lie, I didn't think it was a bad thing to tell at that time.

"Will do." Kristine stood and said to Mom, "I am sorry Lily. It seems the trip, the rush of changes going on because we are in a new home, and Julilah's choice to leave have all clouded my perspective." She bowed deeply. "Please understand I meant no harm."

Mom laughed, it was clear her tension had broken, too. "It's fine, Kristine. We're all going a bit batty under the pressure." She looked at my bedroom door. "Though we should be mindful of where we discuss things in the future."

Kristine's attention turned to Veronica whose ears dropped in response. "Please use this as a lesson on respecting other people's privacy. I expect it won't happen again?"

"No On-ma, it will not."

Kristine cupped Veronica's cheek. "That is good, mu-tos."

Huh, mu-tos means *daughter, but from the perspective of her on-ma. Weird.*

"Anessa," Mom said, making me stand up straight. I couldn't tell from her tone whether she was upset or amused, and I was facing away from her.

"Yes mommy?"

"Don't mention the things you overheard," Mom said. "In either conversation."

Turning toward her I said, "Okay."

In talking to Kristine, my eye level went to normal. When I looked at mom, I forgot to return my eyes to their faces, and was reminded that their outfits were a bit revealing.

My gaze was level with Mom's midsection, which gave me a full view of her garments below the belt. Now, I'd taken several baths with Mom in the past, but today I saw something that was definitely not there before.

My eyes widened and I instantly looked down to her feet in my embarrassment.

"Mommy," I said. "You are a g-girl, right?"

"Of course, honey. Why?"

Nicole whispered into her ear, "Your ring, Lily-li."

"Oh heavens," Mom replied in vexation, and removed her ring.

Though I was "looking" at her feet, my eyes were raised enough so I could see "it" retreat, like a snake entering its burrow. It gave me the willies. *What the hell? I really hope I imagined that.*

"I'm sorry honey," she said. "You can look up now."

I looked up at her face to avoid any suspicion that I was looking anywhere else other than her feet.

"What was that?" I asked.

Mom said, "Do you actually want to talk about it?"

"Not really," I confessed.

Nicole piped up in an apparent effort to be helpful, "It was Everyday magic!"

Mom sighed. "Nicole, she isn't going to fall for that."

I said, "It looked more like a–"

"Sword," Oliver interrupted, having just opened his bedroom door.

Everyone glared at him, wondering what he was talking about, and why his comment was so on point.

Was he eavesdropping too?

He then took a look at Mom and Nicole and shut his door. "Why are mommy and big sis almost naked!" He shuffled around the room for a time then added, "Lom was cleaning Rufus earlier, and I haven't been able to find either of them. I was wondering if anyone has seen my sword."

His perfectly timed word was all we needed to further diffuse the tension in the air, and we all began to laugh.

"What's so funny?" Oliver said behind his door.

That only served to make us laugh harder.

Once we'd had our fill, Nicole said, "I'll talk to Oliver."

Kristine shook her head. "Let me, you need to get dressed."

Nicole looked down at herself and blushed, finally realizing her attire. "Yeah, I guess so."

"Why don't you and I have a little chat, too," Mom said to me.

"Do we have to?" I asked, knowing it was about the peculiar sight a few minutes ago.

We entered my room and Mom closed my door. "Now then."

I sighed and hopped onto my bed.

She said, "Are you familiar with the Ring of He?"

"The what of whom?" I said blankly.

Mom presented the pure white ring to me and gestured for me to pick it up. "I'm handing you this to look at only," she said sternly as I motioned to pick it up. "Do not put it on."

It was striking, though familiar. Along its outer perimeter was an intricate pattern that wasn't a language so much as it looked like a pathway for a circuit.

"This ring is special," she explained. "It allows women who are in love with one another to have a child."

I'd been turning it around to look at it and stopped. *Oh. That explains why they were—* I shook my head to clear the vision that came unbidden.

"What were you and Mama-Krissi arguing over, anyway? It seemed to involve Nicole." I paused to think my next words over and vermilion spread across my face. "I'm pretty sure I know what you were doing."

Mom coughed, then pulled a sheet from my drawer and wrapped it around herself. It seemed my comment had made her a bit self-conscious of her state of undress for the first time.

On top of the same dresser was my teddy bear, and my eyes widened as it hit me. He was wearing a white band on his arm – the ring I'd found when Julilah and Kristine were fighting. I didn't much like its color, so I put it on my toy, once I saw that it would resize to fit the target.

"Mommy," I squeaked.

"Yes?" She sat beside me and put a hand on my back.

I dropped her ring back into her hand, and said, "I think I found one of these when I overheard Mama-J arguing the other day."

Mom whispered to herself, "Is that where it's been?"

Pointing at my teddy bear I said, "Teddy has been using it as a bracelet."

She stood and walked to my dresser. Before she removed it from his arm, she took a moment, and curiously pulled back his little britches. Her face blushed a bit and I gasped.

No way.

"Anessa," she said in an accusatory tone, "you *do* know what this ring does, right?"

"Well, I do now." Flailing my hands in front of me I added, "but I didn't know that when I put the ring on him!" I thought, *I didn't think to check his pants. Who would!?*

Mom smiled at my response. "I believe you. Though Kristine will never believe it." She held up Teddy, "Do you mind if I borrow him?"

"If you need him for an example," I asked cautiously, "Could you use a different toy?" Then I thought about it. "Or maybe, better yet, could I get a new stuffed animal?"

She nodded. "Of course." She put the ring back on his wrist and checked again, "That makes more sense."

Sorry Teddy, you've got a new life as an educational example. Also, I knew that I could never look at the toy the same again.

"Now then," Mom said. "You have a new step mommy in Nicole. Though, daddy and I agree she'll basically just act like your big sister. It shouldn't change anything. Are you okay with that?"

"I'd prefer that," I said, and thought, *Polyamory is hard to get used to coming from a mostly monogamous world. Anfang is weird not seeing an issue with adding a daughter of one of the members to the extended circle of a different member.* Recalling their attire earlier I realized that wasn't a sight I would soon forget. *I wonder if they have anything like therapy on this planet?*

CHAPTER THIRTY-FOUR

A GRAND RITUAL / GATHERING

Septaday, Lokandae 21st, 1735
[July 14th, 2028]

THE NEXT MORNING Sarah woke me up at first-nine, an hour before she usually did.

"Arms up," she said.

A sleepy grumble accompanied my compliance.

She teased, "Come on now, it's not that early."

"It's early enough," I said.

"Let's go get your hair ready. Make sure you're presentable."

I guess this is the first church service we've been to since we moved. For a fleeting second I thought of the amber-eyed girl from last time, and had a hint of regret that she wouldn't be there today.

"What can you tell me about an 'Awakening' Ceremony?" I asked.

"Not much, I'm afraid. I can tell you that it's done in batches of three months. So everyone born in Evantaiae, Lokandae, and Jothariae will be there, if they're aged two Anfang years like you, four, six or eight like Veronica."

Weird. Anfang years still seem wrong when talking of ages. I know it's because of the planet's orbital period. Then I corrected in my head, *when they're aged four Standard years like me, eight, twelve and sixteen like Veronica.* I'd asked Sarah to start using Standard years all the time since it was confusing to think of an "eight-year-old" as an adult. She was trying to accommodate me, but often forgot.

"So it's always on the twenty-first of Crotariae, Lokandae, Ylldriae, and Polarae?"

She nodded and tied a ribbon around my waist, behind my back.

It was far closer to my usual attire from before we arrived in the Redwood Kingdom, which made me happy. Though I half-expected a rabbit to show up during the service and whisk me away. "Heh."

"What's funny?" Sarah asked.

"Nothing." Having my internal thoughts break out like that made me blush lightly. *Don't think about such weird things. My life is strange enough without being portaled… a second time!*

Hoping she would let it slide, I pulled out some white leggings, and she shook her head. Then she pulled out some white mid-calf socks.

"I miss my hose," I said, and sighed. Then I smiled despite myself. It's what Trish used to say about girls she didn't like.

"Maybe if your ceremony today goes well," Sarah said with a hint of a smile, "they'll let you wear them again?"

Trying not to smile at the unexpected memory of Trish, her words made me grab onto her arm and I said, "Really?"

With a weak smile Sarah replied, "Maybe. I'm honestly not sure. But it would be a good time to ask."

"Great!" I said, and then worried about my not-sister. "I hope Veronica's ceremony goes well. It's her last one, isn't it?"

Sarah said, "Yes. She's eight." After a pause she corrected herself for me. "I mean she's sixteen-Standard-years-old."

Since we were going to church, I asked, "Should I pray for her?"

Sarah responded by clasping her hands and closing her eyes. "It couldn't hurt."

Oh, right now? I thought and moved near my cloud overcast window, onto my knees. I thought of the only goddess who seemed to strike me, Eloria. Not as the goddess of death, but in the guise of her calmer persona as the high goddess of craft. *I don't know if this will have any effect, but… Eloria please look after my not-sister Veronica Nu Carlyle. She's shown me nothing but compassion, kindness, and affection. She doesn't wish to be with the Emperor of the Redwater Empire, and her awakening is key to her future. Uhm… Amen?*

Behind my closed eyes, the light brightened. It got my hopes up that someone was someone answering my prayers, but upon opening my eyes, I saw that the clouds had merely parted. *Damn.*

"Are you ready to go now?" Sarah said.

"Yes!" I said and stood, smoothing out my dress. "I'm excited to finally see what these ceremonies are all about."

Leaving your home to go to church should be a simple affair; however, when you're the Imperial Duke's daughter, the expected pomp and pageantry means nothing is simple. On my way to enter the carriage, no fewer than thirty people lined up on both sides to see me off. Though I honestly didn't really count.

Sarah stopped at the door to our estate.

"You're coming too, right?" I asked.

She shook her head. "I'm afraid I am not going to join you at church today." Pursing her lips she added, "I will be there, mind you, but not with you."

"Please at least follow me to the carriage," I said, then whispered to her, "This is a little scary!"

It seemed my plight didn't concern her too much because she giggled, but she followed by my side anyway, for which I was grateful.

It looks cool in Japanese anime, but walking through a corridor of people who tower over you is strange! I saw maids, manservants, I'm pretty sure a gardener and cook – or two – but most of them were guards.

Except for the guards, the men were all giving me a half-bow and had their hands firmly behind their backs, and the women were holding a curtsey pose, which looked uncomfortable. They'd relax as I passed and not a one had a hint of malice on their face.

The guards were looking straight ahead, though their eyes seemed to shift about. It reminded me of dad's comment on our way to the estates: *"It's not that we expect any danger, we should just always plan for it."*

At the end of the line was one of our many carriages. Already they'd painted our newly-minted family crest on it. *The speed at which they work is insane. How much money are we spending just rebranding all of our stuff!?* The sense that we were poor before and had to "find the money" for a tutor, if needed, gave me a mental whiplash.

Next to my ride was a familiar face I didn't expect to see: Daughter Hy from Rhinebur.

It seemed she was there to swap out with Sarah. Daughter Hy opened the door and entered after me.

"Nice to see you, Your Imperial High Grace," she said.

"Your what now?" I said arching a brow at her.

"What do you mean by that title you called me by?" I asked.

Daughter Hy covered her mouth. "Oh! Have they not told you?"

My right eyebrow twitched. "Let's assume I am completely lost by your comment."

"I'm not sure if I should," she said and looked away.

"Daughter Hy, I've been kept in the dark my entire life. Please just tell me why my title is so similar to my daddy's." I sighed. "Before I get upset."

"Well," she started with a bit of levity. "It's part of the reason why I am here." She waved off her comment as though it was nothing. "Don't get the wrong idea, I'm not actually important. But when I was told who I was requested for, I decided to oblige." She bowed. "Your mommy, Lily, wrote a letter and asked me to be here for you. A familiar face to make the day go smoother. I would have rejected her, but she said you were quite important, as your brother is."

Her words wound around for a while before she got to the point, and she dropped her voice to a whisper, "As a backup heiress to the throne, your usual 'Rang en Absentia' doesn't apply. Instead your status grants you a slight bump in rank." She paused for a moment before saying, "Do you know what it means to have 'Rang en–'"

It had been a few Standard years since I read about it. Giving her a flat stare I said, "Humor me."

"It means to be granted an honorary title beneath your parents, that is valid only in their absence. In their presence, you would generally have no title."

"So you're telling me that I outrank my own daddy? That's preposterous. Besides, doesn't that effectively out me as a backup?"

Daughter Hy waggled her finger at me. "Not necessarily. Anyone seeing your rank would assume it's because you're the daughter of an Imperial Princess. Nothing more. Most people believe Lily's ineligibility applies to her children, but they would nonetheless expect you to at least outrank your father."

"A few things. You're acting way different than before, why? What's it mean for Oliver? Is there any actual expectation placed on me for outranking my daddy?"

She gave me a broad smile. "I'm acting differently because my role has changed. Before I was your scripture teacher, now I am your Daughter Envoy. Oliver's title is the same, I would expect. Your father would of course still be able to discipline you, and override any order you gave that would be seen as harmful, since he is your guardian." Giving me a light bow she said, "Before I joined the church as a member of the Scripture's Children, I was also a low noble."

Did she have to add in a reason to believe her words? It only makes her more sus, not less.

Our carriage came to a halt. As was customary, we waited for someone to open the door. Thankfully the entourage that greeted us was a little less daunting here. There were only ten soldiers, though that was on each side. They lined a path that led straight to the door of the church.

There were a few onlookers but glances from the lineup seemed to suggest I was the least interesting person there. As we walked down the "aisle," everyone I looked at avoided looking at me.

Great. So much for meeting new people. Will my entire life be like this? Before it felt as though I had some personal freedoms, but now… even talking to someone seems like it would be a problem. Heat boiled in my chest. *I can't even bloody wear pants!*

I'd stopped without realizing it, leading Daughter Hy to say, "Is everything okay Anessa?"

"I'm *fine*," I said, though my frustration may have leaked out in my tone.

Inside the church was much the same as the one at Rhinebur. We were seated in the Imperial Perch, on the third floor, above the nave.

This entire structure is built around separation, class, and generally making sure you stay within your lane or caste. I sighed. *It's suffocating.* Taking a few breaths I calmed myself as I took my place between Oliver and Veronica.

"Hi," I said in a whisper to my not-sister.

"What's wrong?" she asked.

"Hm?"

"You look and sound upset," she said.

"Oh, it's nothing. Tell you later."

She nodded, and smiled. "I'll hold you to it."

Though it might upset Mom or Kristine, I took a moment to give her a hug. To my surprise the little violation of protocol didn't even garner a reaction. I may have hugged her for a minute.

"Okay, that's enough," Veronica said and giggled.

"Sorry, I needed that."

Oliver looked at me like I'd just kicked his puppy, so I gave him one as well. Though it was decidedly shorter, since his grip was stronger and I was worried he might break one of my bones or something.

We then sat through the usual sermon, and then the priest said, "Will the lay children and their families come forward a row at a time for their chance at awakening."

I'd all but tuned out by this point, but the shift in tone perked my interest.

My interest waned fast as I saw the children and their parents minutes later merely walk down the central aisle of the nave and exit.

What is this, some sort of—

"Praise be! Iola of the Farthen family has a light Divine Link with Hana, Huntress of the Wind."

What? Who's Hana? The name seemed familiar, but I couldn't quite place it. *The hell is a divine link?*

Iola's family, or so I'd assumed by the stark difference in how they treated her, walked down the aisle with her on her father's shoulders. The family was all smiles.

A joyous occasion? Does that mean she awakened as a cultivator? Why the hell do they keep this information from us!?

I spent the next few hours brooding, largely ignoring those below us. It wasn't as though I viewed them as unimportant, but that the secrecy over something so seemingly trivial, over four years, added to my stormy mood.

What broke me out of my funk was strange. A sensation as though someone draped a warm cloth over my shoulders made me raise my head and look around, only to find nothing but my family. I couldn't see any reason for the sensation. A second later we all stood to go to the nave below.

Am I just imagining things? The odd warmth stayed with me as we descended. Before us, the local Imperial Baronet's family went, or the King of Redwood and his son.

The boy stepped forward into the sanctuary and stood there for exactly one minute. There was even someone there timing him. Once he was done, he sat down in the pews. It was an odd contrast to the commoners, who left immediately.

That's it?

There were far fewer Imperials present, making our wait fairly short. Unlike the lay folk for whom the priest announced a Divine Link, there were no additional pronouncements.

When it was Veronica's turn, I whispered to her, "Good luck."

She merely turned to me and flashed a smile. For most of the time she stood stock still until about fifteen seconds before the minute was up, she raised a single hand toward the statue with a bow.

The name of the being depicted in stone instantly came to me. *Hana, Huntress of the wind, she's a goddess…*

"Praise be! Veronica of the Imperial Carlyle family has a middling Divine Link with Hana, Huntress of the wind, and a light Divine Link with Lokar the lesser God of War."

I'd been so shocked that I hadn't even noticed her other hand raising towards Lokar with seconds to spare.

On my side I saw Kristine had started to weep silently.

This Ceremony is about connecting with the gods? Holy crap!

The revelation left me as a ball of nerves. They led Veronica off to the side, out of sight.

Because I was so busy watching her, I totally missed who Oliver had "resonated" with.

Taking a closer look at the statues, there was Hana to my far left, then Lokar, the very god our red moon of war was named for. On my right was Mercury, then a buxom figure that depicted Fandar, the goddess for whom the blue moon of hope was named.

There were other gods visible in the stained glass before us and off to the sides, but my gut told me people were expected to form a Divine Link with one of the four statues in the front.

A priest with a gold and silver studded vestment placed his hand on my back and guided me up a set of stairs. He then squatted next to me. "Hello my child. In a few moments you will step forward onto the spot of awakening. If the heavens deem you worthy, one of the pantheon before you will channel themselves through you."

After a brief pause he said, "Do you understand?"

"Y-yeah," I lied. Of course I didn't understand. But what else was I supposed to say?

"Very good. Please step forward."

His instructions were plain and simple, but my legs were like jelly. When I looked at the "spot of awakening" I realized that it had been marked with tape.

Seriously? Are they pulling the wool over our eyes?

Stepping forward I thought, *Did Veronica just point to who—*

The instant my left foot rested next to my right foot my eyes closed. Pinpricks assaulted me from my head to my toes. Before I knew it I was opening my eyes once again.

I hadn't pointed at any of the four statues in front of me. Instead I'd raised both hands towards the biggest figure in the room, looming over all in the impossibly large stained-glass window: Eloria, the Goddess of Death.

A glance behind me showed a different reaction than Veronica's. Nobody was weeping with joy or relief. What I saw instead was gasps, wide eyes, and absolute shock.

Shit.

CHAPTER THIRTY-FIVE

CHOSEN

DAUGHTER HY CAME forward and took my hand. She said nothing until we were off the main sanctuary. "Congratulations."

"What just happened? I couldn't control my body, and my mommy's response was shock, not excitement." Then, curious to know the answer to the lingering question, I asked, "Does this mean I'm a cultivator?"

Her voice was calm and she smiled. "Whether you are a cultivator or not," she looked back to the stained-glass window, "is up to Eloria." In a quieter voice she added, "There hasn't been anyone who's resonated with Eloria in decades."

Her words, while I'm sure were intended to be calming, only made my stomach tumble further. "Am I in trouble?" Looking back to Daughter Hy from the window I whispered, "She's the Goddess of Death, right?"

We walked further into a less populous, and quieter, area of the church. Veronica exited the room through a door on the right, beaming. Her own Daughter Envoy met her before I could say anything and they returned back to everyone else.

"Now then," Daughter Hy said. "To answer your questions. You are not in trouble. People were surprised by two things," She held up one finger, "The fact that you had a Divine Link with Eloria," then another finger, "and that it was a perfect Divine Link."

"What's that mean?"

Daughter Hy pressed her lips together. "Perhaps it's better if *she* were to tell you, instead of me."

She, she who? I wanted to say but was fearful I knew the answer.

"This way," Daughter Hy said and opened the same door through which Veronica had exited. "Sit down, pray, and call out her full name."

Inside was a white room with a single window, a pedestal and a nondescript statuette. In front of the pedestal was a plain unadorned pillow. I sat down on my knees and clasped my hands in prayer. *Eloria Kirzington von Addenal* entered my mind. I most definitely hadn't known the rest of her name until that moment.

"Hello child," her soft, and warm voice spoke to me.

It's like she's in the room with me.

A fleeting giggle punctuated the air. "Open your eyes."

Doing as she requested I saw a tiny figure of the goddess had replaced the featureless one from before. In full color and everything.

"Oh, so you are here," I said then wondered, *What made her laugh?*

"You did," she said plainly.

Oh so you can, I thought then said, "Read my mind?"

"Of course. I wouldn't be a very good goddess if I couldn't hear my followers' prayers, would I? My angels share this ability, through me."

Oh, is she the one who sent the angel?

"I am. No, she didn't get in trouble for passing out."

Her uncanny ability to guess what I was going to ask made my eyebrow twitch.

"It's not so much predicting the future as it is knowing you very well."

"What do you mean?"

The tiny statue woman hopped off her pedestal. "I've been watching you since you were born." She grinned. "Don't you think it's funny that you could talk from day one?"

I gasped. "You did that?"

She straightened out and buffed her fingernails on her robe. "I had something to do with it, at least." Her eyes looked past me. "But right now, let's do something about that hair."

Pulling a lock of it into my fingers, I said, "What's wrong with it?"

Eloria shook her head. "Nothing's wrong, per se, but I think this would suit it better." She snapped her fingers and the sensation of a hundred fingers moving across my scalp made me freeze up. "There."

The lock I'd held before was now a small braid. Feeling along the side of my head, it was akin to a single Dutch plait. Somehow I'd been given a ribbon to tie it off.

That's neat. Reminds me of when Mama-Krissi fixed the floor.

Eloria huffed and crossed her arms. "Materializing a ribbon from nothing takes a lot more effort than adding more of something to what's already there."

Her reading my mind is scary.

"Yeah, because you can't hide anything from me." She waved her annoyance off. "Anyway. While chatting is fun, I should probably get down to business."

Her comment made me sit straighter, dispelling the jovial atmosphere.

"I am Eloria Kirzington von Addenal," her voice gained an ethereal quality to it that would need an electronic synthesizer to reproduce, "Principal Goddess of Death and High Goddess of Craft on Anfang. I call on you Anessa Jean, of the Imperial Carlyle Duchy, to become my champion."

All I could do was blink at her. *Crap.*

Her regal air shattered when she snickered at my thought. "What's it with you and animal excrement?"

The bluntness of her call-out made my cheeks heat up. "I don't know. You're not asking me to be the Champion of D-death are you?"

A teeny pair of hands clasped my arm. "Oh heavens no! Of Craft, Craft! I wouldn't wish the moniker of Death on anyone."

Sighing I said, "Oh thank the gods…" Realizing I had one in front of me, I amended my statement, "I mean, thank *you*?"

Eloria laughed. "Yes. I swear I'm so glad I br–" She coughed. "I mean, I'm so glad you're on Anfang. Your perspective is a rare highlight on an otherwise dreary and monotonous world."

Was she going to say "brought you to Anfang?"

In response to my thought she placed her finger to her lips and did no more than shush me. Unlike Mom and Julilah's glares to keep quiet on a topic, hers had a weight to it. As though there would be very real consequences for not keeping quiet.

I nodded emphatically. "Do I have to say I accept being your champion? Are there dangers to it?"

She materialized a pair of – I assumed – unnecessary, glasses and placed them on her face. She was now also holding several sheets of paper. In a pompous voice she said, "Your participation is mandatory, and the only dangers are idiots who covet the title."

Taking the glasses off she added, "Though that applies with anything someone might envy." The paper and glasses vanished in a flash of white light. "Do not mention that bit in the church though. They're a bit fanatical."

Tapping the end of her chin she said, "In fact, to keep them occupied." She conjured a hammer in the same magical way as the glasses, then held it above her head. "Give this to them."

I reached for the hammer, only to find it rooted in place, and the statuette had returned to stone. Though instead of a featureless doll, it now had her color and the pose she struck before leaving it behind.

Oh bother.

Assuming it was my time to leave, I leaned forward to lift the statue, only it was far too heavy to lift.

Another laugh rang out and my eyes automatically went to the pedestal the statue was on originally. "Leave it there, silly." Eloria said, once again before me, though in her full height. "Someone else will come and pick it up. Since it's stone, it weighs twice as much as you do."

"Okay. Hi again?"

"Yes, hello again."

Pointing to her statue and then herself I asked, "You don't need the statue to be here?"

"Of course not. It's just a convenient way to talk since it's built as a divine vessel. Coming here in person is a bit more expensive, is all."

Expensive? I thought.

"Yes. Think of it as an expensive [airplane] ticket." She changed topics, which threw me a bit, along with the English word for airplane. "Were you a fan of A. A. Milne?"

"Who?" I blinked.

"Never mind." She mumbled to herself, "Must've been a memory she lost."

What?

"Nothing. Anyway, for your first awakening, I will bring out your essence vision." She tapped near her eyes. "You've actually almost figured it out for yourself already, but the full thing is much more potent."

"Okay?" I said, unsure to how it would help me.

"Your confusion is fair, I suppose." She bit her lower lip. "Let's see." Holding out her palm, a white circle formed on top of it. "This is an Art. Typically, when you mediate you see a faint color. That color is the element that it resonates with. This here, is light essence."

I nodded along. "I'm with you so far."

"If I were to put it in terms from Earth, each element is its own field, which are all around us, at all times." Eloria snapped her fingers and the world lit up in a static like I'd seen many times before, though it was transparent, allowing me to see around me.

"The static you've been seeing represents excitations in those fields. They don't interact with normal matter, until…" She tapped her palm, with the white disc and the essence of the same color in the room rushed toward her palm. "You Will it to do so. Arts can have Will within them, which means you don't have to think when using them."

She motioned toward me. "Essence vision allows you to perceive all of this. Though, I think yours is a little *too* sensitive." Motioning with her hands like she was turning a knob the static mess faded. "There we go."

So this is a goddess. Casually changing how I perceive what's around me. It was terrifying.

"The cultivator light that Veronica saw, and that you saw before your essence vision, was more akin to…" She turned her focus elsewhere and held a hand up. "Ah! A mild radiation. Technically, a mortal *could* see this light, but by that point the excess energy being given off would be fatal for them. Cultivators are generally immune to that radical energy."

I raised my hand.

"Yes?"

"This feels more like a science class than information about magic," I said flatly.

"Your Mama-Krissi told you that cultivation is not magic, didn't she? These are the basics. Imagine what it takes in your head to stimulate the dead cells in woodgrain, to fill in the surface of a floor?"

That required her to think about it directly? Cells are minuscule, wouldn't it take…

"Yes, hundreds of thousands to a few million for a small scratch. There are shortcuts, of course, but generally a cultivator is responsible for controlling the effect if they aren't using an Art." She made the money gesture with her fingers. "That's why arts are expensive."

A bell tolled and Eloria turned toward it. "It seems my time here has come to an end. Don't tell anyone but your parents about being my champion. They'll make sure it's handled with care."

Before I could ask another question she took a step back into some unseen door and vanished from my sight.

My eyes went to the statuette she'd left behind, and agreed after a quick test that I was not moving it anywhere.

Once I'd exited the room I found Daughter Hy. "Eloria left the church something in there."

Her eyes widened and she peeked inside the room. "Father!" she said frantically and walked away.

Oh, so there is a "Father" figure in this Scripture's Children hierarchy. Big surprise.

The middle-aged man who told me what to do on my Ceremony followed her back. He looked inside too and locked the door. Then both he and Daughter Hy prayed for a few minutes.

"C-can you find your own way back to your family?" she asked.

"Sure," I said, and set off. *What's the big deal about redecorating a little statue?* Then I remembered Eloria's words that they were a bit fanatical. *Oh, right. This will keep them busy.*

Though I should have expected it, the hubbub between the nobility quieted as I returned to everyone. There were no issues with me getting through, as everyone made way for me.

Great, now it's weird again. It's her moniker as the Goddess of Death, and I resonated with her. They don't ask for clarification, instead they shrink in fear.

Mom saw me and ran to receive me, picking me up. "Everything okay?"

"Yeah, but I have something to tell you and daddy when we get home."

She smiled. "Okay," then kissed my forehead, then held my braid in her free hand.

I asked, "I apparently have essence vision. Does that mean I'm a cultivator?"

"It does, and it's not common." She sat me down. "This next part of today's events might seem strange to you, but don't be alarmed."

Veronica found me moments later and pulled me into a hug. "I awakened, I can't believe it!" She held my hand and squeezed it tightly. "On-ma said I will have the Right to Choose if I progress well over the next Anfang year."

Seeing my blank stare, she moved closer and whispered, "It means I probably won't have to marry that Emperor."

I broke out into a grin. "Congrats!"

The priest from earlier stood near the sanctuary. "We will now begin the Choosing for Imperial nobility."

In an instant, everyone huddled around Oliver, and started pushing their children toward him.

What in the nether are they doing?

CHAPTER THIRTY-SIX

OLIVER'S CHOICES / A SILENT COMPANION

"OLIVER," A LARGE and portly nobleman said, "Please meet Pia and Roa. They're twins like you."

The two girls both gave him a curtsy. Given they were taller than him, I'd assumed they were older than he was.

"Hello Your Imperial High Grace," they said in unison, which was a little creepy.

Each girl had straight brown hair and bright blue eyes. Their white outfits mirrored one another, with Pia having a simple line of gray flowers embroidered on her left side, and Roa on her right.

They're cute. What's this "Choosing" all about? Moving closer, this time the nobles paid me no mind. They were seemingly over their shock from before.

Oliver's face briefly reddened before he said, "You're both pretty." He stuck out his hand. "I'm Oliver."

The girls both chuckled. It seemed their mannerisms were mirrored too. One raised their left hand to her mouth, the other raised her right hand. They were definitely a team act.

Those two are trouble, Oliver! I thought knowing he'd be putty in their hands when they got older, assuming they ever got to know one another.

Mom approached their father and the two started to talk. The two girls stood off to the side and another woman moved forward with her son.

"Hello Your Imperial High Grace, this is Van. He–"

Oliver cut her off, "No boys."

What's he mean by that? He only wants to befriend girls?

His decisiveness made me laugh, and there was a momentary bit of shuffling as nobles separated the children by gender. The boys all sat in the pews.

This almost seems like rapid dating. Very strange.

In the end, they finished up and he only interacted with one other girl, Mina. She was much taller than the rest, and had platinum blond hair, with oddly orange eyes. She gave the twins a run for their money all on her own.

I was jealous. *She's so tall! At least as tall as I used to be on Earth.*

With the meet and greets done, the three girls and my brother went over and started to talk. I can't imagine Oliver's discussions were very deep, but they sure were spirited. Based on his gestures…

They all looked over at me and giggled as Oliver gave the impression that he was carrying something. His face was serious for once.

Their attention at first made me blush, but then I realized, *Ah. Our encounter with the treant. He's quick to make friends, I'll give him that.*

The remaining nobles refocused on the Redwood Kingdom's prince. Though he didn't awaken, it meant he was a mortal, around Veronica's age. He did have a strong jawline and a physique many would envy.

Huh, actually all of these nobles are pretty. My lack of attention bothered me a bit, but I wasn't unfamiliar with such treatment by others. I had no friends my age, in this life, and only two in the last. I was never a very social person.

What was different now was the deliberate effort to avoid me. If a child tried to approach me, whether boy or girl, their parents would swoop in and pull them away.

Rude. Why did Eloria choose me? Frustrated by my isolation, I moved to sit in the pews myself.

There seemed to be a class separation here, too. On the right the noble children were decked out in the best clothes. Oliver and I were in simpler garments by comparison. Those to my left were still well dressed, but there was far less gold and silver present.

There was more space on the right, but the left was more homey and consistent with our upbringing. I saw an opening in the back next to a boy reading. It was a book on the kingdom we were in.

"Do you mind if I sit here?" I asked.

"Suit yourself. Mom's moseying about with the other adults."

His comment was odd. While the spot was free, none of the adults in the section were out and about. *How long has he been reading that book?*

"Anything interesting in your book?"

He lowered it enough for me to see his brilliant green eyes and his dirty blond hair.

For half a second, our eyes met and I looked away, feeling my cheeks flush. *What was that? Why am I blushing? He's just a little boy.*

"Not much," he said. "The first through sixth prince are listed here." Motioning with his book he added, "Though there's no mention of their ninth prince." He sighed. "The least they could do is say their names before they step forward for their Ceremony."

Nine princes? My eyes drifted to the boy and his father. The man was at least sixty by his hair color. *Huh. Virile.* "They should totally say their names before they step forward," I said to the boy, and wondered why I bothered to say anything at all. Glancing his way I caught sight of his green eyes again, focusing back on the book. *Stop looking into his pretty eyes.*

"Anessa!" Oliver called, but it was barely audible over the chatter.

Hopping off the pew I glanced back at the nameless boy as I left, more confused than ever, I waved to the emerald eyed boy, who just focused back on his book. *I had some odd emotions in a dream with Trish, and now this? Am I more suited to this world's sensibilities than I realize?*

When I reached Oliver, he introduced the three girls.

I gave them a curtsy and introduced myself, and they returned the greeting.

"Oliver tells us that you survived a run-in with a treant?" Mina said.

"Yes, it was scary! It smacked Oliver into a giant boulder, but he got back up and shook it off."

They looked at my brother in tandem and his cheeks gained a rosy color.

He scratched his head. "It's what anyone would do for their sissy."

Roa repeated quietly, "Sissy, huh?"

Her sister asked an awkward question. "You don't want to marry your sissy do you?"

He'd mentioned over and over, how he'd make sure I never marry anyone. It had never occurred to me until this moment that he might have an ulterior motive behind that sentiment. So I was very thankful to hear him say, "No. That would be weird."

I sighed in relief, then asked, "You've introduced me to these girls, are you looking to be their friends?"

He straightened his back and said with confidence, "I intend to marry them in the future."

A smile broke over my face at his childish innocence. *Yeah, it's a bit too early to–*

"Oliver, good news," Mom said from behind me. "I've talked it over with their parents, and your engagements are set."

The turnabout made me face-palm and I thought, *Good grief.*

"Woohoo!" Oliver shouted and jumped five feet into the air.

His joviality was lost on me. "Why would you want to be engaged to someone at your age?"

My brother's answer was concise, "Daddy has three wives."

Though I waited for a more detailed explanation, none came. Looking around at the kids that had formed small groups, not a one was holding hands, nor were they all that much closer than when they initially met.

Ah. Are they playing engagement? I turned to ask Mom, but she'd vanished amongst the other nobles again. *Great.*

"Anessa," Mina said. "Is it true that you bested Oliver once in the past?"

Ah. She meant my Gift Burst, I thought. "Not really. There was an accident at church and I reacted to defend myself."

"Yeah and I went zoom!" He gestured toward the ceiling, all of our eyes followed him up. "Daddy had to follow after me, because it put me to sleep."

The twin girls looked at one another and nodded. They each cocked their head to the side, mirroring one another again. "Are you in the Sky Realm?"

"No, I'm… hold on," I said and closed my eyes, entering my Personal Space. Inside, I checked, twice. The results made me sigh. "Still don't have any dantians. That puts me in the Nascent realm?"

Mina nodded. "Few children get their dantians at your age." She put her hand on Oliver's shoulder. "Oliver's quite the exception."

The young boy looked up at her and blushed again, then took a step away from her. Us four girls laughed at his innocence.

He's so cute, wanting to be like his daddy, but not understanding what situation he put himself in. Looking over the girls he "chose" made me wonder if they would actually stay with him in the future. *I guess time will tell.*

It seemed the attention was too much for him, because he dashed off with apple-red cheeks. The girls nodded at me and followed him at a leisurely pace.

My ears caught Mina trying out her name with Carlyle attached to the end. At sixteen she seemed to be the most aware of the situation. She then sighed and said to herself, "We'll see in twelve Standard years."

Her admission that there was over a decade for them to wait gave me some solace. *That's going to be interesting if he reacts that way every time they come over to visit.* Then I realized, *If they come over to visit. How does this all work, anyway? Surely, they aren't engaged for real… right?* The oddity of the culture of Anfang never ceased to surprise me.

To think an Anfang year ago the people here wouldn't have given us so much as a thought.

Looking around for Mom I found her with a bunch of older women. Kristine and Veronica were off having their own conversation, while Oliver was still playing tag.

It's just me, huh? Looking back at the pews I saw the same seat was free, and figured I'd see if the boy knew any more about this ceremony than I did. *At least he has nice eyes.*

"Is this seat still open?" I asked.

He pulled down his book and said, "Mhmm. Not sure where my mom is, she's probably still schmoozing."

I said, "My name is Anessa, you?"

"M–" he shook his head. "Gideon."

"This is such a weird day. Why do they keep the details of these ceremonies so quiet?"

"It's something to do with favor," Gideon said. He pulled his book away from his face, revealing his baby-face. "The favor of the gods."

"What about the nonsense of pushing kids to form fake relationships." I gestured toward my brother. "That's just weird."

"Agreed." Our eyes met for a moment and he lingered before covering his face again with his book. "They say on the same day you can create a Divine Link with a god or goddess, your Soular Kinship shows." He sighed and tilted his head toward the people at the far end of his pew. "My brothers had someone picked out before their ceremony. They say your Divine Link and Soular Kinship are the same. So picking someone for yourself is an affront to the gods."

The men he was talking about strongly resembled idealized, mature versions of Gideon. If their chiseled jawline, six and a half feet of height and toned arms were family traits, he'd be fending girls off with a stick in a decade or two.

Shaking my head I thought, *Stop it Anessa, why are you thinking about how some random boy will look as a man?*

"Marion," a woman called in our direction.

None of the people in the pews reacted, and a minute later the voice called again. "Marion, I know you can hear me, come here."

To my right Gideon had started to bury his nose into his book and his ears were pink.

"Marion!" The voice chastised.

"C-coming," Gideon said.

Oh, he did start to say something starting with M earlier, so that's his actual name?

"It's my first name," he muttered. "But my friends call me Gideon."

He hopped off the pew and dashed over to one of the middle-aged women Mom had been talking to. She had moved on from that group.

"Anessa," Mom called from the sanctuary.

When I joined her I was glad she called me away. "Did you enjoy your chat with that little boy?"

Her words stole my tongue and I was unable to say something for a few seconds. "I feel more comfortable over near the non-Imperial nobles. They seem more relatable somehow."

Mom bobbed her head in understanding. "I see. It doesn't hurt that he's cute, does it?"

"Not at all–" I started and stomped my foot, "Hey!"

Mom folded her dress beneath her and caught my eye-line as she squatted to speak to me. "I'm only partly teasing you. Would you mind talking to him more often, after this get-together?"

"He seems smart enough and he didn't say anything untoward." Realizing that I had in fact zero friends, because we'd largely lived in isolation at Fleure's estate for a few Standard years, I said, "It wouldn't hurt, I guess?"

Mom stood and said, "Great!" She turned her attention to someone else and nodded.

Her change of focus made me think, *Why do I sense a disturbance in the force?*

A few moments later, Gideon's mother approached us with the distracted boy in tow. He was more interested in his book than the social event around him.

If I weren't so concerned about this, I'd say he were a man after my own heart, but...

"Gideon," his mother said.

He replied without even dropping his book, "Yes mama?"

"Put your book down," she chided.

He sighed and lowered it.

Every time our eyes met it made me flush and squirm a little. *Should I find it's this* "Soular Kinship" *causing this, it stinks. A four-year-old shouldn't have these kinds of sensations!*

He said nervously, "Oh, hi again." Then he looked over at my mom and his book tumbled from his fingertips. "Mama, that's the imperial princess." He whispered to her. "Why is she here?"

Gideon's Mom gave a laugh-snort, "She's Anessa's mommy. Didn't you read the details about the families in attendance, in the documents I gave you last week?"

"N-no." He looked back to me with wide eyes. He bowed. "Sorry, I had no idea."

"Mommy," I said. "He's acting weird all of a sudden." Though I could easily guess why. It seemed he wasn't expecting my mom to be someone of importance.

"Anessa." Mom called. "Una and I were talking when we saw you two together. You also said you wouldn't mind getting to know him better."

"Okay?" I said, drawing out the word.

"Their family were visiting Redwood from Rhinebur, the nation where you were born."

I spun my hand to tell Mom to get to the point.

"It would be very difficult for him to visit from that distance." Mom smiled. "So we thought it might be helpful if he were to stay here for a while."

Both Gideon and I said in tandem, "Crap."

Sadly, our parents focused on the timing, eating it up, and they laughed.

"We have some details to figure out," Mom said and began to walk away with Una.

"What the nether!" I said, but made sure Mom was out of earshot.

Gideon fidgeted. "Sorry about this."

"It's not your fault." I exhaled. "It's this whole crazy culture."

He cleared his throat. "Perhaps I should formally introduce myself?" Picking his book up, he gave me a lighter bow with his hands behind his back. "It is my pleasure to make your acquaintance. My name is Marion Gideon Varn. Third son of the Varn Baronetcy."

Playing the part, since there was no harm, I replied with a curtsy. "The delight is all mine. I am Anessa Jean Carlyle, Daughter to the Imperial Duke Roland Carlyle, also daughter to Lily, an Imperial Princess. Titled Her Imperial High Grace." I laughed despite myself, not knowing if my introduction was even accurate. "Though that is quite the mouthful. You can call me Anessa."

Gideon's response was to stare at me blankly.

Crap, did I mess it up?

"You're an Imperial High Duchess?"

I shrugged. "That's what Daughter Hy told me. But so much has changed over the past few months I'd answer to 'hey you.'"

He visibly relaxed and mirrored his mom's snorty laugh. "You're silly. Acting like a noble is tiring. In fact, many of my friends are commoners. I hope you don't mind me saying that you act more like they do than the daughter of an Imperial Princess."

I smiled. "I'm glad you said that. You should see the clothing they made me wear the first day we set off to Redwood." Straightening out with my arms at my side, I said, "I felt more like a stuffed turkey than a duchess."

He repeated his laugh and we returned to the pew.

"What do you suppose they're arranging anyway?" I asked. "Logistics on how to retrieve some of your things to stay a few days?"

Raising an eyebrow at me he said, "No." He turned away. "They're probably arranging the details of your dowry."

"What?" Looking forward the room spun. "You're joking." I turned back to him and leaned forward. "Please tell me you're joking."

He shook his head.

Inside my head I screamed. *What the hell!? Want to make a friend? Yes. You have to become engaged first. What the f—*

"Are you okay?"

Leaning back against the pew I let the back of my head tap against the wood. "No."

"I mean," Gideon said. "I'm just guessing about what they're doing. Usually you don't visit someone eleven thousand miles away from your family unless they were thinking about a longer-term arrangement."

I blew a stray hair out of my eyes and thought, *He's right, and I totally missed it.* Another sigh escaped, and I said, "You're pretty smart for a boy who is four-Standard-years-old."

"Um…" he said. It reminded me of the sound someone makes right before saying… "Actually, I'm almost twelve-Standard-years-old." He crossed his arms. "All Varn men start out small. At least that's what mama told me."

"Yeah," the gravity of being engaged hit me. "Okay." I leaned forward and put my face in my hands.

Mom chimed in. "Ready to go you two?"

She wasn't my favorite person at the moment and I snapped. "Why didn't you tell me the focus was my *'engagement'*?" My voice must've been a little louder than I intended, and there were suddenly several eyes on me.

Mom was not pleased, and her lips formed a straight line.

"Sorry," I said. Dropping my voice I continued, "But isn't my opinion kind of important here?"

Mom held out her hand for me to take it, without saying a word. She led me outside to a carriage, into which we all three of us climbed, apparently we were riding back together.

Inside the carriage Mom was silent for another good ten minutes before she said, "I didn't tell you because it didn't involve you."

Didn't… involve… me. My own engagement didn't involve me?! I couldn't even shout. It left me dumbfounded. *I mean I remember hearing stories about nobility deciding marriages for political reasons…*

"Also," Mom said in a doubly-cross tone. "If we are in a public scene with other nobles, I fully expect you to not give an outburst like that again." She gave me a few seconds to process her words then added, "Is that clear?"

All I could muster was a quiet voice to say, "Okay." We sat in silence for a while longer. The heat around my collar was all but unbearable.

Gideon was at my side and he said nothing.

There was nothing to say.

"Mommy," I said.

Her tone was back to normal, "Yes honey?"

"Could you let me know about other social customs I might not be aware of so I don't freak out like that in the future?"

She nodded.

Feeling it important, I pressed, "Veronica told me she could earn the Right to Choose by becoming a cultivator. Eloria said I am a cultivator. I will only have one husband in my life." I put my hand to my chest. "I'm certain of that. And you took that Right from me."

She frowned for a moment and furrowed her eyebrows. "I should have told you more. There are many times where decisions are made for the family that are for the good of the family, and for the empire. This was one of them."

The subtext in her words wasn't lost on me. She hadn't said *"Gideon was one of them,"* but that *"this"* was. Looking over at Gideon I sent up a prayer to Eloria. *Let's hope things go well in the future with Gideon.*

CHAPTER THIRTY-SEVEN

BOUNDARIES, PROTECTION AND FRIENDSHIP

THAT WAS A silent, awkward carriage ride after that. As we reached our halfway point Mom said, "Let's talk about what's bothering you some more later. When we get home, there'll be a celebration for Oliver and your birthdays." She smiled. "I think they should even have something prepared for Gideon."

The boy pointed at himself. "What do you mean? How would they even know about me?"

"Gideon, if you're a Carlyle in the future, your 'acp hoth' is a big deal." She pulled out a translucent green cylinder and tapped its side with her finger and put it back in her pocket. "We have kept in touch."

"Acp hoth" I repeated in my head. *Literally meaning "child pact", so it sounds like there is a difference between this arrangement and a normal engagement.* It was a little consolation, but not much.

"Right, of course you'd have a communication jade," he said, then bowed his head. "Thank you for taking care of me."

"It's our pleasure." Mom gave him a faint grin. "Una tells me you were here taking a look at the Maaka Institute. The new semester begins at the start of Mankae. You're a cultivator, but you actually got in on your mortal academic pursuits, is that right?"

"Yes ma'am," he said and smiled.

Mom's smirk broadened, "Please, call me Mama-Lily."

Gideon gulped. "Okay."

She had me interested. "What subjects are you good at?"

"Maths, science, and history mostly," he said. "Oh!" he said. "Did you know we recently found an old archaeological site on our land? Some old sect lived there at one point. There's no records of it at all, so it's a real mystery."

"Really?" I said, imagining what amounted to pyramids on Anfang. *What would they even look like here with cultivators?*

Glancing at Mom netted me a wink and I realized she'd started the conversation for our sake. It made me both happy and frustrated.

Gideon went on about the site for a while.

When he was finished, I said, "What about your other subjects? I'm partial to math myself." Grumbling I corrected myself before Mom did, "Maths, I mean." I thought, *It's silly for math to be maths. Where are we, Europe? Though I guess math would be short for mathematic, not mathematics which is admittedly weird.*

"Yes, I've mostly finished up my times tables over the past year, though I have a ways to go."

"Times tables?" I asked, confused at its simplicity.

He nodded. "I'm still stuck on the rote of doing three-digit numbers."

"Three digits?" said with a gasp. "I guess I'll have to study harder then." My mind went to Julilah when she was my teacher, and I realized we may have skipped past the basics too soon. *There's almost a hundred thousand combinations for three digits. I thought knowing some two-digit combinations was decent!*

"I know a few patterns that show up which might help," he said. "Oh! Before I forget, please don't tell anyone about that dig site. Apparently they want to do a survey before it's recorded officially."

An odd thought about keeping it quiet wiggled its way into my head. *Don't tell anyone…* I looked at Mom who avoided my gaze. *If I was traded for some dirt, I'll scream.*

Once we arrived the usual protective detail was present. Gideon following us like a lost puppy told me his reaction was much like mine the first time, both wonderment and fear.

We collected Oliver and his "fiancées" in the foyer. It seemed he'd become more comfortable sharing his personal space, because Mina was on one side and Roa and Pia on the other. We proceeded into the dining area. Upon entering, several servants either set off poppers or threw confetti directly towards us.

Oliver beamed from ear to ear. "Cool!" He dashed into the room and started talking excitedly to the staff as though it was any other day.

I wish I was as optimistic as he is. Shaking my head I watched the bits of paper rain down off of my head. It made me realize how much I wanted to cry, though I knew it wasn't the time for it. *Maybe it can be called off, or I'll find I get along with Gideon.*

"You okay?" he asked.

Shaking my head again, I said, "Not really. Still wrapping my head around lacking a choice in the whole thing."

With a sigh, he said, "I know what you mean, we're in the same boat there."

Realizing that I wasn't the only one who felt this way gave me some solace. "Thanks," I said and motioned forward, "Let's try to enjoy this party."

Una met us at one of the dinner tables along with Oliver's fiancées' parents.

It took everything Oliver had for him to remain civil at these events with his excessive energy.

After we all prayed Mom proposed a toast. "To the birthday, the union of our families, and most of all the wondrous attention of the gods! May the future continue to bring us fruitful outcomes."

Over the table the adults said, "Hear hear!"

They then broke out into Happy Birthday.

Veronica came over and hugged us both. Before she returned to her seat she whispered to me, "If you need anything, let me know." Her affection at that time was welcome, and I hung onto her for a minute before she pulled away.

Mom would occasionally look my way, watching me closely. Thirty minutes into the festivities she picked me up out of my seat and held me close.

"Sorry everyone, it seems our little princess is a bit tired. Please enjoy yourselves," she said.

Kristine stood and commented about Veronica's news. "My mu-tos had two Divine Links today, she…" Her voice cut-off as the door closed behind us.

To my surprise Oliver, and his trio followed, so did Gideon.

"Oliver," Mom said and looked his way. "Follow Yllia to your cabin. She'll get you four settled." Turning to Gideon she added, "Come with us. You're in Oliver's old room."

The whole time her hand was on my back and neck. All I could do was hug her tightly.

Gideon entered his room, and a manservant they'd just assigned him greeted him. Oliver's effects had been removed and a different aesthetic had taken its place. It was reminiscent of Rhinebur.

How did they put this together so fast? I thought, then realized at the moment I didn't much care.

Mom sat me on my bed and said, "Let's talk about that archaeological site."

Mom's words hit me like a ton of bricks. *She did trade me for dirt. Holy shit.*

Before I could explode in rage at her, she placed down a red S-ROB and tapped its top. The frown on my face must've been pretty severe because she reached out for me. "Calm down. Let me explain." Taking the chair that Sarah usually used to plan my day she sat. "One of the first cultivators of Anfang started a sect, tens of Anfang millennia ago. She was known as the most prolific to be seen in our planet's history. Undine. She was *born* at the peak of the Sky Realm."

"What's that have to do with who I marry?" I said flatly. *Right now the last damn thing I would care about is cultivation!*

"I'm getting to that. Her sect was rumored to be over a hundred thousand miles from here." She shook her head. "But it's not, it's in Westwood's borders. The riches within could raise an army of Olivers or Rolands, and those are the footmen."

"So it's a power play?" I asked, doing everything I could to control my emotions.

"In a manner of speaking. Because of how valuable the sect was, its details were secreted away to only the highest of nobility. Una didn't know what she had, and…" she pursed her lips. "If I'm honest, it might even be greater in value than the Empire itself can hold onto."

She's saying, in effect, it's more valuable than even I am. I'd never felt more alone on Anfang, than at that moment.

"With your hand in marriage secured, we do not get the information that they uncover, nor a share of what they find, but we do get full control and complete ownership of the site." She paused and her tone said she was excited. "We get everything." Taking a moment to compose herself she said, "I realize that in your situation that's not much consolation, but I'll make sure that any resources we receive escalate you to at least Undine's level when she left Anfang behind."

I'd looked down at her lap, thinking about her words. Mom pulled my eye-line back to hers with her finger under my chin.

"She was a goddess."

Her awareness of this and the implications made me question, "I thought mortals like you didn't know anything about cultivation?"

Mom gave me a sad smile. "Your mommy has many roles to play. As a mortal wife I must be ignorant; however, as an Imperial Princess, I know what I need to know for the sake of our empire."

"What about Gideon?" I said, with anger in my voice at my lack of a choice. "He was happy to talk about it, isn't that a problem, and what about telling me?"

She hugged me. "Don't worry about your future little prince. He won't say anything." Taking a breath she whispered, "And you won't either, because I'm sure you know how dangerous it would be." Keeping my hand in hers, she pulled away.

She's not threatening me, so much as telling me it's a dangerous topic. It's possible if she didn't act, a higher noble would've just taken it from the Varn baronetcy anyway. I nodded slowly. "Okay. I won't say anything. I'm still not happy though." I squeezed her hand. "I'm quite pissed, in fact."

"I know, but can you imagine if I tried to," she paused and grinned, "wed him to Oliver?"

Imagining either Oliver or Gideon in a dress made me laugh. "No, I can't. That's too funny." My smile vanished. "There wasn't anyone or *anything* else suitable, was there?"

"No. A fixed resource wouldn't work because if they find out its value later it would cause issues. Resources are often bad at lasting the test of time. And a title by itself would have little merit, without a bond backing it up."

The more she said, the more frustrated I got. *It makes sense.* Worse, I didn't know if I would have acted differently in her shoes.

"Well, is it at least okay if I cry?" I asked, realizing the finality of the arrangement. My eyes stung. The indignation I held onto was quickly slipping into sadness.

She smiled. "Of course it is."

I wasn't able to hold my tears back any longer and the dam had failed. It released the tension I'd balled up since Gideon made me realize we were engaged. By the end of it I was sitting in Mom's lap hugging her torso.

"All done?" she asked after a good ten minutes.

"Mhmm." I wiped my eyes and blew my nose in the offered handkerchief. I'd gained a light hiccup from my efforts that I held my breath to disperse. Once I had, I said, "I'm still not happy about it, but I get the feeling that the decision is somewhat final."

Mom kissed the top of my head. "It is, I'm afraid. Do you want to talk about a lighter topic?" Seeing as I didn't say no, she added, "You'll start school in Polarae." She paused and her hesitation said she didn't know if I would take her next question well. "Did any of your dantians come in?"

Shaking my head I said, "No. Mina said that was typical though, since I'm so young."

"Then you'll join the Civilian division of Maaka Institute. Oliver will be part of the Martial division. Probably as a Core student."

"What's a Core student?"

"They're students that excel in their division. If you and Gideon manage to get your math tables up to snuff, you'll probably end up as a Civilian Core student."

"That's unlikely," I admitted.

"Maybe, but you're smart, I think you'll do fine there."

"You mentioned Oliver had a cottage now. What's that about?"

"If he had one fiancée, he'd be down the hall. But given his choice for three, I thought it would be prudent for him to get an idea of what living with them would be like."

I imagined him playing keep-away daily. Oliver would win that one, unless the girls worked together. Curious about the future I asked, "What about when he gets older?"

Mom tilted her head. "What about it?" Her eyes widened and she smiled. "Ah. Right, he lives in the cottage with them, but he has a minder. They will not sleep in the same room until he is at least twelve-Standard-years-old. Even then, there will be a clear divide between him and the girls." She coughed. "For propriety's sake."

So, like the Amish's bed divider? I thought, but didn't say aloud since I was sure that Mom wouldn't know what Amish meant.

Having my mind clear of the stress, I remembered and said, "Mommy, I have something to tell you."

"What's that honey?" she asked.

"I have a message from Eloria."

Thanks for making it this far!

The lifeblood of a series are ratings and reviews. If you have time, please take the time to leave one.

This series will be releasing often, so look forward to the next book!

Thank you to Alice Waites (Damson) for the illustrations in this story. It wouldn't be the same without her help. Her X account can be found @damson_fox

Another thank you to Danny DeCillis, my editor. For making my words not trip over one another.

Thanks to the talented Ashley Gatti for her voices in the audiobook.

My website is cristoph.net and my X account can be found @cristoph_a_t

ESTAR TRANSLATION GUIDE

Days of the week:
Unday - First day of the week.
Deuday - Second day of the week.
Triday - Third day of the week.
Quattoroday - Fourth day of the week.
Midday - Fifth day of the week (midweek).
Hexoday - Sixth day of the week.
Septaday - Seventh day of the week.
Octday - Eighth day of the week.
Finday - Ninth day of the week.

Month names (and their English equivalent):
Runariae - January
Crotariae - February
Totharae - March
Evantaiae - April
Lokandae - May
Jothariae - June
Mankae - July
Ylldriae - August
Hanvarae - September
Fandariae - October
Polarae - November
Zenthriae - December

While Runariae is positionally equivalent to January, that's where the similarities end. Months are 27 days long (three weeks).

Äneaca is Anessa's name in Estar.

UNITS / CONVERSIONS

Standard minute - Sixty-four seconds.
   Standard hour - Sixty-four Standard minutes.
   Standard day - Twenty-four Standard hours.

   Anfang day - Forty-eight Standard hours or two Standard days.
   Anfang Week - Nine Anfang days.
   Anfang Month - Twenty-seven Anfang Days or Fifty-four & 2718/5411 Earth days long.
   Anfang Year - Three-hundred-twenty-four Anfang days, twelve Anfang months, or six-hundred-forty-eight Standard days. With one leap Anfang day every nine Anfang years.

CHARACTER GUIDE

Anessa Jean Carlyle - Our protagonist. Her death on Earth is somewhat of a mystery. She thought at first it was her best friend that took her life, but things might not be as simple as that. Nascent Realm.

Bal Blackwood - Julilah's second husband. Mortal.

Eloria - Anfang's goddess of Death. She was once viewed as the goddess of craft.

Evan Q'Tar - Heir to the Redwater Empire. Late stages of the Ascended Realm.

Fan Mul - Lily's Lady's maid. Her role changes throughout the book. Mortal.

Gilbert Q'Tar - Ruler of the Redwater Empire. Middling Sky realm.

Jorin Q'Tar - His Imperial Majesty, the Emperor of the Westwood Empire. Sky-Realm, half-step in the Otherworldly Realm.

Julilah Carlyle - Roland's first wife. Veronica's on-pa. Mortal.

Kristine Carlyle - Roland's second wife. Veronica's on-ma. Middling Ascended Realm.

Lana Carlyle - Julilah and Roland's daughter. Anessa's older half-sister. Mortal.

Lily Carlyle - Anessa's mother and Roland's third wife.

Lom Carlyle - Kristine and Roland's son. Anessa's younger half-brother. Mortal.

Marcus Blackwood - Julilah and Bal Blackwood's son. Mortal.

M. Gideon Varn - Son of the Varn Baronet from Rhinebur. His family was visiting the Redwood Kingdom around his third awakening ceremony. Anessa's "play boyfriend."

Mina - One of Oliver's fiancées.

Nicole Carlyle - Roland and Kristine's oldest daughter. Anessa's oldest half-sister. Mortal.

Oliver Sil Carlyle - Anessa's twin. Early Sky Realm.

Pia - One of Oliver's fiancées. Roa's twin sister.

Roa - One of Oliver's fiancées. Pia's twin sister.

Roland Carlyle - Anessa's father and the patriarch of the Carlyle family. Late Sky Realm.

Sarah - Anessa's personal lady's maid.

Sir Gerald Orris - An old man that knows more than he lets on.

Una Varn - Gideon's mother, matriarch of the Varn Baronetcy.

Veronica Nu Carlyle - Anessa's not-sister. Kristine and Julilah's daughter.

Yllia - Head maid of the Carlyle family.

CULTIVATION TERMINOLOGY

Realm - A major steppingstone for cultivators to differentiate between one another.

Stage - A portion of a Realm necessary to advance. Typically, a Realm composes many stages.

Step - Denotes an even smaller portion of a Realm and subdivides Stages.

Dantian - A means for a cultivator to store essence within their body.

Divine Link - A connection with a god or goddess during an Awakening Ceremony.

Meridians - Similar to how veins and arteries carry blood, meridians carry essence.

Nexus - An organ within a cultivator that is used to control essence. It's similar to how your heart pumps blood, a nexus pumps essence. Different in that it helps you enact control *external* to your body.

Mortal - A non-cultivator. Equivalent to a normal person on Earth.

Nascent Realm - A cultivator who is in the first Realm. The weakest Nascent Realm cultivator is stronger than the average mortal (usually).

Ascended Realm - The second Realm. Most consider this Realm to be the real start of someone's cultivation journey. The Nascent Realm is like being on training wheels.

Sky Realm - The third Realm. At this stage, cultivators start to understand basic gravity and learn to counteract it. This is done innately, and they slowly move to temper their bodies for what comes next.

Ring of He - An enchanted ring which is capable of providing female couples with the means to have children. Cannot be used by someone under the influence of a Ring of She. Can be used by Mortals.

Ring of She - The opposite of the Ring of He. Cannot be used by someone under the influence of a Ring of He. Can be used by Mortals.

On-ma - The mother of a child in a female-female relationship.

On-pa - The father of a child in a female-female relationship.

www.ingramcontent.com/pod-product-compliance
Lightning Source LLC
Chambersburg PA
CBHW071127200626
46817CB00018B/2346